THE P'TOWN MURDERS

A BRADFORD FAIRFAX MURDER MYSTERY

JEFFREY ROUND

Cormorant Books

**Canada Council
for the Arts** **Conseil des Arts
du Canada**

The publisher gratefully acknowledges the support
of the Canada Council for the Arts and the Ontario Arts Council
for its publishing program. We acknowledge the financial support
of the Government of Canada through the Book Publishing Industry
Development Program (BPIDP) for our publishing activities.

Printed and bound in Canada

Library and Archives Canada Cataloguing in Publication

Round, Jeffrey

[P'town murders]
The P-town murders : a Bradford Fairfax murder mystery / Jeffrey
Round. — 1st Cormorant ed.

Originally published under title: The P'town murders.
ISBN 978-1-897151-28-0

1. Title.

PS8635.O8625P76 2008   C813'.54   C2008-902284-X

Cover illustration: Nick Craine
Interior text design: Tannice Goddard/Soul Oasis Networking
Printer: Hignell Book Printing

CORMORANT BOOKS INC.
215 SPADINA AVENUE, STUDIO 230, TORONTO, ON CANADA M5T 2C7
www.cormorantbooks.com

For Shane

In every drop of water is the ocean.

BUDDHIST PROVERB

1

In a place that's to "die for," no one expects to die for real. At least that's what Bradford thought as he hung up the phone.

The news came just past midnight, the operator's voice twanging over the line: *You have a collect call from Provincetown, Massachusetts.* He'd almost declined the charges when he heard the caller's unfamiliar name. Something made him change his mind.

A throaty voice came over the wire, a cross between Tina Turner and Divine, as though its owner gargled with razor blades.

"Bradford Fairfax?"

"Yes."

"I thought you should know Ross Pretty died of an overdose of ecstasy last night. No one's claimed the body."

The caller clicked off.

Brad felt as though he'd been punched in the gut. He crumpled onto the bed, gripping the edge of the mattress with his hands. *Ross dead!* It was the last thing he'd expected to hear.

It seemed inconceivable, yet somehow strangely inevitable given Ross's lifestyle. *Just crammin' on life*, he'd say with a grin. And in his day there'd been no one more alive: drugs, circuit parties and a sex life to make even Bill Clinton nervous. But all good parties came to an end, Bradford knew. Better to go when they asked *Why are you leaving?* rather than *Why aren't you leaving?*

Brad and Ross had met under the laser lights at a Miami Black-and-Blue ball, surrounded by hordes of Electro-Twinks and Day-Glo Boys with their incredible bodies and their even more incredible pasts. At first glance, Brad dismissed Ross as just one more insecure boy with an irresistible physique and a sweet smile. He was so shy he could hardly catch your eye until you tumbled into bed with him. That's when he came alive and the real Ross emerged — playful, fun-loving and totally in control.

A natural-born hedonist, Ross made sure he got his nickel's worth of pleasure from life. He was a high-flying dancer whose feet seldom touched the ground. Men of all types and social statures sought his company. He was almost never without a companion. Still, it couldn't make up for the lost childhood, the love and acceptance he craved but seldom found, and the family that denied him to this day.

Ross was one of J.M. Barrie's Lost Boys who somehow found himself in a Eugene O'Neill play cast alongside monster parents, abusive siblings and broken dreams. It would be wrong to say Ross resented his family, but in trying to love them he'd paid a huge price.

His was a tale of sadness and loss, of trying too hard to be loved — a cliché but for the fact that Ross had lived through it and come out the other side scarred and mangled, but still hungry for everything life offered. That hunger was what he and Brad had in common — that and having no family to turn to. Ross had possessed the body of a Michelangelo and the face of a Caravaggio. It was ironic to think that in life almost everyone wanted him, but in death no one had turned up to claim him.

And no one would, unless Bradford did.

He went to the bar and poured himself a glass of sherry. Why, he wondered, had it happened now? He stared into the glass as though the answer might lie there. Would Ross still be alive now if Brad hadn't ended things between them? But that was unlikely. Ross was already a wild thing when they met. Courtesy demanded he be returned to the wild when Brad was done with him. To keep him in a cage — even a cage built of love — would have been unfair. Ross was already beginning to look like a captive bird when Brad had let him go. Still, he ached to think of it.

After their split, Brad couldn't understand why Ross stayed in places like P-Town when he had the entire world at his disposal. In the city, a good-looking kid could always find another lover and settle down, no matter what his past. But Ross stuck to resort towns where nothing lasted beyond a week or two, and whatever bonds you made were broken sooner rather than later. The truth was that connections scared Ross. It was as if he preferred the certainty of heartbreak and impermanence to a chance at something better.

Ross's family wouldn't show, of course. Brad was sure of that. The parents who shunned him in life wouldn't embrace him in death. This was one prodigal son who'd never return home. Ross's real life had been with Bradford and his chosen band of brothers and sisters in those few years they'd spent together. Ross had known they would never desert him, shooting star that he was, hell-bent on burning through life before it burnt him. The real question, Brad realized, wasn't why Ross had died so soon, but why he hadn't died sooner.

He glanced in the mirror. There were bags under his eyes already, and it would be another sleepless night. Time for a refill on the cucumber cream moisturizer. Brad shook his head at his reflection. Shallow even in grief, he chided himself. Then again, only he knew how much he'd miss Ross.

He picked up the phone. As the number connected he lifted the edge of his T-shirt, revealing the rippled abs he'd been working on. Few would know the hours of sweaty labour they demanded. With one finger, he traced the graceful outline of a pair of tattooed wings emerging from the waistband of his sweat-pants. And few would know about those, either, apart from the handful of men who got close enough to see for themselves once or twice.

The face ... well, the face was okay. As long as you appreciated the occasional freckle and more than a hint of red hair, that is. In a bar recently someone had told him he was Abercrombie & Fitch material, but the guy was probably just trying to get laid. You couldn't trust a compliment these days.

A voice came over the line. "Yes?"

"Red here. I need to speak with Grace."

Brad waited while the operator checked the list for his name. He wouldn't find it.

"This is an unscheduled call, Agent Red ..."

"I know. I've got a problem."

"One moment."

The line hummed while the call transferred. As he waited he wondered about the others who called this number. What were their names? Yellow, Blue, and Violet? Or perhaps Red was indicative of his hair colour. He hoped not. Maybe the others were known simply as numbers. *How's it goin', 87!* he imagined calling out to some colleague in a dim bar somewhere.

A familiar smoky voice came on the line. "Yes, Red?"

"I've got to go away for a couple days."

"Reason?"

"Death in the family."

He'd never lied to Grace before, but Ross *was* family. He'd come to seem like a delinquent younger brother after their affair ended. And even though they hadn't seen each other in almost a year, Ross still called once a month to let Brad know how he was, where he was: Key West, Frisco, Vallarta ... wherever there were wild parties and good times to be shared with delicious, sexy men.

5

Brad could barely keep up with Ross's globetrotting, but he'd been glad to know the kid was enjoying himself. And when there wasn't a job as barkeep to fuel his constant movement, there was bound to be a rich man somewhere in a background that got shadowier and shadowier with each passing destination.

Time to think of coming home and settling down for a while, don't you think? Brad would ask every other call, testing the waters. *Always time to think of it,* Ross would reply with a laugh. *But doing it's for old age.* They both knew it would never happen.

On the other end of the line now, Grace drew a breath. "New York's too important for us to take any chances, Red. I should check with the folks upstairs."

"This won't interfere with plans," Brad insisted. "I'll only be gone a couple days, and then I can get to New York on schedule."

He held his breath and prayed Grace wouldn't turn him down. He couldn't abandon Ross again. Not now. Not this time! The thing he hated most about his line of work — the only thing, in fact — was being told what he could and couldn't do with his personal life. He'd had to bite his tongue more than once on being informed he wasn't allowed to date just anyone.

The men Bradford liked were of a type: rough, tough and hirsute — what used to be called "Trade." Grace didn't like Trade. *We chose you because you look young and innocent*, she'd reminded him. *And we expect you to play the part.*

That meant dreary dinner parties with preppie couples and self-absorbed career fags who thought *Rent* was the epitome of culture. Try talking about the glories of Nina Simone's dusky baritone, a portrait by Modigliani, or the exquisite delicacies of a Scriabin *étude*, and those wimps Grace approved of just stared as though you'd said you'd gone to the moon. Or farther.

He could feel her deliberating on the other end, followed by a sigh. "All right, Red," she conceded. "But check in with me when you get there. We've got to keep you on schedule."

"Thanks. You're the best, Gracie dear."

"*Red!*" The tone caught him short.

"Yes?" He was deferential.

"This is very serious business. We're counting on you to come through next week."

"I hear you."

She paused.

"I certainly hope so."

BRADFORD LOVED THE P-Town ferry. He preferred it to flying over the harbour or taking the winding drive along the cape. There was nothing like seeing a humpback whale break through the shimmering water right beside you to make you feel totally alive.

The first time he'd made the crossing — or *almost* made the crossing, as it turned out — the wind had picked up twenty minutes out into the open sea and the boat began to rock ominously.

After another ten minutes the windows and second-floor deck were awash in spray.

Before long, most of the passengers were hugging refuse barrels or clinging to table legs bolted to the floor. The acrid smell of vomit filled the cabin. Brad had sought refuge in the open air on the top deck where his sole companion was a young Asian girl. They'd sat and shared a bag of nachos while the others suffered unspeakable torments below.

The swells grew and the crossing deteriorated until the ship was forced to turn back. Undeterred, Brad grabbed a seat on a bus and endured the long ride across the peninsula that curled back toward the mainland like a scorpion's tail. Despite the inauspicious introduction, it would be the first of many trips to P-Town.

It was another three years before he attempted a second crossing. Ross was with him then. It was Ross's first time in P-Town and the experience had just about blown his mind. *This is the gayest place on earth!* he'd declared, watching men holding hands with other men, and women interlocking arms with women right there on the streets. *It's even gayer than Disney World!*

They'd spent the first night together, and then Ross disappeared for the next three. Eventually he returned, looking well used and more than a little satisfied. Brad had been jealous — it was his nature — but he knew he couldn't offer Ross anything others couldn't provide just as easily. He also knew the two of them had reached the end of the line as a couple, though not for the usual reasons.

For a year or more, under the nickname Icarus, Brad had been spending his spare time on an Internet site called *Brunch on Ideas*. BOI was a forum for heated political discussions, both domestic and international. It brought out a real fervour in the chatters, who returned again and again to the site. And despite its acronym, BOI wasn't particularly gay.

A typical evening brought together hundreds of differing voices from across the continent, and farther: *Hey, all you politicos! Houston here. It's a hundred-and-ten degrees outside. Barbies are melting!* came the report from a regular nicknamed Billy D.

Hey, Billy D — Icarus here, Bradford responded. *Good to hear from you. I'm in a somewhat cooler place, myself.*

London checking in, chimed an eager voice calling itself Lola. *Anybody for a discussion of the relative merits of Bush and Gore?*

Lola, you're all wet, came a swift reply with a New York moniker. *Gore will trounce Bush and the world will never hear about that Texan half-wit again.*

Lay off Texas, Yankee! Billy D. retorted. *I think Bush is gonna win!*

Despite rumours of eavesdropping by security organizations, the chatters freely discussed any and all topics: how to sneak into Cuba, Saddam Hussein, Hilary Clinton's sexuality. Here, the forbidden was everyday. They even joked about the likelihood of secret surveillance. *Smile for the camera*, someone was sure to say to remind them of the presence of electronic snoopers.

The discussions lasted for hours. Brad often found himself at the centre of the talks, frequently accepting the role of moderator at the group's request. When most of the others had given up and gone back to the real world, a semi-regular known as Dedalus continued to engage him. At first, Dedalus seemed to be goading him, prodding for his point of view, which he always gave with unfailing politeness. Later, Brad realized Dedalus had been drawing him out. What he couldn't know was that Dedalus had been tracking him.

It would have shocked Brad to learn his nickname appeared frequently in surveillance scans by the National Security Agency's "Project Echelon." With its high-speed artificial intelligence programs, Echelon intercepted and sifted through billions of private messages every day. NSA relied on the disbelief of most Internet users that such operations could actually occur. It was Big Brother, big time, all the time.

No one was safe. Joke about a possible assassination of George W. Bush by Osama bin Laden, and Echelon red-flagged you. Get fancy and encode it as a pun — a secret wish to see the "Shrub" end up in the "Trash Bin," for example — and you might make a terrorist alert list.

As Icarus, Brad was well-known to the NSA, which eavesdropped on BOI's chat rooms. Grace, a.k.a. Dedalus, didn't approve of the NSA, but she wasn't above eavesdropping as well. Grace soon began to consider Bradford Fairfax a worthy candidate for her own security organization, one that was nameless. It was a secret eye in an invisible door.

Grace contacted Bradford, told him he could do great things for the world, and made him an offer. Then she left him to think about it.

At the time, Brad was a freelance journalist specializing in world affairs. He had few close friends and, apart from Ross, no immediate family. He'd been made a ward of the state at fifteen when his father was killed in a car crash. His mother had died eleven years earlier. As far as Brad knew, he had no living blood relatives. For him to disappear from view completely wouldn't take much.

Brad thought over Grace's offer for a month before agreeing to join. Once he'd made his decision, the rest fell quickly in line. Leaving his old life behind wasn't an issue, but he knew it would change him forever. Any sort of personal commitment would be impossible. It was why he'd chosen to set Ross free in Provincetown.

That had been five years ago.

2

The towers of Boston receded as the water churned beneath the big boat. Sunlight winked on the waves. Despite the bright September afternoon, the air was cool. Brad waited till the city had all but disappeared before making his way inside the cabin.

He looked around at the gay men sporting their festive moods and colourful clothes, the stylish lesbians accompanied by well-groomed dogs, and a handful of straight families with fiercely hip three-year-olds doing intergalactic battle on Game Boys. Somehow, these wildly different tribes all managed to get along together in Provincetown.

Over in a far corner, a handsome muscular man sat clad only in a pair of boxers. Brad's eyes played over the sculpted chest, plucked to within an inch of its derma's life. The man's stomach was so flat it was concave. Brad felt a twinge of abdomen envy mixed with a tingling of lust.

Across the table from the boxer-clad beauty, a slightly plump young man leaned forward, frowning with effort as he applied makeup to the demigod.

I'd like to be his blush brush, thought Brad.

The near-naked man turned and caught Brad's eye. His smile flashed fun across the cabin. And maybe something else.

"Don't move!" squeaked the makeup artist. "You'll ruin my work."

Brad smiled. Only on the P-Town ferry! He moved on till he came to the snack bar, stopping to stare at an assortment of snacks beneath the glass. Hardly anything nonfat or low carb, he noted grimly. At his neighbourhood supermarket, Brad shopped exclusively in what he called the "No Fat-No Fun" section. Maybe it was time to live a little.

He decided on an apple turnover, giving himself a mental slap on the wrist. Just one won't hurt, he thought, though he knew that was always how it started.

The server looked at him with concern. "You sure you want this?" he asked, as though he'd read Brad's mind. Brad flushed and thought of his midriff. Was it showing already?

"It might get a bit rough out there," the man said, with a nod toward the water.

Brad smiled. "I like it rough." No reaction from the server. Brad's smile faltered. Definitely straight, he decided. "I'll be okay," he said with a shrug. "I've done this trip before."

"All right," the man said. "Just thought I should warn you."

"I stand warned."

Brad continued through the cabin, settling in to read the *New York Times*, a publication he liked to refer to as "that amusing concoction of lies." Two front-page stories vied for his attention: Hurricane Isabel was threatening offshore Maryland, and Arnold Schwarzenegger was threatening the rest of America in his campaign to become governor of California.

"I'm not afraid of Democrats," Arnie declared in a fervent interview. "I married one."

Isabel was a woman of fewer words, but her 150-mph winds kept the country's attention regardless.

It wasn't until he reached the back page of section one that Brad found a brief write-up on the Dalai Lama's upcoming lecture series in New York. To conclude his visit, the guru-in-exile had scheduled an open-air talk in Central Park the following Sunday. If Grace was so worried about him, Brad wondered, why didn't she just advise him to cancel his trip? Of course there could be any number of reasons, but it seemed the sensible solution.

He'd just finished the article when a loud squawking burst from the back of the cabin. He looked up to see Marilyn Monroe charging through the room. It was the man in boxers, now wearing a platinum wig and false eyelashes. He teetered through the cabin on high heels, a pink boa trailing behind.

"Help! Save me!" Marilyn cried to the room as everyone erupted in laughter.

"Norma Jean, I am not *finished* with you!" the makeup artist screamed as he raced after the charging figure.

The fugitive spied Brad sitting with his paper and suddenly turned coy. He sashayed over and ran the boa's feathery tip across Brad's cheeks.

"Hey, big boy!" he whispered in imitation of a very-Hollywood Marilyn. "How's about a little fun later, just you and me?"

"Norma Jean!"

Brad suddenly found his face pressed into the man's taut midriff.

"Please don't let them take me," Marilyn cooed in mock fright. His voice lowered and Brad thought he heard the man say, "I know who you are. I've got to talk to you about Ross Pretty."

Before Brad could react, the irate makeup artist reached his prey. "I'm not *finished* with you!" he cried, grabbing the unfinished Marilyn by the biceps and pulling him out of the room.

Marilyn gave Brad a last reluctant glance.

"And I'm not finished with *you*, honey," he crowed over the crowd's approving roar. "By the way, everybody," he said, turning to the room. "I'd like to take this opportunity to invite y'all to my show at the Post Office Cabaret, starting tomorrow night!"

Brad watched, intrigued, as Marilyn disappeared in a flurry of high heels and feathers.

3

Every time Bradford stepped off the Provincetown Ferry he felt as though he'd come home. He merged with the circus-like atmosphere of merrymakers, gleeful children, souvenir hawkers, roving dogs, arts-and-crafts collectors, professional escape artists, and the occasional genuine tourist swelling the crowded streets.

Every year, for five long months from May through September, Provincetown endured a throng of visitors so mighty it stopped traffic the entire length of town. The bustle started just after sun-up and lasted all night long, barely resting for a few tranquil minutes at the beginning of each day. If you were straight, homophobic and arriving unawares from the wilds of New Jersey, you might think you'd been plunked down in Sodom. But if you were one of the chosen few, you knew you'd reached the Promised Land.

After visiting Provincetown it was difficult, if not downright impossible, to go back whence you'd come and resign yourself to coping with "normality" again. *I never want to go home*, Judy told her audience that final night in Carnegie Hall. She might have been talking about P-Town. It had an allure that got in your blood and wouldn't leave you alone.

Residents can tell you that anyone who comes to Provincetown will return before long. Bradford was happy to be made a case in point, returning again and again to the gingerbread houses and salt air, the crowded streets and friendly cafés, the buoys and the boys.

On his first trip he was just another twinkie lucky enough to have booked a tiny room in one of the town's myriad guesthouses. He'd lodged at Romeo's then, a nondescript but entirely functional abode where any number of boys with limited means have rested their weary heads after long nights spent carousing and indulging in P-Town's thousand-and-one distractions.

For young Brad, simply being in P-Town had seemed more than enough reason to be thrilled, but whenever people asked where he was staying they looked genuinely distressed by his answer: *Those shoes with that dress? Impossible!* their expressions declared.

He'd just announced the name of his residence to an ebullient crowd partying in the Atlantic House one evening, when a drunken queen in casual wear sidled over and placed an arm over his shoulder. A jewelled finger strayed across Brad's chest, tracing the outline of a boyish nipple through his Banana Republic T-shirt.

"Don't worry, sweetie," the queen cooed over the din of the bar. "We'll get you into a really ..." — the finger strolled across to the other nipple — "... *good* house next year."

"But I like where I'm staying," Brad replied, for he hadn't yet learned to recognize a queen out of drag. "They even have chocolate donuts for breakfast."

He'd thought himself clever, but the horrified faces surrounding Brad told him he'd just committed social *hara-kiri*.

"You know *nothing!*" the queen shrieked, retracting her arm and banishing him with an imperious finger to the outer circle of the bar.

The queen transformed. Majesty and Presence towered before Bradford where moments before there'd been a dumpy sod in shorts and a shapeless golf shirt.

The queen's nostrils flared. "*Style! Grace! Position!* These things *matter!*" she screamed, as though to say he knew not what dangers lurked.

She regarded him, eyes narrowed, as the bar shifted nervously. "But," she purred. And then again, "*But!*" giving the word its fullest meaning. "You're cute. And you're … young."

The queen faltered, for *young* is the one thing before which all queens will allow themselves to weaken.

"So." She nodded slowly. "*Just so*. We will give you another chance."

Breaths were exhaled. The chatter resumed and people laughed again. Brad had been spared. Moreover, he'd been called upon to join the inner circle of a Queen of Some Standing — nothing to snort at for the impudent upstart that he was.

As Brad was to learn, in every young man's passage into The Life there arrives a moment when he realizes that all is not as it appears. To the uninitiated, The Life may seem a hall of mirrors in which one can be lost forever without a knowledgeable friend or a Wise Queen to act as guide.

Just so!

A Wise Queen stands before one, then, disguised in shorts and a T-shirt. A Wizard stalks the glen without his wand. Alice peers into a looking glass and beholds another world entirely. And Dorothy peeks behind the curtain and sees … *well!*

One must take care not to misinterpret such things. The Life can be an uncharted voyage, a bottomless bog waiting to trap the unsuspecting twink who presumes that a modicum of looks and a certain flair on the dance floor are a substitute for style, or that mere panache might be a match for true wit. The Wise Queen in the A-House had been trying to convey just such to her largely undiscerning novitiate.

Meaning is attached to everything, she'd implied. One must learn to read *into*. A label queen is not simply one who knows the price of your outfit at a glance, but sees its social standing as well. True, it takes talent to see "Burberrys of London" rather than "Designer Knock-Off" sewn onto a tag inside a man's long-sleeved linen shirt, but that's only the beginning. A *vrai* label queen can read meaning into that shirt as well.

Has it been donned casually so as to suggest the *vie d'esprit* of the well-to-do, or is it being worn *avec hauteur* to disguise the fact that its owner has gone bankrupt purchasing this exclusive novelty item to wear to uptown cocktail parties? Or! — *Listen carefully*, the Wise Queen advises, *for herein lies the danger* — is it being worn by a young Gangsta Rapper whose world holds its own private associations of meaning and power? The beholder must beware of confusing them! Those stunning mahogany chest muscles bulging beneath that creamy Touch-Me-There Burberry cotton may seem to have been made just for you, but much is at stake if you risk running your hands over them uninvited. And only a real queen knows such things with unfailing instinct.

That evening had been the beginning of Bradford's initiation into P-Town's gay life. And now, more than a decade later, a bag slung over his shoulder, he strode down Commercial Street with something like a hometown boy's pride. Weaving in and out among the colourful crowds, he noted the passing landmarks: Cabot's Salt Water Taffy Store, Whaler's Wharf, and the Seamen's Bank. He paused outside Spiritus Pizza where the handsomest of men gathered in the evenings all summer long, talking and laughing late into the night. There was no place quite so fine as P-Town.

It was here, Brad knew, that America had its first inklings of what it was to become when a gang of unruly pilgrims dropped anchor offshore to make the peninsula's tip their home for a month. They stayed just long enough to write the Mayflower Compact, declare their divine right to annex the New World and finally realize they were straight, and therefore didn't belong in the Gayest Place on Earth, before moving inland to nearby Plymouth and its momentous rock.

As he walked, Brad pictured the drunken queen making her regal pronouncements that long-ago night in the A-House. It was status she'd been trying to explain. At the height of summer, Provincetown's famed homes-away-from-home were all about prestige, in the same way fraternities jockeyed to reach the top social rung on campus and drag queens schemed to have the grandest hairdo at the ball. It wasn't enough to have a gilded birdcage enwrapped in one's wig. No! *One must have the bird as well!* And so, in Provincetown, gay men vied with one another vigorously and openly to stay at one or another of the better houses.

And *yet!* Brad knew that the real prestige came when you left the heavy traffic of the downtown strip and slipped over into P-Town's residential district. While the tourist zone beckoned endlessly with its circus of delights, the far end of town withdrew from all the bustle and clamour. Here, the crowds thinned and silence took hold of the Cape once more. It wasn't quaint or inviting. It stood aloof, like the Pilgrim Monument or Garbo, wanting only to be left alone.

Here was where the status game got mean and tough. Here a good house could cost as much as three or four thousand a week. And it was here, less than half a mile from where the first pilgrims had landed, that Bradford Fairfax stayed whenever he came to town.

He set his bag down outside a stately house set back from the road and framed by an opulent garden. He removed a pen-like object from his pocket and aimed it at the entrance. The tip emitted a red laser burst and the front door swung open.

Inside, he set his bag on the tiles. With a hand clap, light flooded the hall. He stamped his foot and the door closed securely behind him. Here he'd be completely safe and as alone as he chose to be.

While other guesthouses could boast of costly antiques, famous histories, or naked room service, and one well-nigh legendary place even had original 1930s Norman Bel Geddes furniture to its credit, Brad's house offered a combination of solitude and modernity, two surprisingly compatible companions. It came loaded with the latest in technology and security, while providing a serene seafront view from its upper deck.

Brad climbed the stairs and entered an open space where he was momentarily blinded by a profusion of flowers. The scent of lilies filled the air. A card protruded from a basket of blooms. *Sorry for your loss*, it read, signed simply, "G."

He smiled. Good old Grace. She really did have a tender side under that crusty exterior. Not that he knew what her exterior looked like — they'd never met. And under the terms of his agreement, they never would. All physical identifiers, contact details, and given names had been reduced to code words, pseudonyms and fabricated identities. She was simply Grace and he was Agent Red. He might pass her in the street and never know.

Intelligence agents joked that NSA stood for *No Such Agency*. Bradford's own agency had even less to identify it by. Apart from a phone number, his only contact was via an obscure postal address. Thus the organization's nickname: Box 77.

Like all intelligence groups, Box 77 kept a low profile. It vigorously denied its own existence, and from time to time invented fictitious organizations rumoured to operate in its place. The few colleagues he'd met jokingly referred to the organization as *Neverland*.

Training had been thorough and secretive. The inductees were loaded onto a plane with blacked-out windows. Brad and the twenty-four others found it impossible to tell even which direction they'd flown. On landing, they were blindfolded and driven by truck for several hours in the dead of night before being made to walk the final half-hour to their destination. All they could tell of the place was that it was tropical. Apart from the camp operators, they never saw another person or even a road going in or out.

They met their trainers on the first day. The atmosphere was convivial, relaxed. This was going to be an adventure, Brad thought. At the very least, it promised a friendly bonding session. It was the last time he thought anything like it.

The constant physical tests — feats of strength and endurance — were engineered to mould their bodies into finely tuned and highly responsive instruments. The psychological tests were even harsher. After the first day, a subtle and not-so-subtle eroding of egos and personalities began and continued until a number of recruits begged to be returned to their private lives.

Diamonds were being formed from lumps of coal, flaws ruthlessly weeded out. A trainee suspected of having a weakness for cocaine was offered a stash of blow that nearly blew his mind. Anyone who broke simply disappeared and was never mentioned again. Those who remained had their confidence in themselves worn down to the point where they doubted even their own names.

Told repeatedly they weren't good enough, that their lives and the lives of countless others could be in danger due to their ineptitude, they began to feel they'd never make the grade. The trials seemed endless, the routines exhausting. Nothing was as it appeared. The trainees were set one against another until it seemed no one could be trusted. It wasn't until the final day that the camaraderie returned and the remaining six were congratulated for being among the finest cadets ever initiated.

Brad never learned where he'd been or where the organization's headquarters were located. He simply returned to his old life, telling his friends only that he'd been away on business.

The extreme secrecy had seemed a clichéd holdover from the Cold War, but Brad had quickly come to understand the need for it. The agency couldn't afford to be associated with the actions of its own agents. If anything went wrong, he had no knowledge of his superiors' identities and could never betray them. Not for gain, not even to save his life.

Brad glimpsed his reflection in the window where it was superimposed over the dunes. Few knew his true identity. Lately he'd caught himself wondering who he really was. DNA samples were taken from everyone who joined the service and kept in secret vaults until an agent died. Other than that, their voice and retinal prints were the only foolproof means of identification. Box 77 was a shadow operation, its agents ciphers.

Brad unpacked quickly. He wanted to settle things with Ross as soon as possible, in case he was unexpectedly recalled. He hung his shirts and trousers in the bedroom closet alongside a dress jacket, the only formal wear he'd brought. In all likelihood, he wouldn't need it. He intended to have Ross's remains cremated and assumed he'd be the only one at the ceremony. Casual would suffice. Ross would've appreciated a farewell send-off in jeans and T-shirt. A party was a party, after all.

The fridge contained the usual bottles of Dom and a handful of Brad's favourite whites, including a hedonistic little Robert Niero Condrieu. Seductive hints of marmalade layered with honeysuckle came to mind, as did that night at a Cairo hotel alongside a supple Egyptian. A quick glance showed the wine closet to be stocked with several of the better reds. A Château de Beaucastel looked particularly inviting. He'd have it with supper one night — alone, no doubt, as he wasn't likely to be doing much entertaining.

He poured a gin and tonic and took it to the living area where a surprisingly cheerful Wifredo Lam hung over the chaise longue. The dour Cuban cubist complemented a breezy Robert Motherwell above the mantel and a Dali sketch on the far side of the room. At first sight he'd mistaken the Dali, a male nude with scandalously enlarged genitalia, for an early Tom of Finland.

Next to the decor, his favourite feature in the house was the loft bed set under a cathedral ceiling overlooking the dunes. Twilight lent it a soft violet glow, while mornings brought forth a spectacular golden light. It was one of the most soothing and restful views he'd ever woken to.

The marble-tiled bathroom housed a steam room and a mammoth Jacuzzi to complete the set. Plush towels and fine toiletry articles lined the inset shelves. Guesthouses could get more costly, he knew, but not more comfortably luxurious.

BRAD FINISHED HIS drink and sauntered down to the turnoff where Route 6 met 6A. He looked back once at the house perched on a rise, surrounded by beech trees and backlit by the fading daylight.

He crossed the highway and leapt over the guardrail, heading across the salt marsh. Sand dunes rose in squat mounds that shifted year by year as the wind and water pushed them about like restless crabs dragging their shells along the beach.

He climbed a ridge and the ocean came suddenly into view. Once the sun went down, there would be nothing here but starlight glinting off the licorice-coloured water. The air was cooling as he stood looking over the beach where a handful of men tarried in search of love and other narcotics. He could almost taste the air. When he breathed in, it filled his lungs completely rather than simply occupying the space inside him.

He continued toward the lighthouse sitting solitary at the Cape's outer tip. Here the point of sand curled briefly back toward the mainland, as if at the last moment it had doubted the wisdom of getting too far from solid ground just before it ran out of steam. *Pentimento* the Italians called it, when an artist regretted his efforts and began to paint over the mistakes of the past, concealing but not erasing his work. Never erasing. So too with love, thought Brad. You can bury it deep inside, but it never really goes away.

The sun had long since disappeared by the time he reached the breakwater, a mile-long rock extension connecting the peninsula's tip to the western edge of town. Crossing was dangerous in the dark, he knew, but it would be faster than going the long way over the marsh where the incoming water had already reclaimed much of the land.

Brad stepped gingerly across the oversized boulders, taking care to clear the dark crevices between them. He stopped to inhale the salt smell of clams and algae. High tide was approaching, the ocean reaching shoreward. Birds skimmed its surface in search of a flash of fin as the lighthouse scanned the waves. Across the harbour, the lights of town were coming on. The view was calm to the point of being blissful.

25

He was halfway across when something caught his eye, a dark shape pooled in the windward side of the breakwater. It moved gently, playing hide and seek among the reeds and the inrushing tide.

He eased carefully down to the water's edge, pulling the shape back from the current that dragged and sucked at it as though reluctant to give up its prize. The body was that of a boy, probably in his early-twenties. Alive, he would have been stunningly handsome. And judging by his condition, he hadn't been in the water long.

Still, dead was dead.

4

The cop who answered his call was a tall dark bruiser. Identifying himself as Officer Tom Nava, he pulled out a badge and held it in the glare of a flashlight inches from Brad's face.

"Yup, that's you all right," Brad agreed, looking from the ID photo back to the officer. He was *mestizo* — part Mexican and part native — a look Brad found particularly appealing.

They stood on shore at the near end of the breakwater. In the distance, the lights of a police boat flickered as the crew lifted the body from where Brad had secured it to the rocks with his shoelaces.

"What relation were you to the deceased?" Nava asked, jotting in his notepad.

"None," Brad said, wondering if the bristling tuft of hair at Nava's collar extended over his entire chest.

The officer scowled. "Were you two having sex when he slipped in and drowned?"

"I told you, he was dead when I found him."

Nava grunted. "So I guess you can't tell me if he was on any sort of recreational drugs?"

"Obviously not."

Nava scribbled away. Thinking of Ross, Brad said, "Why do you think he was on drugs?"

Nava shrugged. "Some bad party favours going around lately. And besides, it's not that deep here. I'm wondering what would make a healthy young guy like this take a one-way plunge off the breakwater at high tide."

He finished taking down Brad's statement, and then asked the address of his guesthouse. Something seemed to twig at the name.

"Fancy place, I hear."

Brad shrugged. "It's cozy," he said.

The cop had already assumed Brad was gay; the address had probably confirmed it.

Nava put his notebook away. "I may be calling you with more questions," he said.

He insisted on escorting Brad to his house, though it was only a block away. Brad guessed the officer wanted to see if he was telling the truth about where he was staying.

Leaving Brad at his front door, the patrol car backed out of the driveway and down the road. Brad went upstairs and lit the fireplace, pouring himself another drink. He tried unsuccessfully to get the drowned boy's face out of his mind. Finally, he went out onto the upstairs deck overlooking the dunes. Beyond the street lamp all was blackness.

IN THE MORNING, Brad called the coroner's office. He'd been right in assuming no one from Ross's family would show up to claim the body. He made an appointment and got dressed.

Inside the building that housed the morgue, a young man with a soft face greeted him and identified himself as town coroner.

He showed no surprise as he glanced over the paper giving Brad power of attorney over Ross. Brad and Ross had each drawn up documents naming the other as executor of their respective estates. This wasn't done during their affair, but after, when Brad's had turned out to be the one friendship Ross could always count on. Back then dying had been the last thing on either of their minds. This wasn't how the story was supposed to end.

Brad followed the man in his crisp white lab coat down a series of hallways. They entered a room buzzing with fluorescent bulbs. Brad tensed as a drawer was pulled forward, as if hope still remained that it might not be Ross inside. It was.

"Such beautiful muscles," the coroner said, pulling the sheet down around Ross's waist. "He's really a lovely corpse."

Brad ignored the strange remark.

Lying there with his eyes closed, Ross looked sad and alone, as he'd often appeared in life when you caught him unawares. Had the eyes been open, though, they would never have accused Brad of abandoning him. Ross was a wandering soul who believed in the saying that for a bird to soar, the sky must have no boundaries. Brad just hoped Ross hadn't regretted the loneliness soaring brought.

A miniature cobra reared its head on Ross's left shoulder. Brad knew Ross had got the tattoo when he'd converted to Buddhism the previous summer. As he'd explained during a late-night phone call, the snake was considered a protector of the Lord Buddha.

"Buddhism? Won't you have to give up drugs?" Brad said. "The body being a temple and all that?"

"Oh, no! This is a modern sect," Ross replied. "We believe in instant gratification and fast-tracking to enlightenment. It's all about pleasure. Partying is just another way of attaining nirvana."

Despite his flippancy, Ross was serious about his newfound beliefs. He insisted they were helping him become a happier person. Another time they'd had a long conversation about death. With his usual panache, Ross had made dying sound like an event to be looked forward to. On the way to nirvana, he explained, all souls went through a transition state known as the *bardo*. Here, a soul encountered the forty-eight peaceful deities of the heart and the fifty-two wrathful deities of the mind.

"Sounds like some of the circuit parties I've been to recently," Brad joked.

"The first-stage bardo isn't that big a deal," Ross continued. "You simply start to lose touch with your physical sensations — kind of like getting drunk. But in the third-stage bardo it really gets wild. They say you see fireflies coming through smoke."

"Fireflies?"

"I think it'll be like our last night in P-Town."

"Oh, right!" Brad said, recalling the final night they'd spent together on the Cape. "I'll never forget that!"

Back then the conversation had seemed overly fantastic and a trifle silly. Looking down at the lifeless figure now, Brad wondered if Ross had seen fireflies as his soul left his body. He might never know.

Other than his tattoo, Ross was exactly as Brad remembered. He didn't linger in the room, preferring to recall Ross in life rather than in death. He exited to the sound of a drawer sliding shut, and waited outside in the hall for the coroner to rejoin him.

"Cause of death is listed as an overdose of ecstasy. It's a fairly common party drug," the coroner answered in response to his question. "Perhaps not as common as cocaine, but preferred by the younger generation for its mood-elevating qualities. Unfortunately, it can have serious side effects, as in this case."

Brad recalled Officer Nava's remarks about the young man whose body he'd discovered the night before. For someone to die in such a fashion in Provincetown probably wouldn't be given a second thought. On a whim, Brad asked, "Is Ross's the only body you've got?"

The coroner smiled. "Oh, no. We've got a full house today. Evelyn Dover just passed away at 103. People said she stayed alive that long just to annoy her children. She told them she wouldn't give up her estate until they were mature enough for it. Well, they're all over eighty, so I guess she meant it."

Brad grinned.

"There's a heart attack victim in the second drawer. Your friend Ross is in three. Drawer number four is a bit of a mystery. Another healthy young man brought in last night — it appears to be a drowning. Odd though, given his physical state. He looked like he could swim for miles."

"Any chance he was on drugs when he fell in the water?"

The coroner gave him an odd look. "I'm sorry," he said, suddenly reticent, "but that's official business. I can't disclose that information."

He placed a cremation authorization form on the counter.

"And you said no one from the immediate family tried to claim Ross's body?" Brad asked as he looked it over.

The coroner shook his head. "Funny thing, that. I phoned a number the police found in some personal papers left by the deceased. His family claimed not to be related to him."

"Not so funny, if you knew them," Brad said. "That's why he gave me power of attorney. If I hadn't come, no one would have."

"Well, there *was* that other guy," the coroner said.

"Someone else tried to claim him?" Brad asked, genuinely surprised.

The coroner nodded. "Oh, yes!"

"I thought you said no one else had been by when I spoke to you on the phone this morning."

"You said *family*. This guy wasn't related."

Bureaucrats, Brad thought, rolling his eyes. "Who was he?"

The coroner shrugged. "Didn't leave a name. Nice-looking guy, though. Late-twenties. Soft-spoken. He had lovely muscles, too. I gathered he was a friend of the deceased."

There was no telling who it might have been. Apart from that, everything was just as the mysterious voice on the phone had said. That reminded Brad that somebody in P-Town knew who he was. Make that *two* somebodies, he realized, recalling the drag queen on the ferry. What else might Marilyn Monroe have to tell him other than what he already knew, which was that Ross was dead?

Brad signed the form, listing himself as an adopted brother, and prepaid the bill. He thanked the coroner and left. For the second day in a row he'd been preoccupied with helping the dead.

Rather than give in to sorrow he headed out to Race Point, the place Ross had loved most in P-Town. The sun was still high, the sky radiant when he arrived. For a long while he stood looking out to sea, the waves and the wind his only company. Finally, he retraced his steps to town.

31

5

Evening was a pleasant reminder of the summer that had just passed. The air carried no hint of the bitter cold that would soon be all it held. Lighthouse beams flashed across the harbour and out to sea, bringing Bradford a memory of his father. When he was ten, his father had taken Brad on a fishing expedition. As the sun set, they sat and watched it silently without moving. *Always stop to enjoy a beautiful view*, his father instructed. *You'll never have enough of them.*

Brad recalled a few other guideposts handed down to him. Along with the practical ones of looking both ways before crossing a street and not trusting strangers with candy, he counted other bits of fatherly wisdom among his inheritance. *Everyone has a reason for the things they do*, his father once said. *You don't have to like or agree with it, but you'll be better off if you understand it.* Another time he'd said, *Good-looking faces come and go, but there'll always be a market for sincerity.* They may not have seemed like much, but those words had proved useful to him over the years.

His father would have enjoyed P-Town, he knew. The drag queens and leather bars might've needed some explaining, but then again a good tour guide would see to that. He just wasn't sure what his father would have thought of his choice of professions. It would have made for an interesting game of charades.

As he strolled along Commercial Street, Brad stopped to look at a colourful poster. *It's My Party and I'll Sing If I Want To!* it shouted, as a half-dozen faces stared at him. Here was a vamp Bette Davis, a kooky Liza, a manic Madonna, a soupy Peggy Lee, a pouting Marilyn, and a deranged Joan Crawford. The Whitman poem, "Song of Myself," came to mind: *I am large*, its author proclaimed. *I contain multitudes.*

Beneath the faces of the women, and sedate by comparison, was a picture of an attractive man with the name Cinder Lindquist. Brad stared. This was the man who'd pressed his face into his abs and whispered Ross's name to him on the Provincetown Fast Ferry!

Cinder, he mused — a fitting tag for someone who erased his own identity to take on others'. He was curious to know exactly what Cinder, Marilyn, Norma Jean, and the rest of the multitude had wanted to tell him. He would take in a show that evening.

A few doors down Brad found himself looking up at the cheery facade of a new restaurant boasting a sensational-sounding menu and an excellent view of the harbour from an upstairs patio. Buoyed by the promise of good food and a cheery atmosphere, he climbed the stairs and stood in the doorway like a pound puppy awaiting adoption.

The mâitre d' approached, all style and effervescence. He winked at Brad, who followed him to an understated little table for one, *avec* view. Promising to send his waiter right over, the mâitre d' exited with genuine *élan*.

Brad was charmed. That brief overture, however, was the extent of the restaurant's commitment to customer satisfaction. At that moment, an evening that had begun with such promise only moments before took a very wrong turn.

Fifteen minutes elapsed before Brad set eyes on his waiter. The young man approached wearing a tank top and shorts that could only be described as *nubbly*. One look warned Brad that this song-and-dance number wasn't going to be about him, the customer. Rather, it was all about the server.

The young man clearly felt he had better things to do than wait on tables. There was kitchen gossip to share, ex-lovers to dish, patrons to ignore and, somewhere in the midst of all that jazz, annoying orders to be handed over to supercilious chefs who didn't care that *you* might be hungry and paid the bills, because *they* had lives. The customer was merely a jail warden, while the unhappy staff were misfortunate prisoners of conscience near the end of their unduly long sentences.

And so it went. Brad placed his order, fearing even to hope, and waited another half-hour. Between occasional sightings of his waiter, he amused himself by listening in on a couple of dish queens two tables away.

"What's your favourite song?" the first queen asked, playing straight man to the other.

"Favourite song? That's when my trick screams, '*Take it out! Take it out! Take it out!*'" the second queen bellowed, followed by tears and roars of laughter from the first.

Apart from this blithe entertainment, the evening progressed like a sloth crossing a road and falling into a ditch. The meal arrived, a dollop of slop on a hand-painted plate, served with more than a *soupçon* of impatience from the waiter. Had blind Tibetan monks prepared the food, it might have been forgivable. It might even have been better. But in fact, it could not be forgotten soon enough.

Brad attempted a few exploratory bites and draped his napkin over the remains. With nothing to lose, he lingered on the patio as he finished his gin and tonic. He was sucking on the ice at the bottom of his glass for the third time when the waiter's batteries clicked in, humming and bustling and making those Don't-I-Deserve-a-Really-Big-Tip noises all around Brad's table as he delivered the bill.

No, you do not, thought Bradford, stealing another look at those terrifically gymmed legs. You absolutely do not, but you're ... *young*, so I'll give you another chance.

With a sigh, he penned in the substantial tip and signed the credit slip, then exited the restaurant wondering who in the world he had just reminded himself of. Grace? He couldn't place it.

At twenty past nine, Brad entered the Post Office Cabaret. He purchased his ticket and took a seat as far from the stage as possible, which wasn't far in that tiny space. He found himself in the midst of an up-tempo crowd in lacy shirts and spandex biking shorts. Everyone seemed to be drinking some variation of the cocktail *du jour*, a debonair concoction of crème de menthe, tequila and absinthe. The room was full to overflowing. Clearly, Cinder Lindquist claimed a solid following in P-Town.

For the next hour and a half, Cinder and his many faces transformed with that Now-You-See-Me-Now-You-Don't appeal shared by magician's assistants, supercilious waiters and female impersonators. All the usual suspects were there, doing somewhat more than the usual things: Liza strangled Judy, Marilyn pussy-whipped Peggy Lee, and Bette Davis bonked Mae West. Meanwhile, Joan Crawford confided to an aging audience member: *Don't die, dear. They'll dish you!*

With a turn of the head and a toss of the mane, the lives of the famous appeared and disappeared before the audience's eyes.

35

Cinder concluded his act with a risqué pastiche from *Porgy and Bess*, sung alternately by Ella Fitzgerald and Louis Armstrong. The audience was nearly gaga as he slipped offstage.

So the boy's got talent as well as a physique, Brad thought, remembering the tantalizing display of muscle he'd witnessed on the ferry.

The applause exploded as Cinder made a brief reappearance to bid his audience goodnight. Each curtain call brought back another celebrated face. Brad wasn't sure if Cinder had noticed him, but as the curtain fell Marilyn blew him a kiss.

Finally, the clapping died out and the crowd stood to leave. Brad waited. When everyone else had gone, a head peeked out from behind the curtain. Still a fatuous Marilyn, Cinder rushed over and plopped himself down in Brad's lap.

"Honey, was I fabulous?" he squawked.

"To die for," Brad allowed.

"You are *too* perfect!" Cinder proclaimed. "Now come back-stage and help me out of these rags."

In the dressing room, Cinder suddenly turned serious. "In case you're wondering, I recognized you from Ross's picture albums. He had dozens of photos of you!"

"How did you know Ross?"

Cinder looked to the mirror where his face assumed a mask of grief. "We were roommates a couple of summers ago. It's so terrible about his death, isn't it?"

"Yes, it is terrible," Brad agreed.

The expression vanished. Cinder's face resumed its telltale Marilyn skittishness, but his talk was pure Tallulah.

"Anyway, that's how I knew who y'all were on the boat yester-day. And I knew ya'll had come about his death.."

Brad wondered just how much Cinder really knew about him and whether his identity might be in jeopardy. Ross could have revealed a bit too much about Brad's line of work, thinking that a little colourful gossip wouldn't hurt since none of his Provincetown acquaintances would ever meet him in the flesh. Anonymity was easy in a big city where new identities could be put on and discarded again in seconds, but in a small seaside resort, people could know more about you than you knew about yourself.

"I'm flattered you recognized me."

"It would be hard not to recognize a celebrity," Cinder cooed.

"A what?"

"Well, maybe not here, but certainly back where y'all come from you're a celebrity," Cinder said, tossing the end of the boa over his shoulder.

Brad was perplexed. "Who is it you think I am?"

"Why, you're Hartford Coleman!" He faltered. "Ain't you?"

Brad laughed. Cinder had mistaken him for a hard-bitten New York theatre critic with the power to put any stage performer squarely before the public eye. The only problem was, he recalled, Coleman seldom liked any of the performers he saw.

"No," Brad said. "I'm not. I think Ross dated Hartford a few years ago, but I'm not him."

Cinder pouted. "Are y'all sure you're not him?"

Brad nodded. "I'm sure."

"Then who are y'all?"

"I'm Bradford Fairfax," he said.

"*Ahh!*" The name brought forth a smile of recognition. "The bisexual golfing instructor and heir to a small chain of men's retail outlets from Seattle. Ross said you had multiple orgasms that were out of this world."

Brad flushed. At least the multiple orgasms part was correct, thanks to years of Tantric exercises and a mostly unintentional celibacy. The rest was a pastiche of personas Brad had developed over time. Despite a little bragging on Brad's behalf, Ross had kept his true identity a secret. He was safe.

"So y'all can't help me get famous and rich?" Cinder asked, clearly disappointed at having met yet another Miss Congeniality.

"I'm afraid not, but if I give any interviews to *Golf World* while I'm here I'll be sure to mention you. I thought your show was amazing."

Cinder's smile lit up the room. "Too bad you're not a critic," he said. "Or a crime writer. That wasn't true at all what they said about how Ross died."

"What do you mean?" Brad started. "Didn't Ross die of an overdose of ecstasy?"

"Ross *hated* E. He said it robbed him of his erection. He couldn't fuck when he took E, so he only took GHB and sometimes K or H or occasionally V, and from time to time even a little T or C. But never, ever *E!*"

Brad's mind leapt. "But the coroner's report showed that Ross was pumped full of ecstasy!"

"That's just it, honey. He may have *died* of an overdose of E, but I know Ross Pretty and he sure didn't take it willingly."

Cinder moved closer, glancing warily over his shoulder and speaking in a stage whisper. "I think it has something to do with Hayden Rosengarten, his boss at the Not-So-OK Corral. At least that's what we all call it around here. It doesn't have a real name, so far as anyone knows."

"Tell me this again slowly," Brad said.

Five minutes later a picture had emerged of Ross's final months working for an egotistical power broker who sold sex-and-drug-sodden weekends to wealthy men and gay celebrities who wanted their party lives kept out of the public eye.

"Five thousand a night buys anything a body could want," Cinder explained. "And I do mean 'anything.' I know because I perform there sometimes. As an impersonator, I mean. I don't do sex for a living any more."

Brad watched Cinder carefully. "What was Ross's job there?"

"Pool boy and sex slave to anyone who wanted him. And believe me, there were plenty who wanted him!"

Brad could well imagine that.

"Do you have any idea why someone would want to kill Ross?" he asked.

Cinder shook his platinum locks. Suddenly his face took on a look of realization.

"What am I saying? Of course I do," he said. "It's like they take over me. When I'm Marilyn, I really am a ditzy blond."

"That's okay," Brad said. "Take your time."

Cinder frowned in a pantomime of concentration.

"Actually, I thought Ross might have pissed off some of the other boys by getting in a little too tight with Hayden. There was a real good-looking boy named Perry who used to be the boss's favourite, but something happened not long after Ross showed up. There was a fight and Perry left and never came back. Maybe he got even with Ross. I hear he works at Purgatory now."

"The Gifford House bar?"

"That's the one."

Brad made a mental note of it. "Anybody else?"

Cinder thought for a moment, and then snapped his fingers.

"There was a drug dealer," he said. "He got in a nasty argument with Hayden. I think Ross used to buy party favours from him now and then. Maybe he gave Ross an overdose of E to get back at Hayden. Kind of like a gang warfare thing, if you know what I mean."

Brad wondered if he was dealing with the overactive imagination of a small-town drag queen, but Cinder's story had the salt air tang of truth. Brad thought again of the drowned boy and the cop's suspicion that he'd been on drugs when he fell in the water. Had the coroner been concealing something? He'd have to look into it quickly. Once the body was cremated, there wouldn't be much call for anyone to investigate further.

"Cinder, are you sure of everything you're telling me?" Brad pressed.

"Sure as shootin', big guy," Cinder said, trailing off into a whispery Marilyn again.

"How can I meet this Hayden guy?"

"Honey, you don't want to meet him — believe me!"

"All the same, I need to," Brad said.

"Well then, you need to spend a night at the Not-So-OK Corral," Cinder said.

"Can you arrange it for me? I'd like to see for myself where Ross worked."

"Uh-huh. Sure I can set it up for you. I'm performing there for the next few nights after my show, but it'll cost ya."

"I'm good for it."

Cinder smiled and blew back a platinum lock. "I've heard," he cooed.

Cinder's fingers crept up Brad's thigh, making his crotch stir. He hadn't dated a woman since Leslie Anne Morphy in grade six, but then it wasn't every day that Marilyn Monroe gave him the eye.

"And now, Sugar, Marilyn would like to give y'all a private performance y'all won't evah forget."

6

During the night Brad dreamed he was making love to a blue-haired alien with a spectacular erection. As he gazed into the creature's eyes, he felt as though he was staring into the very depths of the ocean.

The dream was a recurring one, but it never made much sense. He always started out alone, but soon became conscious of being drawn toward the alien, who smiled down at him from somewhere high above. Eventually, the distance between them shrank until they found themselves lying on a beach. At some point their clothes dissolved, the alien penetrated Brad with his erection and their bodies merged. That was usually where it ended.

Last night's dream had gone farther. They were riding a winged Lipizzaner that climbed with them into the air over Provincetown. Clinging to the alien, Brad felt an indescribable sensation of pleasure overtake him and woke to find he'd drenched yet another expensive set of sheets with his wet dream.

Morning light filtered in over the bed. Brad's heart ached at the memory of having been joined so completely with another being. It was something he'd never experienced in real life, not even with Ross, though there had been moments when they'd come close.

Except for his father, he had never trusted another man completely. He always kept a guard between himself and his lovers —

a guard he couldn't drop. And as much as he'd wanted Ross to be free, Brad had been threatened by his desire to be with other men. Something in Brad wouldn't allow him to commit all the way with someone who still had so much exploring to do.

"I can't give you the kind of relationship you want," Ross told him candidly when they moved in together. "But I can tell you I'll love you for as long as I live. Even longer, if that's possible."

When they'd separated, Bradford had accepted the lifetime promise to love each other as friends. Now that was over too.

He looked out the window to the dunes. To some men, the dunes *were* Provincetown, that incredible swath of wilderness where you could just let go and shuck your clothes and explore your innermost self with a beautiful stranger. It was a gay Eden. He watched as two buff men cycled down the road past his house. The pair stopped at the edge of the salt marsh and dismounted, chaining their bikes to a wooden fence and walking hand-in-hand toward the beach.

Gays tended to collect lovers rather than cultivate relationships, Brad knew. Their lives often resembled an unplanned garden bearing an explosion of different flowers. Under such conditions nothing could really stand out, making the whole seem little more than a riot. And while riots might occasionally be useful for changing the social order, how cultivated could they be?

While many gay men looked down their noses at the traditional concept of marriage, Brad believed they could learn from their straight friends the simple doctrine that, to a certain degree, less is more. With relationships, as with gardens, a well-cultivated handful shows better than a hodgepodge, tilt-a-whirl of sexual theme-and-variations.

43

One thing he knew for sure through conversations with his own friends, it's not *more* that gay men wanted, but *better*. Still, the straight camp could stand to learn a thing or two from his tribe. With a divorce rate of something like thirty percent, the hetero dream of suburbia was largely hollow, not to mention undecorated. Land of bad perms and ski jackets, there were no fireflies coming through the smoke in any stage of the suburban afterlife. Their nirvana had failed them.

That, Brad knew, was because straights dreamed exclusively of the pleasures of idleness while gays dreamed of a never-ending circus of delight. To the gay man the suburbs are death, an endless desert of nothingness, but the straight man often doesn't figure this out till it's too late and his life has turned to dust. Nevertheless, one must consider the alternative: drowning in a sea of mediocrity.

That was why The Life needed a cutting edge, and that edge was constantly moving. Who would choose to become the victim of social decline like the procreating hordes that married and moved to the suburbs, never to be heard from again except at Christmas? To do so was to declare oneself *Out! Passé! Over!* Yet a cutting edge is best danced upon with friends and lovers of some standing, not mere add-ins to the wedding scene in a mural of jolly peasants frolicking on a pig farm in Lower Bohemia. After all, Brad thought, it's *better* we want, not *more*.

Besides style, the most important thing straights could learn from gays is choice. Straights will tell you that deciding *when* and *whom* you marry is a choice. *Wrong!* That's simply a rose-coloured view of the assembly line. But for a woman to choose to live with her husband *and* her female secretary while cultivating relationships with one or two others *is* a choice, because it's not a given.

So often choice means going against the grain of expectation, yet it doesn't mean simply inventing bizarre alternatives to the norm. That's merely being different for the sake of being different, which is mere reaction and ultimately a bore. Marrying an orangutan is not a choice, unless you're Michael Jackson, in which case it might be. No — choosing means considering the alternatives and perhaps creating a few for yourself.

45

So many unimaginative people think of striking out on their own as being something akin to "celebrity." *Oooh!* they say. *She's so different!* Meaning *bizarre*, rather than *unique*. Meaning Christina Aguilera or some such, with braids and a quavery voice. But that's not really different. It's just more variety. Being Christina Aguilera or Britney Spears is *not* a revolutionary act. But being Che Guevara or Harvey Milk *is*, for the very reason that leading the revolution is hard work. For another thing, you may be the first to be shot.

So for gays, choice is at the root of everything. Brad was acquainted with one young man of an exotic sexuality who found it exceedingly hard to stay with his lovers after capturing them, but even harder to give them up. More than once the young man — Justin — faced an *It's me or him!* imperative delivered by a jealousy-stung boyfriend. Eventually, he instituted a friends-first policy to his encounters, taking great pains to bring all his former and current lovers together two or three times each year.

To his delight, Justin discovered that everyone got along splendidly once they realized each was as heart-achingly beautiful as the next. There was no need to feel left out, for there would always be a succession of lovers in Justin's life, like a rotating royalty policy. Many of them even found eventual long-term happiness in pairing with each other.

Unlike Justin, however, Brad found himself alone as he entered his thirties, the decade all gay men dreaded as a threshold to diminishing dates, shrinking hairlines, expanding waistlines, and a time of swapping disco for karaoke.

Brad recalled another friend, a neurotic writer much concerned with aging. To stave off the inevitable, this friend had thrown himself a fortieth birthday party to mark the passing of his thirtieth year. That, he declared, had given him a decade of grace and moisturizing lotions, at the end of which he would hold his thirtieth birthday and declare himself thirty-something for ten more years.

Still, it wasn't age Brad feared so much as growing old alone. Watching the couple trudging over the dunes made him acutely aware of his loneliness. Something deep within him made Brad long to share his life with another, even while he realized he might spend his remaining years on his own. Who really wanted to be the partner of a secret agent for a nameless security organization? No one he'd ever met. It demanded too much.

In the first place, there was always the possibility that Brad's life might end suddenly, leaving his partner to deal with the loss. In the second place, there was an additional risk to the life of any potential partner. Often the families of such agents were easier targets than the agents themselves. Risking their lives to have sex was already daring enough for most gay men.

After joining Box 77 Brad thought he'd be fine on his own, but as the third year of loneliness wore on he found himself craving some sort of emotional intimacy. Of all the men he'd dated, there was one he'd found irresistible, someone so good and upright even Grace might have approved of him. Against all the rules, Brad had come close to disclosing his secret life to this man, a gentle, caring teacher of children with developmental problems. But after one-too-many broken engagements on Brad's part due to work complications, the man dropped him, suspecting he had commitment issues.

Brad was shattered. He did have commitment issues, but not of his own making. He just couldn't avoid the demands his work placed on him. Nor could he offer much of a home life to someone else when he might be sent off anywhere in the world at a moment's notice. It was better not to explain.

47

From that day on he'd resolved to walk a solitary path. He'd have no one to report to, no one's birthday to remember and no one to please. And on most days, that was just fine — unless he thought about it too hard.

He watched the couple disappear over the dune on their way to the beach.

THE PHONE RANG. Brad sprang up, bumping his head on an exposed beam over the loft as he grabbed the receiver.

"Hello?"

"Hi, Mr. Multiple Orgasms," the voice gushed.

Brad blushed.

"It's me, Cinder. I can't talk long. I've arranged for you to come to a *soirée* this evening at the Not-So-OK Corral. You can see for yourself what goes on there. Be sure to bring your spurs and lots and lots of cash."

Brad wrote down the address — or rather the lack of one, as Cinder said the house had no number. He'd know it when he got

JEFFREY ROUND

there from the widow's walk on the roof. It was also the oldest house on the street.

"Just a word of warning, cowboy," Cinder said. "It might be better for both of us if no one knew you were acquainted with either Ross or me. Mr. Hayden Rosengarten is one mean fairy godfather, as you'll get to see. He'd as soon shoot you as screw you out of half a million dollars, which is apparently what he did to his last business partner."

On that curious note, Cinder exhaled a breathy farewell.

7

A little old-fashioned research seemed to be in order. Brad showered, then threw on his favourite Old Navy T-shirt and a pair of hiking shorts. He stuffed a bottle of Dasani water, some passionflower suntan oil and a pair of binoculars into the bottom of his knapsack, then he stepped into his sandals, clicked his heels and set off for the dunes.

It was too early to check out the bars, but if anybody knew of Provincetown's notorious guesthouse it would likely be someone in the sandy playland at the ocean's edge. If he was lucky, he might even find a source that could tell him about the infamous Hayden Rosengarten.

Sure enough, a parade of able-bodied men strutted up and down the beach. A cautious few were fully clothed, while others wore only bathing trunks. Still others wore considerably less. Men of every age, size, and bandwidth were on the prowl. Here were circuit party boys, leathermen, cha-cha girls, divas, cowboys, twinks, opera queens, silver foxes, urban lumberjacks, preppies, young hustlers, old wolves, gym queens, muscle tykes, clones, devastatos and even a few rare beach sightings of the mysteriously intense alternativos. Together they comprised the glories of the Rainbow Nation, and then some.

Brad noted the comely muscles and shapely dicks swinging back and forth as their owners strolled like proud dog walkers exercising their frolicsome pets. As he trudged along, he had to remind himself more than once to keep his mind on the job, recalling Grace's admonition to take his work seriously.

Up ahead on an open patch of sand, an Accessories Queen with spiked orange hair and green earrings sat perched on a portable chair beneath a multicoloured umbrella. A Walkman emitted a frantic can-can from the centre of a yellow Eminem beach towel where an assortment of tanning lotions, lip balms, toe creams, CDs, a cherry cola six-pack, four paperbacks, even more towels (that somehow managed to look oddly sinister) and three pairs of sandals completed the scene. The whole thing resembled an over-earnest lawn sale.

Brad looked up and down the beach. There was no one else within fifty feet of this circus act. Maybe he was expecting overnight guests?

Whenever he found himself alone in a town, Brad always looked for the loudest, brashest person he could find. That would guarantee direct access to the latest gossip, best dish, and seamiest invitations to be had. A loud queen is an all-knowing queen, and he'd just scored a bull's eye.

A swathe of gold medallions lay nestled between a pair of hairy breasts book-ended by nipples of the pencil-eraser variety. Bracelets jangled on the man's excitable wrists and a rivulet of oil ran down his stomach to pool in the crevasse of his navel. The face was bulldog ugly. If God had created this man in His image, then Brad was in no hurry to meet that God.

The queen's eyes roamed over him. Fingers scratched suggestively at a bulbous crotch straining beneath a skimpy pair of bathing trunks. Brad smiled behind his sunglasses. I'm a whore for my job, he told himself.

"Nice day," Brad said.

"If it don't rain."

Brad scuffed at the sand.

The man patted the ground beside him suggestively. "Have a seat, studmuffin."

"Neighbourly of you," Brad replied, sitting cross-legged at his feet.

"Could get more neighbourly." The queen shifted a stubby leg in a spray of sand and coconut oil, bringing his foot to rest on Brad's crotch.

"What brings you to these parts, cutie?" he asked with a leer.

"Oh, just escaping the wrath of Isabel and Arnie."

The face contorted. "You a Democrat?"

Oops! Brad thought. Hush my big mouth!

"Nope," he said.

"Republican?"

Brad shook his head. "Nope."

"You gotta be one or the other!"

Simpleton, thought Brad. "I'm an abstainer."

"Hmpff! Never heard of them. Me, I'm a Republican and I *like* Arnold. I think he'll make a great governor."

"How's that?" Brad asked.

A ringed finger flashed imperiously. "Number one, he's rich." A second digit rose to join the first. "Number two, he's an actor. And that's what makes for a good show!"

And God help us all, thought Brad.

A fat pink tongue ran over the queen's lips. "I'm in insurance. What do you do, sweetheart?"

"Travel writer. I'm researching exotic ways to spend a weekend."

"It don't get much more exotic than this," the man said, flinging his arms out to encompass the dunes, the beach and the entire ocean view. Hands fluttered back to the hill of his stomach, hooking both thumbs under the waistband of his trunks. The leer returned with a vengeance.

"If you know what to do with it, that is ..."

Brad felt the man's toes grope his crotch with genuine agility. Not in your lifetime, he thought.

"Actually, I was thinking more in terms of exotic guesthouses. Know of any?"

"Probably more than I should. I've stayed at a few in my day. Ever been to El Rancho? There's plenty goes on all night in that little rodeo. I've been known to get pretty exotic there myself."

Brad knew about El Rancho. It was a long way from the Not-So-OK Corral in both location and reputation. He let his gaze travel suggestively down to the man's crotch.

"I was thinking more of the private part of town. I heard there was a place that costs as much for one night as most other houses cost in a month."

The man's face showed genuine surprise. "Really? How much?"
"Thousands."

"And what do I get for my 'thousands'?" he asked, running a hairy paw across his chest.

"All you can eat, snort and blow in one night," Brad answered, resisting the temptation to call him "monkey nipples."

"Book me!" he cried. "I never heard of it, but I'll try anything!"

Brad ran a finger up the inside of the man's thigh. The spandex swelled and twitched. He lifted the man's foot from his crotch and dropped it onto the sand.

"I'll let you know if I find it," Brad said, rising.

"Why, you're nothing but a cocktease!" the queen snarled.

Here, it seemed, was the inverse corollary to his father's advice on good looks and sincerity: if you want someone to go away, disingenuousness works best.

Brad turned back. "I guess I'm just an actor at heart. I could run your country for you, but I can't be sincere for the life of me."

HE LINGERED ON the beach for another hour, asking every man he met about the mysterious guesthouse. Most of them were genuinely friendly and he didn't even need to flirt to start a conversation. Knowing how gay men loved their gossip, however, he was amazed to discover that no one had heard of it. Obviously, Brad thought, it's as exclusive as it's meant to be. Probably why it's successful.

He sat on a piece of driftwood and brought out his binoculars, scanning the beach. The passing parade of men kept its eyes peeled for Destiny. Like most children, and Blanche DuBois at the end of her tether, gay men still believed in Magic. They were all waiting for the one magnificent man who would come to claim them and transform their lives from a shabby beach shack into a seaside palazzo complete with interior fountains, marble mantelpieces, perfect brunch guests and a history that included 'the day Madonna came to dinner.' On straight beaches, where dreams are downplayed, they're mostly just waiting for lunch and the next beer.

Brad caught a flash atop one of the dunes. He focused the lenses and, to his surprise, saw a pair of binoculars trained on him. Right, he thought. Now I'm someone else's prey.

He watched the glasses watching him. After a moment, their owner laid them down on the sand. Brad could make out a lithe young man in a baseball cap sitting cross-legged on top of the dune.

Brad turned back to the shoreline and continued to scan with his binoculars. The whole time he felt the hair on his neck rise with the presence from above. He turned and looked back. The figure sat there, arms outstretched and palms turned upward as though waiting for rain. The brim of the boy's cap obscured his face.

Brad stood and made his way toward the dune. He scrambled upwards, stumbling now and then as the sand shifted and pulled him back down. Once he fell into a thorny bush and scratched his leg, but he brushed himself off and kept climbing till he reached the top and stood before the figure whose position hadn't changed.

The young man sat in a contemplative pose, head cocked toward the beach and the brim of his cap pulled way down. He was completely and splendidly naked, right down to the bare chest that had never felt a razor in its life and the notable dick resting on the sand between his legs. The tattooed outline of a horse's head embellished his trim stomach.

Whoa! Now here's a guy I could really go for, Bradford thought. Research be damned!

"Hi," he said, the beginning of an erection tenting his shorts. "I noticed you staring at me from up here." There was no response from the seated figure. Brad suddenly felt awkward, aware that he was now the one staring. "I like your ... tattoo."

"You're bleeding," the young man said.

That's certainly an original opener, thought Brad. He looked down. Sure enough, his calves and shins were smeared with blood where he'd been scratched by the thorns.

"Wow, I didn't notice. Thanks."

"No problem."

"So what brings you to these parts?" Brad ventured, extending a hand.

The head lifted till he could see the boy's face. An aquamarine eye caught his own. "Hello, Bradford."

Brad felt his erection subside.

55

"Ah, hi ..."

"It's Zach," he said. "I guess you've forgotten."

"Uh, sorry, I ..."

"Never phoned back?"

Brad felt anger surge where a moment before there'd been only simple straightforward lust.

"You told me you had a boyfriend!"

"I told you I was leaving him."

"You weren't fast enough."

"I dropped him the next day."

"Too late!"

Zach continued looking up at him. "You don't have much patience, do you?"

"I don't go in for serial monogamists."

Zach sighed. "I fell in love with you. What do you want me to do?"

Brad stepped back. "Nothing. Don't do anything. Just ... stop following me."

Zach's face darkened. "Just because you fucked me once and I said it was the best thing that ever happened to me doesn't mean I'm following you. I come to Provincetown every year at precisely this time, so get over yourself like I get over myself every time I think about you."

"Whoa! Slow down there, little buckaroo. I'm sorry for accusing you of following me. I'm sorry we ever met, in fact. Though if you recall, that was *your* doing. Now if you'll excuse me, I have a lunch date."

With that he turned and marched along the dunes toward town, getting stuck in the marsh once before looking back to see that Zach was no longer watching.

8

The morning progressed into a languid afternoon. Brad forgot about the unpleasant encounter with Zach. In town, boys in shorts and T-shirts walked hand-in-hand along the streets. As he passed one attractive couple, Brad unconsciously squared his shoulders and thrust out his chest. The shorter one turned to whistle at him. Brad looked back in time to see the boy being dragged off by his boyfriend.

He stopped for lunch on Commercial Street. In a waterfront café, he found himself eye-to-eye with a mesmerizing gaze. A charismatic man with a shaved head gazed at him from a poster. Brad recalled his father's earliest bit of advice: *Always stop to enjoy a beautiful view.*

The face was arresting: from the distinguished brow and memorable cheekbones, to the full lips and hypnotic eyes that burned holes in the casual onlooker. He could have been the love child of Jackie Chan and Vin Diesel.

According to the poster, the man was a visiting Tibetan dignitary closely associated with the Dalai Lama. Brad smiled and thought of Ross's rather sudden conversion. Obviously, there was something to Buddhism after all!

After lunch the first stop on Brad's itinerary was Purgatory, the downstairs bar at the famed Gifford House. With any luck he might uncover something useful about Perry, the former employee who Cinder claimed had left the Not-So-OK Corral after an argument with Ross. Sometimes a bit of smoldering rivalry was all it took to spark a jealous rage that could end in murder. It happened all the time between husbands and wives. It might occur just as easily between two hot men flirting with the same boss.

Gifford House bristled with sex appeal as Brad approached. A circuit party crowd lingered on the outside deck, hanging over the railing to watch new arrivals coming up the hill. Brad marvelled at the homing instinct that brought so many delightful, provocative men to places like this. Like him, they'd all ventured a long way to reach this end-of-the-line seaside resort.

To a gay man, Provincetown wasn't so much a geographical destination as a psychosexual one. Each had already made a difficult inner journey to arrive at this place. To get here, they had tested and spread their wings in nondescript little clubs and taverns all across the continent, listening for that inner voice to answer the rainbow's call. It was the same voice that spoke to all gay men, one patient syllable at a time, until they were ready to hear it. It began with a secret thrill every time the handsome class president in high school passed you in the halls, or when you felt that inexplicable urge to attend the homecoming game — despite how much you hated football — so you might cheer extra hard for the devastating fullback as he scored a touchdown.

Look! it commanded. *Feel!* In time it progressed to full sentences: *It's all right to touch. Do you like this? It's called pleasure!* Only years later did it give rise to the understanding you'd felt all along but simply hadn't realized at the time: the class president had secretly yearned for the hunky fullback until that fateful camping trip and the first drunken *bonk!* that would resound forever in their imaginations, the unassailable love waiting beneath the palms at the end of the mind.

At some point every man encounters the spectre of these youthful lovers, though never fully measuring up to their ghostly perfection. We live in a world of shadows, Brad thought, recalling desires of his own that he'd long ignored. And then one day, to no one's surprise but yours, you found yourself walking entirely uncloseted and without a second glance over your shoulder into a bar in Provincetown, of all places! The caterpillar's transformation to a butterfly was complete.

Brad made his way through the Porchside Bar toward the indoor stairway which a sign declared the entrance to Purgatory. In a far corner, Patsy Cline crooned an off-hours set. She would serve as his Beatrice, Brad decided, as he descended to the darkened basement.

Downstairs, a handful of men stood watching a washed-out porn video. Desire lingered in the shadows, afraid to speak its name but unable to leave. Brad's gaze travelled across the room to a bar with one of the sexiest men he'd ever seen. With his dark shaggy hair and puppy-dog eyes, wearing only a pair of coveralls that set off his V-shaped chest and sculpted shoulders, he could have been a poster boy for the world's most elite gym.

Brad winced at the sight. He hadn't been to the gym in a week. He was half convinced his muscles would begin to lose their tone in another day or two at most.

He wandered over to the bar and took a seat. The bartender acknowledged him with a friendly nod as he polished a glass.

"What's your pleasure, friend?"

A night in your arms, Brad thought. "A gin and tonic, please."

"One G and T, coming up."

Brad watched the languorous muscles stretch and flex as the bartender prepared his drink. All those hours in the gym just to be able to look like that when you poured booze, he mused. But it was worth it!

The bartender set a glass filled to the brim in front of him.

That's a nice tall drink, Brad thought. Just like you.

"Run you a tab?"

Brad's eyes traced a vein along the man's forearm, across his shoulder and neck, right up to that winsome face. He could stay there all night watching him move from one side of the bar to the other for as long as he could think of things to order. Perfection was so hard to resist.

"I'd better pay up now," he said, handing over a bill. "I'm not the sticking-around type."

The bartender gave a soft laugh. "I've been married to you, then. Several times, in fact."

Brad watched him turn and glide over to the register where he leaned forward to deposit the bill, his sculpted butt protruding invitingly. That ass, Brad thought, is a work of art.

The bartender felt Brad's eyes on him. He turned with a smile. There was something about him that reminded Brad of Ross, an amiable playfulness that said, *Come closer — but not too close!* He sensed something wounded beneath the friendly surface. He'd seen that look before. He was pretty sure he could guess what it was.

Nimble fingers laid his change out on the bar. Brad pushed it back. "It's yours," he said.

"Thanks!" The barkeep flashed a devastating smile. "Name's Perry, by the way."

Bingo! This was the man Cinder had mentioned.

"Frank," Brad said. They shook.

"You in town for a few days, Frank?"

"A week or so."

Brad picked up the glass and sipped. It lay just on the wry side of jet fuel.

"Whew!" he said. "Can I get a little tonic to go with that gin, Perry?"

Perry picked up the drink and returned it only slightly watered down.

"Funny, you don't look like the easy-over type," he said.

Sex appeal in spades, Brad thought. "Depends who's doing the flipping," he said with a wink. "But I don't want to kill the night before it's begun. Truth is, I don't take many vacations and I like to remember them when I'm done."

"Where are you from, Frank?"

"Little town up north. Nothing to brag about. Haven't been back for a while."

Perry shrugged. "I hear you. We're all escaping something, and it's usually the past."

"Here's to escape!" Brad said, raising his glass.

"What do you do, Frank?"

"Inventor," Brad answered, knowing how it loosened people's tongues when he gave himself an interesting profession.

"Cool!"

Their conversation was interrupted by the approach of another customer, a baby-faced cowboy in training. The young man had that small-town gay-boy-becoming-a-man look of being slightly unsure how things worked. He could be staying at Romeo's Guesthouse right now, Brad thought, enjoying his first time ever in the gayest place on earth.

The boy stared at Brad and the bartender in turn. Perry popped the top off a beer and pushed it along the bar, taking his cash without any interest. The boy's open face said he knew what he wanted but was unsure how to get it. He drank and wiped the foam from his mouth with the back of his hand.

I'll bet he's a Hoosier, Brad thought, remembering a fond encounter with an Indiana native and his lasso one winter's night.

The boy's gaze got stuck on Perry as he turned to go back to the far end of the room. Every few feet he looked over his shoulder to see if the handsome bartender would return his attention.

"Beautiful kid," Brad offered when he'd gone.

Perry smirked. "You can have him. I've had my fill of beautiful young men."

"I guess it's pretty much the same thing day in and day out around here," Brad said. "One beautiful guy after another."

"You got that right," Perry replied.

"I've met a few of them myself," Brad said. "In fact, the last time I was in town I had my heart broken by one of the best. Some guy who said he lived here, actually."

Perry's face showed interest. "Yeah? Who was that? I might know him. You get to know everybody after awhile. There aren't that many of us townies."

Brad frowned. "You'd think I could remember his name, but after he dumped me I tried hard to forget it."

Perry laughed. "That bad, huh?"

Brad shook his head. "Naw, it's not coming to me. All I

remember is that he worked at some swank guesthouse out near the dunes."

Perry's eyes flickered. "Lotta guesthouses in town," he said with a shrug.

"Yeah, but this one was special. It had no address."

Perry's ears twitched, as though he'd heard something at a distance.

"Ever hear of a really elite place out by the dunes?"

Perry frowned. "As I said, there're a lot of different places in town. It could be any one of them."

"Actually, I think I remember the guy's name ... Ross Something-or-other."

Perry looked blankly at him.

"Ring any bells?"

"Nah," Perry said, picking up a glass and retrieving his dry cloth.

Liar, Brad thought.

Perry looked him in the eye. "What did you say you did again?"

"Inventor."

"Yeah, right," he said, returning to the far end of the bar. "No, I never heard of a guy named Ross who worked at any guest-house here."

"Well, no matter," Brad said with a smile. "I've had my heart broken by better men than him."

After that, the handsome barkeep found one excuse after another to avoid talking. Brad could see he was getting nowhere, so he downed his drink and left.

9

Brad stopped in at the police station. Tom Nava sat with his feet up on the desk, eyes hidden behind mirrored sunglasses. He was dressed like a motorcycle cop, the kind some men fantasized would stop them for speeding out on some deserted road and teach them a lesson they'd never forget. And never want to.

Nava stirred and turned his head at Brad's entrance.

"Good afternoon, Officer Nava," Brad said, watching himself approach in the cop's lenses.

Nava nodded. "Mr. Fairfax. To what do I owe the pleasure?"

Brad smiled. Take it slow, he reminded himself. Cops were always looking out for what you didn't tell them.

"I haven't been able to sleep after what happened the other night. I'm curious to hear who the boy was or if you've learned anything about him. I thought it might give me some peace of mind."

The cop lifted his feet from the desk and stood with the sleekness of a cat. His chest strained the fabric of his uniform. His shoulders were massive, the waistline narrow, like an oversized Tom of Finland doll. A holster strapped to his belt displayed the handle of a hefty gun. The man was dressed to kill in more ways than one.

"There's not much to tell," Nava said. "Boy's name was James Shephard. He'd been in town all summer doing odd jobs. Bit of a wanderer, from what I gather. We tracked down some people who knew him from another city."

Brad shook his head. "A real shame, a young kid like that."

Nava grunted. "It happens. People think it's just water, but the ocean isn't the same as a swimming pool. The tide can play tricks with you. It's hard to know what he was doing out there on the dunes at night. Just a guess, but I'd say he was cruising. We found his clothes about a half-mile up the beach."

65

"You think he was looking for sex?"

Nava looked him over before answering. "That would be my guess. Lotta moral degenerates around this town," he said.

"Why 'degenerates'?"

The cop snorted. "It's one thing to be gay; it's another to fuck anywhere at random."

"The dunes after dark is hardly random," Brad said with a shrug. "But I guess you'd need to understand the mind of a gay man."

"I *am* a gay man," Nava said.

Whoa! thought Brad. "Then you should understand the urge to explore the sexual side of things."

Nava removed his sunglasses and Brad caught his powerful eyes in the light for the first time.

"I may be gay," Nava replied, "but I'm not a moral degenerate."

So you've got a narrow personality range and a penchant for being a power broker, Bradford thought. *Big deal!* Being unimaginative doesn't make you morally superior.

"I guess you don't need to live your life in full colour, like some men," Brad said.

The cop stared at him for a moment and then laughed. "Do I look beige?" he asked, and suddenly Brad had to laugh as well.

Brad could see Nava wasn't the type to avoid a fight, but he was probably smart enough to avoid starting one. He could imagine him as a boy trying to make it in white America, full of resentment and envy. As an outcast, you sometimes tried harder than others did. Brad could relate. As a ward of the state, his own life had been shattered into a thousand pieces. Whatever he'd had as a child of a single parent had been lost completely when his father died. Ever since then his journey had been to find those pieces and put himself together again.

Where others in his situation might just let everything go, thinking it hopeless, Brad persevered. Meanwhile, the courts quibbled over the contents of his father's will, stealing the greater part of it. When Brad turned eighteen they awarded him the crumbs, like a discharged prisoner being handed his belongings in a bag at the end of his sentence. He knew he didn't have a lifetime of funds, and decided to make do with what he had. He'd enrolled in journalism school and in four years had the makings of a career. That had stood him in good stead till Grace intervened and spun his life in a whole new direction.

"Were there any drugs in his system?" Brad asked.

Nava stared at him. "Why?"

"I didn't get much of a chance to talk to you last night ..."

"You told me what I needed to know."

"But I didn't tell you everything. Does the name Ross Pretty mean anything to you?"

Nava's eyes narrowed. "Yes, it does. I was the investigating officer on that one, too. Pretty died of an overdose of ecstasy."

"I just wondered if the deaths could be related."

"I doubt it. This kid didn't OD — he drowned. There were trace amounts of THC in his system, which means he probably smoked up sometime in the last week. But he wasn't on anything when he died."

Brad felt deflated. He'd hoped to discover some similarity, no matter how small, between the two deaths.

"What do you know about Pretty?" Nava asked.

"I've come to claim his body."

"You his lover?"

"No." Brad shook his head. "I was once, but that was years ago. He gave me power of attorney when we split up. That's why I'm in P-Town. But a little bird whispered in my ear that his death might not be accidental."

Nava cocked an eyebrow at him. "How so?"

Bradford told him what Cinder had said regarding the circumstances of Ross's death.

"We know about Rosengarten," Nava said scornfully. "He's a real piece of work. One day he'll cross a line and get himself arrested. He just hasn't come close enough yet."

Brad wondered what Nava would think if he told him he was going to Rosengarten's guesthouse that evening. He decided against it.

"In any case," Nava said, "I can't get too excited by the accusations of a professional drag queen. I've got enough to keep me busy making sure the tourists don't do things to get themselves killed. We've also got a category five hurricane headed up the coast and I'm trying to get prepared in case it hits."

Something occurred to Brad. "Where was Ross's body found?"

"In his apartment at the east end of Commercial. He was slumped over a shrine of some sort in his bedroom. Lot of incense and orange peels scattered on a board propped up on a stack of bricks."

Brad nodded. "Ross was a Buddhist," he said.

"In any case, the Ross Pretty investigation is officially closed. I don't see any reason to reopen it."

"Who told you to look for Ross's body?"

"A call came through to the office."

"Scratchy, ragged voice?"

"Yeah. That's right. Why?"

"That was the same person who called me at home. Sounds like somebody knew something. I'd say you might want to check into it a little more."

BACK AT HIS guesthouse, Brad phoned Grace to let her in on the strange turn of events. The operator put him through immediately.

"Good to hear from you, Red," she said.

He gave a rundown of the happenings of the previous two days, beginning with his discovery of James Shephard's body, Cinder's unexpected revelation about Ross and his intention to visit the mysterious guesthouse that evening.

"I thought you were attending a family funeral," Grace broke in.

"Ross *was* family to me," he said defensively. "He was the closest thing I had to a brother."

This much was true and it was all in his records. Brad was pretty sure Grace knew about his past, but she'd allowed him to come to Provincetown regardless. Still, she could have jumped all over him for lying if she'd wanted to.

Grace drew a breath. "I don't know how you do it, Red, but you always seem to end up where the shit flies."

"If it's all right with you, I'd like to stay here another day or two. My gut tells me these deaths are connected."

"I might be able to let you stay a little longer than that."

"You mean I'm not going to New York?"

Brad held his breath. As far as he was concerned, New York was less habitable than the dark side of the moon, though he hesitated to admit this to his gay acquaintances. New York was the litmus test of gay style, but even a few minutes in the town of towns assaulted his senses and left him reeling.

Everyone he knew who moved to New York came back changed beyond recognition, if they came back at all. One friend, a soft-spoken lesbian named Sally, moved to Manhattan to study acting. In a month, she was having phone conversations at the top of her voice. Within two months, she was uttering every thought that passed through her head. She'd completely lost her subtext.

On a good day, Brad simply said New York didn't work for him. On a bad day, he thought of it as the Calcutta of the West. In actual fact, he didn't believe New York worked for anybody apart from a handful of snobbish culture queens and one know-it-all author of gay bedtime stories and opera quiz books who was so unpleasant he had to live there because he'd have been murdered anywhere else. If *they* didn't live in New York, there'd be no one left apart from a colony of immigrants who never made it upstate and a tribe of singer-actors straight off the farm who didn't know any better.

The first time Brad had been assigned to New York for a two-month stint, he pleaded with Grace to take him off the case.

"Why?" she'd demanded.

"It's like that, uh, movie with Judy Garland?" he began, unsure how familiar the reference was outside of Gay. "And she goes to this place that everyone says is the most fantastic place ..."

"Are you talking about *The Wizard of Oz?*"

"Yes! You know it?"

Grace grunted. "Doesn't everyone?"

"Well, anyway ... by the time she gets there she's decided she hates it. It doesn't work for her, you see. Just like it doesn't work for me."

"Oz?"

"New York."

"Oh, I see. An analogy."

"Anyway ... that's how I feel about it. A lot of fake wizards hiding behind curtains, when we all have what we need already ..."

"'And there's no place like home, there's no place like home ...'"

Brad was stunned into silence.

"Shall I change your code name to Dorothy?" Grace asked.

"If you'd like to be Aunty Em."

"Fine, but no dice. You're going."

Luck was with him this time, however. Grace had decided to keep him on the coast.

"I know how much you like the Cape. For now, stay where you are and see what you can dig up. Something may develop."

"Will do. And Grace ... ?"

"Yes, Red?"

Once again Brad found himself wondering who in the world this person was with whom he'd shared such intimate details of his life.

"Thanks ... for the flowers."

"You're welcome. By the way, how much is that visit to the guesthouse going to cost us?"

"Five thousand."

"Egad! Well, you'd better be extra careful. At that rate, I can't afford to send you flowers personally if anything should happen to you."

10

Brad stared over his laptop toward the dunes. He'd struck out with his earlier attempt to get information on Rosengarten and his guesthouse. Even the police didn't seem overly concerned about the place. Maybe he needed to dig a little deeper. He wondered if the house itself might be the key to whatever was going on.

Finding information about a specific address on the Internet was a crapshoot, he knew, but finding information on a specific house *without* an address might be just about impossible. He looked up "Historic P-Town Houses." Several thousand sites came up immediately. He breezed through a dozen without finding anything useful. He needed a new strategy. What had Cinder said? That it was *really old.* Of course, to a drag queen that could mean just about anything.

He typed "Original P-Town Houses." That brought up considerably more sites — in fact, there were far more sites than there were houses in Provincetown. He scrolled through a number of entries. Articles from the *Times*, *Fodor's*, and various travel guides topped the list. Halfway down the third page he found a site telling how in the early-1800s some of the houses had been rowed across the harbour from Long Point back when the town's inhabitants were seamen who followed the schools of fish almost literally. Because of their tendency to change locations, one newspaper of the day declared the houses "subject to the most unnatural of laws, not being anchored to any land."

Brad laughed out loud. It was probably the first reference to anything unusual about a place that was in time to become noted for the unusual. Photographs showed a few of the original houses still in existence. What else had Cinder said? That it sat on the crest of a hill north of Bradford Street in the east end. It also had a widow's walk.

He narrowed it down to three places, all located at the crest of a hill. One house had originally been a storage place for huge blocks of ice cut in winter and sold in summer to preserve the season's catch. It had been dubbed "The Ice House." Brad clicked on the thumbnail print and watched it size itself into view. There was a widow's walk!

The Ice House had a colourful history, having been variously a tavern, an inn and a popular whorehouse where two presidents were rumoured to have visited. By the mid-1800s, the house had become the basis of underground railroad operations on the Cape, providing an escape route for runaway slaves. A series of double closets were employed to hide escapees from southern marshals who came looking for them. Dozens of escaped slaves were hidden there before being shipped north through Maine and on to Nova Scotia. Near the end of the War Between the States the house mysteriously burned one cold winter night, killing six runaways and four members of the owner's family.

Brad went back to the search engine and typed in "Ice House, P-Town." It yielded two results. The first simply gave a brief mention of the house. The second site offered a more detailed account of its history. In 1870, an eccentric entrepreneur named

Jeb Lacey had rebuilt the Ice House for his mother's retirement home. A wood exterior was scored with chisels to make it resemble stone and then overlaid with paint and plaster to give it a New York brownstone look. Lacey had the interior decorated with exotic wallpaper from places as far away as Paris and China. Tin ceilings and marble fireplaces were installed throughout. The second floor was famed for housing a fossil display and a collection of Arctic memorabilia from one Admiral Donald MacMillan.

74

Lacey did everything to make his mother comfortable while he plied the lumber trade up and down the New England coast. He had a cupola and a widow's walk built for her to watch his schooners sailing in and out of the harbour. By the time it was finished, the house was so different from the rest of Provincetown that it was ridiculed by the townspeople. To make things worse, Lacey's mother came to be known for her strange attire, her big-city affectations and the peacocks tut-tutting through her gardens. Both she and the house were shunned.

Jeb's visits to sea grew longer. Ignored by the locals and left alone for months at a time, Maud Lacey retreated to her cupola with its superior view of the harbour. One day she was found pacing the widow's walk, emaciated and dressed in peacock feathers, mumbling as she stared out over the harbour. Jeb had his mother hospitalized, never to return to her home.

After her death in 1901, there were frequent reports of strange occurrences and unusual noises around the house. Locals of the time believed her ghost haunted the place. Several claimed to have seen a woman's figure stalking the widow's walk on stormy nights. Others suggested it was Jeb Lacey, also gone mad, obsessively restaging his mother's weary vigil like an early Norman Bates.

Lacey died a reclusive bachelor in 1925 and the property changed hands once again. A genteel couple ran it as a boarding house for the elderly. While not particularly profitable as a rest home, the house did exceptionally well as a liquor smuggling operation during Prohibition. The famed slave closets, faithfully reinstated by Lacey, proved useful for hiding contraband as it became a safe house once more.

Another quarter of a century passed. In the 1950s, a wealthy Bostonian named George Taft purchased the property. While Taft had no need to open his doors for economic reasons, he nevertheless ran his bed and breakfast as part of a group nicknamed The Triple L or *Lovely Landlady's League.* For the third time in its history the Ice House became a different kind of safe house, providing refuge to the emerging community of homosexuals who had begun to discover P-Town in earnest. It wasn't long before the Ice House became renowned as one of the first gay-owned guesthouses on the Cape.

Taft ran it until his death in 1976 at the hands of a churlish houseboy who drowned his employer in a goldfish pond in the adjacent gardens during a fit of pique over a banished disco record. At that point the house went to two men from New Orleans who saw it as their dream home. They prospered until the dream turned to a nightmare during the HIV epidemic. Both owners died a month apart in 1986.

After that, the house disappeared entirely from the town annals. It might have been burned to the ground a second time and never rebuilt. No mention of it was to be found from that date till the present, as though a conspiracy of silence had successfully concealed its notoriety.

Bradford closed his laptop and sat back. The house's history was certainly fascinating. But why had it disappeared for the last seventeen years? Maybe he'd find out on his intended visit that evening.

He headed to the bathroom, peeling off his clothes and leaving them in a heap on the floor. He showered and re-emerged from the steam, wrapping a towel around his waist. Next, he shaved and dressed in Bergdorf Goodman chic, glad he'd brought his jacket, and taking care to insert false business cards into his wallet.

Done, he turned to the mirror. The results met with his approval. *If you're going to walk with the lions,* he told himself, *you have to dress like one!* It was the sort of thing his father might have said.

It was a warm September evening as Bradford Fairfax made his way along Bradford Street, Provincetown's *other* thoroughfare. It always made him grin to stride along the road that bore his name. *Yes, they named it after me*, he could hear himself teasing Ross way back when.

Silence and darkness reigned as he approached this part of town. Most of the homes were shuttered, abandoned for the season. Here and there, lights gleamed from cheery windows where small gatherings of men prepared dinner and amused themselves with impassioned tales of adventures in the dunes, notable fashion faux pas sightings and other such fancies as young men are prone to.

Brad felt a pang of longing. He missed the physical togetherness that comrades brought, that sense of having a *family* of friends. How he'd love to arrive at such a house bearing a favourite bottle of wine, throw open the door and enter the fold to cries of, *Here he is at last!* from his pals gathered round the table.

That, at the very least, should have been his due as a card-carrying member of Gay, the rightful legacy of every post-Stonewall queer. It was for this very sense of belonging that each gay man stormed his own inner Bastille, breaking down the barricades for liberty and love. But in his line of work, Brad knew, he'd never achieve anything remotely like that. He'd have to be content to enjoy a limited acquaintance with his own kind at a discreet distance.

While others his age were off having romantic adventures, he'd been busy learning surreptitious surveillance techniques. When friends boasted of salacious weekends in Palm Springs with Mr. Leather USA or of renting a villa in Capri next to a renowned Met opera conductor and his guest, the tenor *du jour*, Bradford had been getting briefed on the latest spying methods. His friends would have been astonished to discover that not only could he have told them what they did in their bedrooms at night, but also what they'd cooked for breakfast and whom they'd had for lunch. When they were learning to speak Gay, he was off studying Russian. "Could you *just!*" they cooed. "Abso-*lu-lu!* How too-too de-*lish!*" When asked what he'd been up to, Brad would wink and say, "Yah schpi*on.*" *I'm a spy.* It was all in the syntax.

In the midst of his regret, he stopped and looked around. He'd arrived at a neighbourhood that was nearly as dark as the unlit coast. The houses on either side of the road seemed little more than derelict fishing shacks. It was odd, but he couldn't recall ever having been in this area of town before. Overgrown hedges obscured street signs as the wind moaned in the trees.

As Brad stepped from the curb a car raced silently toward him. The vehicle appeared so suddenly that he barely had time to register the danger. An outstretched arm hauled him to safety at the last second. Brad fell to the curb as the car screeched around the corner, vanishing as quickly as it appeared. Looking up in astonishment, he saw a cowgirl peering at him through a pair of rhinestone-encrusted cat's eye glasses. She shook her head.

"Let me guess — you're not from here, are you?"

"N-no," he stammered.

She helped him to his feet. "You gotta be more careful, honey. They'll mow you down like wheat around here."

"Wow," he said, looking down at his saviour, who stood barely five feet tall. "Thanks for being on the ball."

"You're lucky I was," she agreed. "Name's Big Ruby."

"Bradford Fairfax." He brushed the dirt from his pants.

"Well, Bradford, you sure don't wanna end up dead on Bradford Street, now do ya?" she chuckled. "Why are you wandering around in the dark?"

"I'm looking for a guesthouse. Apparently it's got no name or number. Do you know of it?"

Even in the dark he could make out Big Ruby's scowl. "I know it!" she snapped. "Nothing but trouble and evil-minded types go there. If you're one of them, I'm sorry I saved yer skin. I won't bother next time."

Figures, thought Brad. If you want to hear about bad news in the community, a politically correct lesbian will know about it miles ahead of any gay man.

"What's so bad about it?" he asked.

"I told you. Nothing but rich, troublemaking scum goes there. The bastard who runs it ... well, I got no words for him."

Brad's gut instinct said he could trust Ruby.

"I'm trying to find out what happened to a friend of mine

who works there. Or at least he used to, until he ended up dead a couple of nights ago."

He could feel Big Ruby soften.

"I'm sorry you lost your friend," she said. "But if I were you, I'd stay far away from Hayden Rosengarten and his *guest*house."

There was that name again.

Ruby shook her head. "You could end up the same way, if you're not careful."

Brad remembered Cinder's warning. "You make him sound pretty awful," he said.

"If I ever got my hands on him, I'd kill him myself. That'd be one progressive step for humanity."

"Sounds pretty drastic," Brad said.

"Sometimes drastic is what's needed," she said ominously. "And I can be drastic when I need to be."

Brad wondered if she really meant what she said. "Well, thank you again," he said, dusting off his clothes. "I'll keep that in mind, but I've got to get into that house and see what I can find out."

"I'm telling you, honey, it's nothing but trouble!" She paused for a moment, considering. "But if you're set on finding it, take the next right. You'll come across the place at the top of the rise. Big scary-looking place. You can't see it from the road because of the belladonna hedge, but it's right there if you know where to look."

"Thanks."

"Honey, if you ever need us, the galfriend and I run Coffee Joe's on Commercial Street."

"I know it!"

"Just ask anyone. They all know me. You take care of yourself now."

Brad watched Ruby walk around the corner and out of sight.

11

Bradford turned right and found himself at the foot of a hill. He trudged upward into a darkness thick enough to carve with a knife. As he got closer, he saw that Big Ruby had been right. Even lit up, the house was impossible to see from the road.

An iron gate hemmed the yard in behind a thick hedge. *Belladonna.* From his training, Brad recognized the flowers and black berries also known as the Devil's cherries. A couple could make a man deliriously happy. A few more would send him on a permanent trip around the universe. Even the leaves and roots of this plant were dangerous to touch.

In the distance, the dunes were a shadowy moonscape. From far off came the soft shushing of waves. Brad peered through the hedge. The house seemed to float eerily above the horizon as though it might cut loose from its moorings and drift off into the night. Though that might not be all that unlikely, he thought, given the "unnatural" history of P-Town's houses.

Whatever the myth of it, he emerged from behind the hedge now and stood face-to-face with the actuality. The house wasn't spectacularly large or imposing, just forbiddingly self-confident. Perched high atop was the widow's walk. With a pair of high-powered binoculars it would afford a good view of the entire town. He wondered if there might be some reason the present owner required such a feature.

Brad was conscious of eyes trained on him — security-camera eyes. He rang the bell and a gate clicked open. A hand-lettered sign stood off to one side of the walk. He'd expected to see a friendly WELCOME or even the name of the guesthouse. Instead, it read forbiddingly: NO DOGS OR BULLDYKES IN THE GARDEN. *Yikes!* No wonder Big Ruby hated him.

As he reached the porch the front door opened and a tall, thin man with baleful eyes towered over him: it was Ichabod Crane crossed with Jack Nicholson.

"Good evening," Brad said, extending his business card. "Sebastian O'Shaughnessy."

"We've been expecting you, Mr. O'Shaughnessy," the man replied, his lips curling into a smile that looked about as welcoming as a crack in the sidewalk.

Ichabod stood flanked by two Dobermanesque bodyguards in black leather and gleaming silver studs. He accepted the five crisp thousand dollar bills Brad proffered under the wary eyes of the watchdogs. *No credit cards, no strings attached.* That was how Cinder had put it. That, apparently, was the way they liked things here.

A massive chandelier twinkled above a grand staircase whose polished oak railings swept upwards and out of sight. The house had probably looked much the same a hundred and fifty years earlier. A portrait of a woman with bulging eyes and red hair piled high on her head glared down at him. It was Maud Lacey, he knew, without needing to ask.

The thin man rang a hand bell and a faun with blond curls appeared from out of nowhere.

"Quentin, please see Mr. O'Shaughnessy to his room," Ichabod commanded.

Brad followed the boy to a private room with a four-poster bed. His young escort opened the mirrored doors of an armoire and retrieved a vermilion dressing gown trimmed in gold. Deft hands helped Brad out of his jacket and into the robe. He could appear downstairs for dinner anytime after ten o'clock, Quentin said. Brad checked his watch. It was just past nine.

"Will there be anything else, Mr. O'Shaughnessy?"

Brad was tempted to ask if he could knot a cherry stem with his tongue. He handed the boy a tip. "No, that will be all."

The boy brightened. "I'm at your service all night," he said in a way that made Brad blush. "If you need anything, don't be afraid to ask. Your pleasure is my pleasure, sir."

With Quentin gone, Brad turned to the room and proceeded to open all the drawers and closets one at a time. He discovered an assortment of creams, lotions, potions, powders, body scrubs, lubricating jellies in a variety of flavours, an artfully arranged collection of condoms presented in order of size, colour and texture, as well as leather harnesses, rubber body suits, whips, clamps, chains, veils, eye patches, boots, straps and hoods, plus a variety of ingenious-looking instruments of arcane purpose. It was a veritable arsenal of kink.

Brad stood before the mirror. He'd already decided Mr. Sebastian O'Shaughnessy would be a casual smoker. He reached into his pocket, withdrew a cigarette from an elegant case and lit up.

"Good evening, Mr. O'Shaughnessy," he intoned in a deep voice, taking in his reflection from different angles.

"And what is it you do, Mr. O'Shaughnessy?"

He watched himself ponder the question as he exhaled a wreath of smoke.

"Why, I'm a forensic accountant," he replied. "And you, sir?"

He waited till he was convinced of his new identity and then went out into the hall. From somewhere nearby came a stifled whimper. Curious, he tried one door after another, but found them all locked. He put his ear to a final door and heard the sound again. It was impossible to tell whether it was a whimper of pain or pleasure. It might have been someone in the throes of a drug overdose like the one that had killed Ross. It might also have been the sound of a ritualistic sexual fantasy being enacted under the baroque rules of gay S & M.

Brad imagined two queens engaging in a fierce battle of style and one-upmanship: "Oh," says the first queen, hands-on-hip Bette Davis-style. "You haven't seen *Hairspray, The Musical?*" The effect on the rival queen would be as if she'd arrived at cocktail hour smelling like a barnyard, only to have her worst enemy point this out to everyone. "What do you mean, you haven't seen it?" Brad imagined the aggressor hurling at his hapless victim, the submissive M quivering at each harsh syllable. "What are you waiting for — the *book?*" cries the sadistic S. "Wherever did you get that dress — at a McDonald's jumble sale?" For *shame!* And then comes the *coup de grâce:* "Who does your hair — Posturpedic?" At which the M would crumble.

Coarse? Crude? Devastating? Yes, yes, and yes again. But such tactics, Brad knew, are not designed merely to intimidate and ridicule, crush and destroy. In fact, there are clues for those who will see. One has only to observe the clothing: is the intimidating S any more smartly dressed than his victim, the M? *No!* In fact, it might even be seen that a Wal-Mart queen is abusing one attired in perfect Bloomingdale's *couture*. So who is really in charge? Who is the victim and who the perpetrator? Who is abusing whom and why? The answers might surprise. But far from blaming the victim for the crime being visited upon him, it may even be observed that there is no crime at all.

For herein lies the mystery, the subtle interchange of need that exists between the bull and the flag, between the dancer and the dance. For gay S & M, as Bradford knew, is not private play so much as public *dis*play. Here is role-playing as formal as anything to be found in Kabuki. It's not that it's fake — it's stylized! It's über-gay!

With this in mind, Brad braced himself as he reached out and turned the handle. Through the crack he watched a scrawny gnome staring in a mirror. The man could have been an aged elf, one of Santa's best, but for his attire: a black leather harness and a gold snake bracelet coiled around his biceps.

The elf gazed at his reflection and sniffed. Perplexed, Brad watched him flex a sinewy muscle. The snake quivered slightly before falling to his wrist as the man relaxed his arm. He saw Bradford in the mirror and shook his head.

"This was once the body of a god," he said. "But now?" He pointed to the snake. "They always fall!"

"Excuse me," Brad said, backing away. "I was looking for the laundry."

12

Mr. Sebastian O'Shaughnessy arrived late to dinner. He hadn't been trying to make an entrance, despite the gold-trimmed vermilion robe. And, as it turned out, none was made. Not in this circle that had been, done, seen, sniffed, tasted, rimmed, flambéed, and casseroled everything it possibly could.

There was no *nouveau* here, no *entrée* or *ingenue*. But for all its worldliness, it wasn't so much jaded as pale, flat and stale. It was bread without yeast, diamonds without sparkle, the Supremes without Diana. Worse, it was a surfeit of experience without imagination. And imagination, as Oscar Wilde knew, was the magic ingredient that could turn an eggs-and-bacon sort of life into a scrumptious soufflé of an existence.

Brad lit a cigarette and sat at the end of a long table alongside a dozen other guests, all wearing similar dressing gowns. At the far end, a rugged Marlborough man dominated the room. Silver hair framed his tanned face, the lines of which made him appear powerful rather than aged. This, Brad presumed, was their host, Hayden Rosengarten.

Two guards flanked him. On his left stood a handsome Nubian, mirrored by a spectacular specimen with almond eyes and golden skin standing to his right. The pair made attractive bookends.

The man next to Brad turned and introduced himself as Ted Palaver, a Chicago stockbroker.

"Sebastian O'Shaughnessy," said Bradford, as they shook. "I'm a forensic accountant."

"Oh, very good!" said Ted, staring deeply into Brad's eyes. "I just made half a million this morning. Perhaps you could tell me where to hide it."

Ted stroked Brad's palm. "You have lovely hands," he said. "And no nicotine stains. You must be a careful smoker."

"Very careful," Brad answered, suddenly worried about his cover.

He caught a world-weary gaze across from him. At first glance, the man appeared to be nearing sixty. On closer inspection, however, he looked considerably younger.

"Sebastian O'Shaughnessy," Brad said, reaching across the table.

"Enchanté," replied a voice that combined the cultivation of Noel Coward with the hopelessness of Kurt Cobain.

He declined to shake. Brad withdrew his hand. The man mumbled something that suggested he was a singer. He was definitely a diva, but his ennui defied any attempt to imagine him on stage, except perhaps as the aging Sarastro in *The Magic Flute.* Brad concluded that he was a culture queen, the most meticulous of queens to converse with. He'd have to trot out the Proust and sprinkle his conversation liberally with references to Arvo Pärt and the Kronos Quartet.

A door opened and a familiar face entered the room. Flashing a brilliant smile, the man took his place at the table. Is that who

I *think* it is? Brad wondered. He was certainly short. Brad looked again. It's *him!* he realized with a start. He was in the presence of Hollywood royalty!

Various film roles in which this man portrayed a pool shark, helicopter pilot, samurai warrior, an everyday dad and even, once, a rabbit, flashed before Brad's eyes. And here he was now, taking on the role of gay sybarite. The rumours were true!

All those cretinous tabloid accusations of tell-all hustlers and betrayals by the dumbfounded ex-wife were based on fact! How many times had he seen this man on daytime talk shows, uttering nonsense about his ongoing belief in the Easter Bunny and other inane, nonthreatening remarks. Oprah had treated him like an Elmo doll. He'd made bland seem like a respectable choice.

Of course! Nobody could be that colourless unless he had something to hide. For the world to know this man was gay would rend the heart of America's Disneyfied conception of itself. He was an icon, an archetype! He was the fantasized purity of America itself. And he was a lie! Then again, Brad reminded himself, just because a man had a wife and kids he could prove were his with a quick DNA test didn't make him straight. Anybody could afford a marriage licence and a turkey baster these days.

Off to Brad's left, someone yawned. The actor's entrance had hardly registered. To the world he might be a megastar and a hetero hunk, but to the lot in this room he was just an overrated Muppet.

Brad looked at the men around him. From their conversations he knew they counted among them a cattle baron, the CEO of a multinational IT corporation, and a Nobel Prize-winning physicist. And to his shock, he'd also recognized Gifford Freeman, a garrulous Texan senator renowned for his vitriolic and very anti-gay public stance. To Brad he'd always seemed the epitome of double standards and sleazy politics. He'd just had those feelings confirmed. And, just as they'd accepted the presence of the star, no one in the room seemed the least bit surprised or outraged to find this political chameleon in their midst, either.

The room embodied a wealth of power, prestige, and influence. Yet for all that, the gathering was tawdry and sad. The men with power seemed lonely, the ones with prestige looked insecure, and those who had it all were the worst of the lot, acting bored and dejected as though life's promise had failed them.

These men, Brad knew, were the real power brokers in the room. The others — the *famous* others, like the megastar seated down the table from him — were mere actors and entertainers. Though their names carried the weight of legends, they were of little interest to the power elite.

What intrigued Brad most was how each of these men had risked something by being there — if not their families, then their careers and reputations. Their lives were a grand illusion perpetrated before the public's blind eye, with a history of closeted behaviour reaching back as far as King David's passionate love for his "friend" Jonathan.

So many gays had struggled to be what they were: men who could have sex with other men, and look themselves in the mirror the next morning knowing they weren't immoral or damned, but simply actors in the Theatres of Carnality and Love. Yet the men in this room cowered from the real world, thrashing about in gilded cages that separated their public selves from their private desires. It wasn't enough to have the bird in the cage, Brad knew. *The bird needed to soar!* That was something Ross had taught him.

Brad glanced over the elegant spread. A voluptuous floral arrangement grouped an impressive variety of orchids, ranging from the tiniest fingernail-sized blooms to others as big as a fist. Similarly, the wine boasted labels so exclusive they weren't even listed in most sommelier guides. The half-finished *Cos d'Estournel* sitting before him must have cost at least four or five hundred dollars. A French superstar of wines, it was the Bordeaux equivalent of the celebrity seated just down the table. Brad had been curious about both for years. At least the bottle would be available for sampling.

The food, too, was as extraordinary as it was delicious. A warm bear liver salad was accompanied by a succulent emu pâté, though he passed when it came to monkey brains *à l'orange*.

The evening's entrée, wild boar stuffed with Asian truffles, was carried out by a bevy of spectacular servers clad only in aprons. Conversation stalled each time they made an entrance, and seemed unable to revive till they left the room again. Perhaps that was what all the exorbitant prices were about, Bradford mused: this conspicuously decadent consumption and these overprivileged men playing at being bad boys.

He found himself stealing glances across the table at Hayden Rosengarten, *auteur* of this risqué engagement. Their host sat smoking a cigar and chatting with his guests. Brad was drawn to the man's forcible presence and the steel blue eyes that quietly took in everything around him. What exactly, he wondered, could there be to fear from this man?

The team of muscled servers entered yet again, bearing gleaming trays of oysters on the half shell. As one overeager Adonis passed, he stumbled and nearly crashed into the table. With a snarl, their host plunged his burning cigar into the boy's bare chest, pushing him aside with a single action.

"Clumsy oaf!" he bellowed.

"My fault, sir!" the boy mumbled, terrified, as he hurriedly retrieved his tray and ran from the room.

None of the guests seemed startled by the incident. Clearly this wasn't unusual behaviour in their social circle.

"Useless servants," Rosengarten griped. "What do I pay these people for?"

"Careful, Hayden," the senator warned, "or they'll be calling you a Republican."

"I've been called worse."

"What's that — a Democrat?"

"You're all the same to me," Hayden snarled. "The bottom line for everyone in this room is power, one way or the other."

Here, Brad saw, was a man clearly unafraid of the wealth and influence surrounding him. His curiosity was beginning to get the better of him. Ross had worked right here during the final months of his life. What part had he taken in this Roman circus? Had Hayden Rosengarten ever burned him with a cigar?

Money and fame might distinguish the men in this room from the rest of the world, but it didn't make them interesting or principled. It was a gala of the unglad, hosted by the ungracious, for the undeserving.

When the meal was over, the apron-clad beefcakes returned with a variety of chemical substances on trays. The old-looking young man across from Bradford helped himself to three differ-ent powders.

"You might want to be more cautious about mixing those," Brad suggested.

The man turned his gaze toward Brad and blinked. His pupils

were so dilated the irises seemed to have disappeared. He waved a cigarette in Bradford's direction, as though it were an extension of his arm for making public pronouncements.

"They way I see it," he drawled, "I'll either die happy or have a really good time trying."

He bent to take another snort. His name hadn't rung any bells when he'd introduced himself earlier, and for the life of him Brad couldn't remember it now.

Brad felt a foot steal into his crotch for the second time that day. He looked up to see the old-young man leering across the table. He appeared to be on the verge of a drug-induced coma. How'd you ever get so lost? Brad wondered, feeling like a world-weary mother.

A tray passed before Brad. Beside the lines of noxious substances sat a small dish of groundnut toffee for those who preferred sweet to the savory. Food, sex, drugs — there seemed to be something for every taste. Just how far would the Ice House go to satisfy its guests' desires? Could 'murder most foul' be on an unwritten list of diversions available for a price?

His thoughts were interrupted by his host.

"What's your pleasure, Mr. O'Shaughnessy?" he heard Rosengarten ask.

To know yours, Brad thought.

A smile played over Rosengarten's lips. His eyebrows arched like an eagle waiting to swoop down on an unsuspecting rabbit.

"I trust we can provide whatever you require in the way of pleasure this evening," his host stated.

"I'd rather hold off for a bit," Brad replied, squirming as the singer's foot meandered over his crotch. "I'm planning on making it through till the wee hours."

"Just like an accountant, harbouring even time itself," Hayden said. "Perhaps you'd prefer a more mundane indulgence to start?"

He indicated one of the servers, turning the boy abruptly by the elbow and running a hand over his globelike buttocks.

"This delightful flower is named Athens."

"He's practically an acropolis in his own right," Brad said.

"If he doesn't meet your fancy, we have more than a dozen others."

Brad's eyes moved to the almond-eyed bodyguard in the doorway.

Hayden followed his gaze. "His name is Johnny K., and I can tell you that his penis is legendary. In fact, I believe he has your name tattooed on it."

There were guffaws around the room. Brad managed a smile. "Sounds tantalizing," he replied, "considering the length of my name."

"He's yours for the asking," his host said. "All you have to do is say what pleases you."

"And what if what pleases me most is you, Mr. Rosengarten?"

The smile froze on his host's face. "Ah! Sadly, I would have to disappoint you. Though I thank you for the compliment."

A clock chimed midnight. A curtain parted and the spectre of Marilyn Monroe wavered before them. It was Cinder, of course, but judging by how little interest she stirred up, even the return of the real Marilyn would have created less than a ripple of curiosity with that crowd.

The platinum bombshell shimmied through the room in a torrid rendition of "Heat Wave," fastening herself to Senator Freeman, perhaps the closest thing to a Kennedy she could find. She notched up the temperature with "Fever," wafting feathers and dripping diamonds. Not once in his routine did Cinder betray a hint that he'd noticed Brad among the guests.

Despite the bravura performance, the act ended to tepid applause. Her momentary reprise from purgatory over, Marilyn withdrew like the ghost of Hamlet's father at the cock's crowing.

The curtains reopened on another resurrected legend, this one a rugged '80s porn star dressed in a Roman toga. Bradford could recall any number of trenchant performances the man and his famed appendage had given in their prime. His favourite was *Flesh Gordon*. While time had done little to diminish the star's awesome physique, the drugs he'd imbibed over a lifetime of devotion to his art seemed to have done noticeable cranial damage.

The oversized cretin appeared to have no idea where he was or what he was supposed to be doing until a wisp of a youngster appeared beside him. The boy lifted the giant's robe, exposing his legendary member to a round of applause. This part of him, too, Brad noted, had sadly been affected by the drugs and seemed equally ignorant of its purpose before them that evening.

The young man became absorbed in his quest to waken the sleeping giant. Eventually, he was able to inspire a respectable erection in the aging star, eliciting gasps from several of the men at the table. Aroused, it seemed, the beast was still truly formidable.

A small cheer rose from the crowd. The boy smiled as though he'd managed a great feat, but the greater was yet to come. The star, finally seeming to grasp why he was there, grabbed the boy, who squirmed and let out a scream. The giant slapped a hand over his mouth and began his assault on the young man's sphincter.

"Some people roast a pig when they have guests to supper,"

Brad heard Hayden say. "I deflower a virgin."

Just then, the thin man from the front door appeared and leaned down to their host, whispering in his ear. Hayden looked up sharply and nodded. He rose.

"Gentlemen, I'm afraid I must leave you for the briefest of moments."

Rosengarten disappeared with his bodyguards, while Ichabod slipped back out the way he'd come.

Brad was curious to know what had made his host leave so abruptly. He looked around the room to see who might be watching. The singer had gone into a drug-induced haze. Ted, meanwhile, had fallen asleep with his chin on his chest, dreaming of blue chips. The others were absorbed by the onstage spectacle.

Waiting till it seemed discreet, Brad slipped through the door after Rosengarten.

13

Bradford started up the grand staircase after his host's receding footsteps. He passed the portrait of the unhappy Maud Lacey, still awaiting the return of her peripatetic son. Next to her was an original Botero, the painter's famous fat men looking lustfully mischievous in garters and negligees. They'd always made Brad laugh. Now they reminded him of nothing so much as the roomful of ninnies he'd just left.

Upstairs, three separate passageways led off from a circular landing. Brad peered around a corner and saw Johnny K., the almond-eyed guard, posted outside a panelled door. A loud voice came from inside the room. Clearly, that's where Hayden had gone.

Brad peered down the second hallway. At the far end, a ladder led upward. In all likelihood, he realized, it ascended to the cupola. It would be useless to go up there now. He chose the third hallway and found himself treading a darkened passage to a set of double doors where a sign read, "Arctic Collection of Admiral Donald MacMillan."

He turned the doorknob. All was dark. He slipped in, closing the door behind him with a soft click. He fumbled in his pocket for Sebastian O'Shaughnessy's matches and struck one against the box. As it flared, a ghostly white shape lunged at him out of the darkness. Brad stifled a yell and fell back with a thud. The room plunged into darkness and silence again.

He lay there listening. Nothing moved. Had it been the ghost of Maud Lacey, still haunting her house after all these years? Brad wasn't sure he was ready to believe in ghosts. Still on his back, he struck another match. Towering over him, a polar bear reared on its hind legs, claws menacing the air and teeth set to tear apart anything that got in its way. Thankfully, its time for destruction was long past.

By the light of the fading match, a row of stuffed puffins sat laughing silently at him. They'd known all along it wasn't Maud Lacey's ghost. Off in another corner, a ship's anchor had come to rest. The match died again. Brad stood and lit another. He moved softly about the room whose walls were covered in maps and charts that once belonged to Admiral MacMillan and his crew. They'd been seeking a new world at the top of the globe, but somehow all routes had led to Provincetown.

A wall hanging caught his eye. Three silhouettes crossed an ice flow as a flock of geese winged silently over an igloo. A boat waited in the distance. Something protruded from behind the weave. Brad ran his hands over the hanging and felt the wall shift. He gave a quick push and a panel opened.

He was in the secret slave closets! The darkness ahead was pierced by pinpricks of light. Brad eased his way along till he found himself peering through a hole into a sumptuous bathroom with smoked glass walls. Whatever else it might contain, his host was noticeably absent. He continued on to the next peephole.

As he inched forward, his host's voice came booming through the wall.

"Are you threatening me?" Brad heard him snarl.

He could see Hayden pacing around a large oak desk, the phone pressed to his ear.

"Try me, you son of a bitch!" Hayden spat into the receiver. There was another pause. "Well, join the parade. Lots of people would love to see me dead!"

Shifting his gaze, Brad saw the Nubian bodyguard standing inside the door.

"You listen to me, you little worm!" Hayden sneered. "You're a fake and we both know it. I'll expose you to the whole world if you try anything else!"

Rosengarten hung up violently just as a knock came at the door. Ichabod entered wearing an agitated look.

"Yes, Jeremiah?"

"It seems one of our guests has vanished," the thin man said, his gloomy gaze roaming the room. "A certain Mr. O'Shaughnessy."

Oh-oh! Brad thought. *Gotta scram!*

Rosengarten motioned to the bodyguard. "Cyrus, take Johnny K. and find him. He can't be far."

Brad watched as Ichabod exited behind the guard, then he hurried back down the darkened passage to the Arctic Collection. He peered out into the hallway in time to see Ichabod descending the stairs along with the two guards.

He waited till they were out of sight before slipping from the room and across the landing. He'd just reached the top of the stairs when he heard footsteps coming up. He froze. It would be impossible to return to the Arctic Room without being seen. Gauging his chances, he decided to take a risk.

He sprinted down the hall to Hayden's door and stood in the

doorframe, smiling invitingly. A hand lingered suggestively over his crotch.

"Hi there!" he called out. "I was hoping to catch you alone."

Hayden's steely eyes took in his guest. *"Ah!* My young friend with the father complex. I seem to have become something of an obsession for you."

Whoever had been coming up the stairs arrived at the door right behind Brad.

"Yes, Joseph," Rosengarten snapped. "What can I do for you?"

The young man stopped in his tracks. "I was ... just coming to see if everything was okay, sir," he said.

"It's all right," Hayden said. "Mr. O'Shaughnessy was just expressing an interest in my ... well-being. You can go back down."

"Yes, sir!" The boy disappeared down the hall.

Rosengarten waited, his eyes on Brad. "Please come in, Mr. O'Shaughnessy," he said, leaning against his desk and picking up a cigar.

Brad retrieved his matches and lit it for him. Rosengarten puffed several times, and then looked over at Brad. "How are you enjoying your evening so far? I trust you're having a memorable time?"

"Very memorable, thank you. Interesting guests, tantalizing food and delectable service."

Brad looked around, quickly taking in the room — filing cabinets, bookshelves, a standing lamp. There was nothing out of the ordinary.

"And then there's the house itself," he continued. "I'll bet the history is fascinating. Am I correct in thinking the hedge outside is belladonna?"

"Quite correct!" Hayden said, breathing a cloud of smoke. "You're not only handsome, but observant as well."

"Don't you worry about, uh, poisoning your guests?"

Hayden shrugged. "There are things *inside* this house that are far more deadly," he said. "Not to mention tempting. It's amazing what money can buy."

Brad nodded. "I'm no stranger to the things money can buy," he said. "And I know all pleasures have their price."

"Of course! As do all men. But I pride myself on offering the things that money can't buy."

100

"Such as?" Brad asked, alert to the answer.

Rosengarten fixed his gaze on Brad. "Discretion, for one," he replied simply. "It can be a priceless commodity when you have need for it. Personally, I find it a necessary complement to both the deadly and the tempting. You must have recognized the good senator sitting in our midst?"

"Of course."

"How do you think he'd feel if word got out that he was seen frequenting a resort like this?"

"Not very happy, I'm sure," Brad said.

"Exactly! Especially as he has plans to run for the presidency in the near future. And we are also graced with the presence of a very big star this evening. He has some highly irregular tastes, to say the least."

"'To each his own,' as they say. I'm sure you must get all types here," Brad said.

"All types, yes indeed. Politicians, movie stars, religious figures ... even Mafia heads."

And all in good company, Brad mused.

"Why, just two nights ago we were host to a very queer fish indeed ..."

Rosengarten brought the cigar to his lips and seemed to ponder the memory, as though it disturbed him.

Two nights ago was when Ross was murdered, Brad realized. Just how *queer* was this fish and what did it have to do with Ross's death, if anything?

"That's why these men spend thousands coming here instead of going elsewhere. Absolute discretion," Hayden continued, punctuating the air with his cigar, "is my guarantee when they walk through this door. Why, the names I could name ..."

Brad leaned forward.

Hayden pulled back. "But I would never," he said. "I'm not free to disclose trade secrets. If anyone thought I was trying to blacken his reputation, I'd be putting myself in a very dangerous position, indeed."

"My lips are sealed, Mr. Rosengarten."

"And such lovely lips they are," Hayden said, tapping ash into the palm of his hand.

Brad looked directly into Rosengarten's eyes. I'm flirting with my ex-lover's murderer to entice evidence out of him, he thought. How obscene is that?

Keep your mind on the job, he could hear Grace say. Brad's eyes lit on a paperweight on Hayden's desk, an ugly obelisk with a starfish embedded at its centre. He reached over and picked it up.

"That was a present from an admirer on my fortieth birthday," Hayden said. "The late Andy Warhol threw a party in my honour."

"Sounds like a great time."

"The only thing that marred it was the music. He was going through a lesbian phase at the time and hired all women singers. It was one depressing wailer after another ..."

Rosengarten shuddered.

"But why are we talking about this, Mr. O'Shaughnessy? What would make this night memorable for you? A blowjob from James Dean? Montgomery Clift in a sling? These things can be arranged. A little makeup, the right wardrobe and lighting, and *presto!* You can have anyone you've ever wanted. With muscles, even."

"Now that you mention it, I've always wanted to be lassoed by the Marlborough Man," Brad murmured, his gaze travelling down Rosengarten's chest.

Hayden's face feigned disbelief. "Why would you want me, with all those strapping young lads downstairs?" He made a deprecating gesture. "I know I may seem a little rough on them at times, but they're like family to me. *Suffer the children,*" he intoned, piously.

"Some kids like it rough," Brad said with a wink. "And a few of us even enjoy a little 'suffering' now and then."

Come on, Brad was thinking. Show me how far you would go.

"In fact, Mr. Rosengarten," he continued, "I think you and I might share similar tastes. Certain *dark* tastes for forbidden things."

He was staring right into Hayden's crystal blue eyes. He could feel the man's breath on his shoulder. Okay, so sometimes I have to do more than keep just my *mind* on the job, Brad told himself. Grace might not approve, but Grace didn't have to know everything.

Hayden smiled and leaned back on the desk as though considering something. That's when they heard the first gunshot.

14

The dining room was in chaos as they entered. Ichabod stood by the doorway, hands on his hips, looking furious. Most of the guests were huddled beneath the dinner table except for the old-looking young man who sat wreathed in cigarette smoke, gazing absently into the distance. The porn star, oblivious to everything, was onstage in the throws of preorgasmic fury.

On the far side of the room a body lay on the floor. It was the man with the snake bracelet. Brad was about to rush over when a second shot tore into the ceiling.

"The chandeliers!" shrieked the irate Ichabod, as a chunk of ceiling fell onto the table and smashed a pot of exotic blooms. "My orchids!"

In the midst of the pandemonium stood Senator Freeman, smirking and waving a Colt .45 over his head.

"What's going on here?" Hayden bellowed.

"I was just saying I had a rod that could rival that gentleman's on stage any time," said the garrulous Texan with a laugh.

"He tried to kill me!" exclaimed the tiny man cowering on the floor.

"This here Yankee faggot called me a closet case," the senator replied. "And I told him my private life is none of his business, but that subterfuge and trickery is how everything works in these here Yew-nited States of America."

"He doesn't deserve to call himself a gay man," moaned the elf. The ghost of self-esteem had raised its head, and it had taken a geriatric gnome to do it.

"Partner, that's the last thing I'd be calling myself!" the senator said, roaring with laughter until his face turned red and he began to wheeze.

"Careful, Senator," Hayden warned, "or they'll be saying you laughed yourself to death in a gay whorehouse."

The elf shook his fist. "I didn't spend my life fighting for respect so this baboon could make a mockery of it!"

"Hold your fire, gentlemen," Hayden spoke up. "This is a private resort, not a public battlefield." He turned to one of the young servers. "Claudio, take our friend here ..." he said, indicating the man lying on the floor. "And cheer him up a little."

They waited as the older man hobbled out of the room on the arm of the younger. "When I was your age," they heard him say, "I was as handsome as you are now ..."

Rosengarten turned to his guests. "That's the end of our scheduled entertainment, gentlemen," he announced, as though the shootout had been part of a floor show.

Within seconds, a bevy of young beauties swarmed into the room.

"Choose the object of your pleasure and feel free to retire to any area of the house." With a meaningful look to Brad, he added, "Except for my upper ensuite offices, of course."

Rosengarten nodded to his bodyguards, who followed him out of the room. Brad was wondering whether to run after them when he felt an arm slide around his waist. He turned to see Quentin smiling at him.

"Shall we?" the boy asked.

Brad allowed himself to be escorted back to his room. Inside, Quentin locked the door and looked at him invitingly. Brad's eyes played over the boy's body. A little physical recreation wouldn't hurt, he mused. Surely Grace wouldn't object. After all, she was paying for his night of pleasure. Perhaps, Brad thought, he might even learn a little about the mysterious Mr. Rosengarten at the same time.

"Shall we start with a massage?" Quentin asked as he untied the sash on Brad's robe and let it slip to the floor.

The boy wasn't much of a masseur, but he managed to offer in pain what he lacked in skill.

"Do you like working here?" Brad asked.

"It's a great place," Quentin replied, jabbing his fingers deep into Brad's muscles. "I get to meet some very interesting people."

"Are they always this excitable?"

Quentin laughed. "Not really. It's pretty laid back for the most part. Usually the yahoos are made to check their guns at the door."

The boy was chatty and well versed in Ice House gossip. According to Quentin, his boss was well nigh fifty-seven years old, despite his remarkable physique. In the '70s, Rosengarten had been king of New York's disco scene when legends like Grace Jones and Margaux Hemingway strutted with the *hoi polloi*. He'd made a killing selling cocaine to the danceteria owners, who passed it on to their best customers. That explained the birthday bash thrown by Warhol, Brad realized.

A decade later, when most of his friends and colleagues were dying along with disco, Rosengarten was just hitting his stride, opening clubs of his own and financing drug cartels under the auspices of some powerful political allies. And thus his open-door policy with the likes of Senator Freeman, Bradford surmised. One hand scratches the other, and indulges both.

In the '90s, Rosengarten had invested heavily in e-commerce in an attempt at legitimacy, but just as he was about to retire the market plummeted. Fortunes went bust and reputations dissolved in a mire of bankruptcies and lawsuits. By then the feds were onto him. He abandoned his former life, took what money remained, and sought refuge on the seventy-mile stretch of cape just south of Boston. There, he started over. Provincetown had seen plenty in its day, but it had never seen the likes of Mr. Hayden Rosengarten, entrepreneur. And it seemed it would never forget him, either.

So that was the story of the man behind the mask, Brad mused. He was little more than a self-made drug dealer — it'd been pretty much the same story ever since Prohibition and the rise of bootleggers. But what of Ross, a good-time boy who only wanted a place to earn a little cash and have some fun? Had his murder been someone's sick fantasy purchased for a price? All of this must add up to something, Brad felt, but he wasn't sure just what that might be.

"Who's the tall, skinny guy at the door?" he asked.

"That's Mr. Jones. As long as you don't mess with his flowers, you're fine."

Brad pictured the reams of delicate orchids throughout the house. The Martha Stewart touch, he thought. Every brothel needed one.

Quentin stood with his crotch tantalizingly close to Bradford's face. "How's that?" he asked.

"Looks pretty good from here."

Quentin grinned. "I meant the massage."

"Damage done," Brad said with a wink.

"Time for the main event." Quentin pulled his shirt overhead and dropped it onto the floor.

Brad's eyes were fixed on the snake tattoo on the boy's left pectoral. "Tell me," he said. "Did you know a guy named Ross who worked here?"

"I don't think so." Nothing in Quentin's expression said he wasn't telling the truth. "But then again, I've only been here a couple of weeks. I might not have met everyone. What does he look like?"

Brad described Ross. The boy's blue eyes brightened.

"The guy who died!" he said. "Yeah, I knew him. Everybody knew him. But he went by 'Brad' in here."

Bradford almost choked. "Do you know how he died?"

"Too many drugs," Quentin said sadly, as though seeing his own eventual fate.

He smiled again and dropped his shorts to the floor. Brad's jaw dropped along with them when he saw the formidable erection rearing before him. His eyes followed a thin trail of hair up Quentin's belly to his chest and the other phallic symbol neatly tattooed there. The deadly *and* the tempting.

"Was Ross your favourite?" Quentin said. "Let's see if I can please you like he did."

A HALF-HOUR LATER, Bradford raised himself up off the bed. The boy had fallen asleep beside him. Brad shook his shoulder. Quentin stirred and stretched his arms overhead.

"How'd I do?" he asked.

"You were spectacular," Brad said as he dressed.

Quentin reached for his shorts and handed Brad a business card. "I also do private massages," he said with a wink.

A real entrepreneur, Brad thought, as he pocketed the card. "By the way, do you know if anyone disliked Ross — uh, Brad?" he asked casually.

There was no reply. Brad looked over to Quentin, whose face had taken on a curious look.

"Goodbye, Mr. Fairfax," a familiar-sounding voice said from behind.

The last thing Brad felt was a *whack!* across the back of his head as the lights went out.

15

He was having the dream again, the one with the blue-haired alien, only this time he was falling from a great height while the alien radiated calming waves toward him.

Brad landed with a thud as an incredible pain split his skull. He opened his eyes. He was lying on his back in semidarkness. Where was he? He tried to think through the pain to the night before. Had he tricked with someone? The last time he'd felt this way he'd met a muscleman named Chet. They'd mixed poppers with champagne, and the result had been disastrous.

His hand crept out from beneath the blankets and felt around. He was alone in a bed — that much was clear. It was starting to come back to him now. He was in Provincetown. He'd come because ... oh, *shit!* He'd come to bury Ross. It returned to him in a flash. But where had he been the night before?

He tried to turn, but the pain made him cry out. It wasn't a dream! He slowly willed himself to roll onto his side. He could just make out that he was lying on a low-slung pallet in a dimly lit room. But where?

There was someone else in the room. A figure wearing a baseball cap sat on the floor in a full-fledged lotus, arms raised at his sides and palms turned upward, as though supplicating the gods.

"Where am I?" Brad murmured.

"In my room at a Provincetown guesthouse."

"Why am I here?"

Zach opened his eyes and fixed them on Bradford. "That's a really good question."

"Should you answer it or do I not want to know?"

"I rescued you."

"Uh-huh," Brad said. "Go on."

Zach lowered his arms and stood in a single effortless motion. "Let me get you some painkillers," he said, making his way out of the room.

He returned with three tablets and a glass of water. "Extra strength," he said, handing them over.

Brad took the tablets and swallowed, aware he was breaking training protocol by accepting drugs — even of the pharmaceutical sort — from someone he didn't know. Or barely knew.

"I was passing the dunes on my bike around one o'clock last night when a car went racing by," Zach said. "I had to swerve into the ditch to avoid getting hit. Man, you guys were travelling!"

Brad handed back the empty glass. "Thanks," he mumbled.

"Someone opened the passenger door and you tumbled out. Luckily, you hit a sand drift when you fell. They left you lying there and took off down the interstate. If another car had come along it would've run right over you."

Images rushed kaleidoscopically past: a mysterious guesthouse out by the dunes, a belladonna hedge, himself posing as Sebastian O'Shaughnessy, the lavish food and drink, fabulous orchids, a gun-toting senator, the megastar and all the others. There was also his brief flirtation with the guesthouse owner, Hayden Rosengarten, and a young man named Quentin who'd answered all his questions but one. Oh, yes! And before that, a cowgirl named Big Ruby had saved him from being run over. Then finally, he recalled hearing his real name being spoken before he could turn around. There'd been something familiar about the voice ... !

It was all beginning to make sense. Someone had pieced together the reason for his visit to the guesthouse and knocked him unconscious. Obviously, that someone knew who he was and why he'd gone there. He was lucky to be alive.

"I've been sending you healing energy," Zach said. "Do you know anything about Reiki?"

"Sure," Brad said. "I know about Reiki. Thanks, uh ..."

"It's ..."

"Zach — I know," he said. "I don't forget things twice."

Brad raised the sheet and gazed at his naked body beneath it. He looked back at Zach.

"I didn't molest you!" Zach said defensively.

"I was looking for bruises. Really."

Bradford could just make out Zach's face under the brim of his cap. "What time is it?"

"Almost one in the afternoon. You've been out for more than eleven hours."

"Whoa!" he said. "Well, thanks for all that. I'd better be going."

He tried to raise himself off the pallet, but a searing pain brought him right back down.

"You'd better take it easy," Zach said. "You're severely bruised, but at least nothing's broken."

"You're a doctor?"

"I told you, I'm a healer. A psychic healer. I did an energy scan of your body."

"You did a *what?*"

"An energy scan," Zach said, holding up his hands as if in evidence. "I heal with the energy in my hands."

Brad shook his head in disbelief.

Zach knelt beside him. "When I scanned you I sensed you'd been hit on the back of the head. It could have been from your fall, but it felt like it was from a metal bar," he said.

Zach reached out and gently touched the back of Bradford's head where the pain was most intense. Brad recalled the powerful *whack!* that had put the lights out for the evening. Zach ran his fingers down Brad's chest to a rib on his left side.

"There's another sore spot here," he told him. "But as I said, it's just a bad bruise, not a break."

Zach pressed lightly on the spot and Brad winced.

"Ow!" Brad looked up. "Are you for real?"

Zach nodded. "I see these things as colours. Whenever I see green, there's healing going on. In this case, it's an ugly greenish-yellow, which indicates severe bruising. If I saw red it would tell me there'd been a break or at least a fracture, but I didn't see anything like that."

"What planet are you from?"

"Neptune, actually," Zach replied with a straight face.

"You're an alien?" said Brad skeptically.

"No more than anyone else," Zach answered matter-of-factly. "I was born on Earth, but I spent time in the energy fields of Neptune and Jupiter between incarnations. That's why I understand healing in this lifetime."

Brad looked away and shook his head. "I'm sorry, but this is totally weird."

Zach shrugged. "I'm a Buddhist. I believe in reincarnation. We've both been around many times. I've known you before. You made me miserable in another lifetime, too."

"What do you mean, 'too'?"

Brad tried to raise himself again. Zach placed a palm on Brad's forehead, ignoring his question.

"But this time you're going to have an opportunity to make it up to me. Just relax and try to connect with my energy," he said, raising his other hand in the air.

Zach closed his eyes and appeared to be concentrating on something. Brad lay back, not knowing what else to do. He sensed his forehead heating up to the point where it felt feverish.

Zach opened his eyes. "Do you feel that?" he asked.

"Wow!" Brad said. "You can do that at will?"

"I told you," said Zach. "I'm a psychic healer."

"It's very cool!"

Zach looked perplexed. "It should feel hot," he said, withdrawing the hand and examining it. "Usually this is my hot hand."

"No, I meant it's a cool talent."

"Oh!"

"I've heard of such things. Where I work they talk about it, but I've never actually experienced it."

"I thought you worked for IBM."

"Oh, that ... !" Brad shrugged. "That was last year. I've moved on since then."

Brad tried to recall who he'd said he was lately. He'd claimed he was a travel writer to someone on the beach. Then he told Perry the barkeep that he was an inventor. And Cinder thought he was a golf pro. Given the size of Provincetown, he'd better keep his stories straight and remember who thought he was what.

"Actually, I'm a pro golf instructor at the moment," he said. "Athletes are always into the latest healing methods."

He watched Zach's face for signs of disbelief.

"You change careers pretty fast," Zach said simply.

"It's hard to keep up with me."

"Is that why you were ejected from a car doing fifty miles an hour last night?"

"I think someone was trying to keep me away from the competition."

"Looks like your competition plays rough," Zach said with a laugh. He bent forward and his cap fell off. He reached for it and looked up to find Bradford staring at him in astonishment.

"Oh, boy!" Brad exclaimed. The curly hair tumbling out from under Zach's cap was blue. "You *are* an alien!"

"It's just dyed. I told you, I'm an earthling like you, only I know where my soul's travelled between incarnations."

"Did ... did you have that ... ? I mean, was your hair blue the first time we met?"

Zach reached up and felt his locks. "No, it's new, but you likely wouldn't remember. It was dark that night."

"Oh, right," Brad said, blushing. "And the tattoo I saw yesterday?"

"New, too," Zach said, pulling up his shirttail to reveal the horse's head covering his taut abdomen.

Calmness suffused the boy's eyes and radiated in his features. Brad felt mesmerized.

"Can you help me get up?" he said. "I've got to get back to my house. I have a lot to do this afternoon ..."

"Your pain will be pretty severe for another day or two. You should probably take it easy. The aspirin will wear off in a few hours, but I don't think you need to see a doctor."

"Thanks for the prognosis," Brad said ironically.

"You're welcome to come back for more healing, if you like. I'd recommend at least two week's worth of treatments." Zach looked away awkwardly. "If you don't want me to do it, I'm sure you can find someone else in P-Town who can."

"I'd better get going," Brad said.

Zach helped him to his feet. Once he'd dressed, Brad stood by the door. Should he just walk away and end it here? That's what he'd done the last time.

"Zach, I ... well, thank you."

Zach extended his hand. "Glad to be of service, Bradford."

Brad hesitated. Surely he owed Zach more than a handshake? He shrugged. "Can I ... take you out to supper this evening?"

Zach's mouth fell open, but nothing came out.

"Unless you've got a hot date already."

Zach looked up sheepishly. "Not even a cool one."

"Meet me at Café Edwige tonight at eight."

Zach grinned. Suddenly he was just an attractive young man with nothing stranger about him than his blue hair.

16

As he limped home from Zach's guesthouse, Brad pondered the recent turn of events. Two days earlier on the P-Town Fast Ferry, a female impersonator dressed as Marilyn Monroe had tipped him off to the probable murder of his ex-lover. That same evening he'd discovered a drowned body at the breakwater. Next, he was almost run over on Bradford Street, but at the last second he'd been rescued by a diminutive lesbian named Big Ruby. Ruby had warned him to watch himself at a disreputable guesthouse where he'd been felt up by a drug-addicted singer with a foot fetish. Then he'd been attacked at the same guesthouse by an unknown assailant and thrown from a moving car, only to be rescued yet again by a young man with blue hair who radiated healing energy through the palms of his hands.

Who knew Provincetown could be so scary?

When he reached his house he tried to phone Grace, but was told she was currently out of contact. It was strange for his boss not to be available, even in an emergency. He left an urgent message saying they needed to talk.

In the marbled bathroom, Brad turned the Jacuzzi on full, tossing handfuls of sea salt into the swirling water. He undressed and gingerly lowered himself into the enveloping warmth. Zach had been right — he felt plenty of pain, but fortunately nothing seemed to be broken.

The water lapped at his sides, massaging and soothing his muscles. As the jets whirred he tried to formulate a game plan. Considering the events of the previous evening, it seemed that much more likely that Ross had been murdered. But why, and by whom? It was clear that someone was aware of Bradford's true identity and possibly even his whereabouts. Unless that person now believed him to be dead, of course, but a quick glance at the morning papers would tell his assailant otherwise.

Who was behind the attack? Cinder knew about Brad's relationship to Ross, but what else did he know? Not only had he arranged Brad's visit to the guesthouse, he'd also conveniently been at the house the same evening. Cinder could easily have tipped someone off to Brad's real reason for being there. But if that were the case, why invite him to the house in the first place? If Cinder hadn't told Brad about the suspicious circumstances of Ross's death, they would almost certainly have gone unnoticed. So why expose a murder one day and then try to kill the person who might help solve it the next? Or had he merely been set up by Cinder in order to implicate someone else in the crime? A drag queen's revenge! Now *that* was possible.

And even if Cinder wasn't involved in the killing, how much could Brad trust a public drag queen to keep things to himself? What was it Rosengarten had said about the need for absolute discretion? That it was *a necessary complement to both the deadly and the tempting*. It sounded like something out of a secret service training manual. An idle word in the wrong ear could have unintentionally led to Brad's discovery. And God knows how drag queens loved their gossip!

So far the only real clue seemed to be the familiar-sounding voice that had spoken his name before he was knocked unconscious. Brad still couldn't place it. Maybe it would come to him.

He reached up to feel the bump on his head. It throbbed. He was lucky he didn't have a concussion, but perhaps he should see a doctor just in case. On the other hand, he couldn't afford to waste time. Someone certainly seemed to think he was hot on the trail of something. If only he knew what!

He tried again to recall the voice. There'd been something throaty about it. Could it have been Hayden's? His head ached with the effort to remember. Cinder could change his tone in seconds from a Betty-Boop falsetto to a Don't-Fuck-With-Tallulah bass. Who knew what he really sounded like?

There was also that kooky singer with the foot fetish. He'd had a reedy tone when he spoke. Yes, it could have been him. But again, why? And what was his connection with Ross?

Brad's mind sifted through the possibilities for a likely suspects list. There was also Big Ruby, now that he thought about it. Brad had told her enough about why he was in P-Town to catch her interest. Obviously, Ruby couldn't have been anywhere near the guesthouse last night. Or could she? It would be a stretch, but she might have followed him there. She could be far more involved than she let on. From the anger she'd expressed toward Rosengarten, he'd bet money she held a personal grudge against him. And by her own admission, Ruby certainly seemed to feel that murder had its uses.

The jets buzzed and whirred as the water flowed around him. He needed a plan. Right now, talking to Big Ruby seemed like a good place to start. He stood and reached for a towel, gently dabbing at his aching body. At least there was no damage done to his tattoo. He flexed his abs, admiring himself in the mirror. The wings rippled as if waiting to take flight.

He glanced out the window to see a man watching him with a pair of binoculars from a neighbouring house. Bradford flashed him and shut the blinds. *Peeping Tom*, he muttered.

He walked naked into the bedroom where he threw on his usual attire of walking shorts, T-shirt, and moisturizer.

His phone rang. He snatched it up, expecting to hear Grace.

"I have some interesting news for you," Tom Nava said. "You asked if there was a connection between the two dead boys. I forgot one thing."

"What's that?"

"Ross died from a drug overdose and the other boy died as a result of drowning. But there was one thing they had in common — a snake tattoo."

"Is that right?" Brad said, recalling the cobra on Ross's shoulder. It had been dark when he found James Shephard by the breakwater, so he hadn't noticed any markings. Suddenly, he remembered the coiled snake on Quentin's chest and felt the hair rising on the back of his neck.

"Any idea what it might signify?" he asked, reaching for his discarded pants and retrieving the boy's business card from his pocket.

Nava paused. "Why do you think I'm telling you?" he asked gruffly. "I was hoping you would."

The cop's growl made Brad tingle.

"Oh!" he said, ignoring the stirrings in his groin. "Ross got the tattoo last summer. It's a Buddhist symbol."

Nava grunted. "Buddhist symbol, huh? Could be they just went to the same tattoo artist."

"I may have a way of finding out," Brad said. "I'm going to call a friend who's an expert on these things. I'll let you know what I hear back."

Brad dialed the number on Quentin's card. After what had happened the night before, he couldn't just announce himself as the client who was knocked unconscious. He'd have to inquire discreetly when Quentin was going to be home and make an appointment under another name. Then he could turn up and find out what the talkative blond knew. The phone rang eight times without an answer. Brad set the receiver down. He pocketed the card to remind him to call again later.

In the mirror, his neck sported a large bruise ranging from yellow at the centre to an ugly greenish-purple around the edges. Unfortunately, they weren't fashionable colours, he noted, and tied a bandana around his throat.

He walked the few blocks to Coffee Joe's. Brad wasn't sure how long Joe's had been in P-Town, but it'd been a local hang-out for as long as he'd been going there. Two men occupied a bench on the outdoor patio. Both had the chiselled cheekbones and bristly moustaches of the daddy-type Brad found irresistible. The first wore a sleeveless T-shirt, showing off his burly arms. The second was a bare-chested Viking. A garden of wiry hair sprouted from his massive pecs. In another era he would have stood guard at the gates to Valhalla.

Brad caught his eye. The man scowled, dismissing him in a glance. Try as he might, Brad couldn't approximate that hard-edged, brooding-miscreant look that would have doomed such a man to the position of bouncer in a straight bar, but in a gay club would immediately elevate him to 'god' status.

In the Hierarchy of Gay, Brad knew, men like this were

endowed by nature with thrillingly wicked — nay, almost evil — thighs that brought about despair in the general populace. And those types slept only with their own kind unless they were having an off-day, having been mortally wounded by some skinny retail clerk at Bloomingdale's with an over-the-shoulder, "In your size? For you, I have only a serape. Try our camping department."

At that moment, three twinks exited the café slurping English toffee cappuccinos and vanilla crème lattes. They were what upscale porn magazines referred to as "hottie boys" and the down-scale ones as "fresh meat." Brad caught himself humming "Three Little Maids from School Are We." They looked as though they never worried about their waistlines or missing the gym for a single moment. In fact, they looked as though they'd never been to a gym. The only thing weighty about them was an overdevel-oped sense of style and irony.

One at a time they glanced up from their straws to look Brad in the eye, giggling and slurping their approval. All three of them combined wouldn't equal Brad's body weight. Why do I always get hit on by underage cha-cha queens? he wondered. Like the muscle daddies on the bench, he just scowled and looked away as they skipped past him down the sidewalk.

Inside, Big Ruby stood behind the counter beside a bald hunk. Tattoos covered the helper's shining scalp in an intricate design of violets and daggers. Brad gave the guy an admiring glance. It was coolly ignored. Strike two.

Ruby waved and adjusted her cat's eye glasses. The rhinestones sparkled in the halogens above the display counter.

"Hello there, friend!" she said, reaching across the counter to shake his hand. "Let me guess — a Tazo Chai Lite?"

"Yeah! How'd you know?"

"Easy! You're the classy type — a little bit country, a little bit gourmet."

"You sure know your customers," Brad said.

Ruby turned to a shiny, chrome-covered machine and quickly whipped up a confection that was one-third froth and two-thirds steam.

"On me," she said when he tried to pay.

"Much obliged," Brad said. He took a sip. "Wow! That's great!"

Ruby beamed. "My best Darjeeling with a splash of Key lime honey. By the way, how'd you make out last night?"

Brad smiled ruefully and rubbed the back of his head. "I should have listened to you."

Ruby's face paled. "What happened?"

"I guess I'm lucky to be alive today. I was ambushed and left for dead out on the highway near the dunes."

Ruby's hand flew to her mouth.

"Ruby, I'd really appreciate it if you'd spend a little time talking to me."

"Halle!" she snapped.

The bald hunk looked over. "Yeah, Rue?"

He was a *she!*

"Take over for me."

"Sure, Rue," the girl said, wiping her hands on her apron.

"The galfriend," Ruby explained with a nod of her head in Halle's direction.

They walked out to the back of the café and sat on a stone wall. Brad started in on the story of what had happened to him after meeting Ruby the previous evening.

"Hang on," Ruby said. She pulled a thick joint out of her

apron, lighting up before passing it along. "This is good fair-trade dope. It'll help ease your pain some," she said.

Brad smiled as he reflected on all the alternative medicine being offered to him in P-Town. He took a toke and passed it back.

"I may be a Buddhist," Ruby said as she took the joint from his fingers, "but if I ever get my hands on that bastard, I'll tear him apart."

Another Buddhist, Brad noted with curiosity. "I've been meeting a lot of Buddhists on this trip," he said. "I wonder why that is."

123

"Well," Ruby began, "the practice teaches that nothing is coincidental. There's probably a reason you're connecting with our energy right now ..."

"Actually, what I meant is why are there so many Buddhists in P-Town?"

"Oh!" Ruby adjusted her glasses and smiled. "The Cape just seems to attract peace lovers — and I am a peaceful gal, despite what I've said against Rosiegarters."

"I believe you," Bradford said, as the joint went back and forth.

"When the Chinese invaded Tibet, a lot of Buddhists left the country — those that weren't thrown in jail, of course." Ruby shrugged. "I've got my own Reluctant Rinpoche just a few streets over from me."

"Your own what?"

"*Rinpoche.* Rhymes with 'ricochet.' It's the name they give to reincarnating teachers who come back time and again to teach the rest of us lowlife types. They could float off peacefully into the bardo for all time, but they sacrifice themselves by coming back to help unevolved souls like you and me. Mine's one of the really big ones, but he doesn't have his own group yet. He just showed up a few months ago and said the Cape was calling him."

Ruby sucked on the joint and held her breath till her eyes watered. She passed it back to Bradford.

"Stuff's not bad, eh?" she said, watching as he took a toke. "Some dope rips the shit out of your throat and makes you feel like you've been sucking on sandpaper, but this stuff goes down real smooth."

Brad thought that was an interesting comment, considering all the throaty voices he'd been hearing lately.

"Anyway, my Rinpoche left Tibet when he was barely a child," Ruby continued. "When the Chinese invaded in '59, the Dalai Lama fled with two children and a handful of holy books."

Brad's interest twigged at the mention of the Dalai Lama.

"My Rinpoche was one of the kids," Ruby concluded. "I've been trying to convince him to teach, but he's not ready yet. Anyway, I'm sure that's not what you wanted to talk to me about."

Brad pulled a picture of Ross from his wallet. "I'm trying to find out what happened to this guy."

Ruby took the picture and nodded. "I remember him well. He was a sweet man, really and truly. Used to come in every other day for a caramel macchiatto. Sometimes he'd sit and we'd talk for a while — nothing special, just shootin' the shit. I never knew where he worked or I would've warned him he was in bad company."

Ruby passed the picture back and shook her head sadly.

"Any idea why someone would want him dead?"

Ruby's eyes narrowed. "You sayin' he was murdered?"

Brad nodded. "I'm afraid so."

"What happened?"

"Drug overdose. But it was a drug he didn't normally use."

"Well, now!" Ruby took a final toke and blew the smoke slowly across her lips. She looked Brad in the eye and shook her head. "It doesn't make sense, a nice man like that. Who would want to harm him? There'd be plenty that'd want to see his boss dead, though."

"Do you think someone who had it in for Rosengarten might have bumped off Ross to get back at him?"

"To send a message, you mean?"

"Something like that."

Ruby ground out the roach under her sneaker.

"Doubt it," she said. "This town's too small. Things like that'd get around faster than a jackrabbit on speed."

"Could he have seen something at the house that made him a target?"

"Now that's possible!" Ruby paused. "I hear tell there's plenty of high-powered, closety political types go to that place. Maybe your friend Ross sees somebody who doesn't want to be seen there — somebody real dangerous — and the guy has him popped."

Bradford had already reached a similar conclusion. He thought of Marilyn Monroe and her deadly tryst with the Kennedy brothers. Where many have cried "conspiracy theory," others simply knew better. Marilyn's death had always seemed too convenient. And who better to have done it than J. Edgar Hoover and his demented band? In their eyes, Doris Day could have been a communist sympathizer and a threat to the government. But it wasn't till the revelations of Hoover's personal life came out after his death that it really began to make sense. Everything had been tossed from that closet, including the dresses the old man liked to wear — all the way from kitsch to kvetch, and just about anything in between. Who would have benefited most from the death of America's love goddess but a dress-wearing, FBI-running, Johnny-come-lately rival? Marilyn threatened to blow the goods on the Kennedys and Hoover came to the rescue, taking the opportunity to get their love doll out of the picture and get himself in good with the boys in one foul move. It was that simple.

"How many other guys work in that place?" Ruby asked.

"Maybe a dozen."

She clucked. "You should ask one of them. They'd know more than me."

"That's what I was doing last night when I got conked on the head," he said. "Can you tell me anything more?"

"Not really, hon," she said. "I avoid the place like the plague. In a small town like this it's hard to stay out of people's way, but I try extra hard with that bunch."

Brad was disappointed. He was sure Ruby knew something that could help. At least the dope was working. The throbbing in his head had begun to feel like a distant ache. He pulled out his card. "Here's my number. Call me if you remember anything."

"Will do." Ruby shook her head and laughed. "My, my! What kind of Karma do you have going on, brother?"

17

Zach was waiting at the café. He wore a tight yellow sweater that focused attention on his boyishly handsome face, while leaving no doubt about his well-formed physique. He'd come capless that evening. His hair had been coaxed into a whorl over his brow, a little peak tilting up and back the way the younger boys styled it those days.

That is one delicious-looking young man, Brad decided, as he crossed the room. Envious eyes followed him to his seat. Anyone watching might think they were a couple. Oddly, that appealed to him.

Their waiter that evening was somewhat more experienced at serving the public than the one Brad had endured the night before. He spread a napkin across Brad's lap and made sure he was comfortably settled before leaving. Every few minutes he would float by the table or wink from across the room, as though the three of them shared a secret. In fact, he was so attentive Brad began to suspect he had designs on Zach.

Zach was forthcoming about himself. As he told it, his family were typical middle-class liberals who embraced the ideals of tolerance, education and self-knowledge. His parents encouraged their children to follow their own paths in life. Zach's sister Anna had recently become a dancer with a European ballet company, while Zach's older brother Harold, a nuclear physicist, was busy making waves in his field.

Zach was the baby in the family. His talents had proven somewhat more esoteric. Apart from an affinity for healing, he'd also come out in his last year of high school. Secure in his sexuality when others were just questioning theirs, he informed his parents of his orientation. *We support you in anything you choose,* was their response. Zach had never looked back.

After high school, he enrolled in university but showed no real interest apart from Asian languages. He dropped out in his second year to tour the Far East. He spent a month rafting on the Ganges and eight more months in the mountains of Tibet learning to harness the healing powers latent in his hands. That, he claimed, had taught him more than all his years in school.

He'd returned home the following spring, but couldn't make up his mind about his studies. He hemmed and hawed about it all summer. At the last moment, he chose not to return to school and had come to Provincetown instead, hoping to discover a new direction in life.

Zach ended his narrative and listened as Brad spoke briefly of his past, and how he'd become a ward of the state at the age of fifteen after the death of his father. He also mentioned Ross's death, the reason for his presence in Provincetown. Zach offered his sympathy.

"We'd been apart for a few years," Brad said. "Still, I wish now I hadn't let him go."

"Do you feel responsible for what happened?"

"In a way," Brad admitted. "Though I always thought of Ross as a survivor. Whenever he fell down, he'd just pick himself up and go on. He never wasted time feeling sorry for himself. And even though he had a family, he thought of himself as an orphan, like me. I just never expected him to end up like this."

"Was he another younger guy who fell for you?"

"Ouch!"

"Sorry. I didn't mean it that way. How long were you together?"

"Two years. Just long enough for me to fall in love and long enough for him to realize he wasn't the settling-down type."

Zach cocked his head. "Most gay guys aren't. They just think they want to be. As soon as anything ties them down, they get scared and start to run."

"Is that experience talking?"

"Exactly."

"You don't seem old enough to have had all that much experience — no offence."

"I'm twenty-one!"

Bradford whistled. "Twenty-one! You'll be old and jaded in no time."

"Anyway, what's age got to do with it? These days most teenagers know more about sex than the pope."

Their server had chosen that moment to return with a bottle of wine.

"Depends which pope," he remarked as he opened the bottle with a soft pop.

Zach grinned. "How's your head feeling?" he asked Brad when the waiter had gone.

"Much better, thanks. Between your Reiki and Big Ruby's fair-trade joint, the pain seems to have receded to a dull roar at the back of my head."

"Well, let's have some wine then," Zach said. "Whatever the

Reiki started, this will finish. Cheers!"

They clinked glasses and sipped.

"Wow! This is really good wine!" Zach declared.

Brad looked up in surprise. Here was a very attractive twenty-one-year-old with blue hair telling him the wine was good. It *was* good wine, he knew, because he'd purposely selected an excellent vintage. In fact, it was *superb* wine. But at twenty-one, not only had Brad not known good wine from bad, he had yet to discover that he liked wine.

Brad found himself gazing with interest across the table. This wasn't the same boy he'd slept with a scant year-and-a-half earlier. Or perhaps he just hadn't given him much of a chance then.

Zach combined the boyish good looks of Tobey Maguire with the sexual appeal of a young porn star. He was a grunge Gainsborough: *Hustler Blue Boy.* Brad still recalled their initial encounter the previous summer. He'd been idling on the Internet one evening when a message blinked in front of him: *I found your profile on GayNet,* it said. *You sound like a very cool guy. Want to meet?*

It was signed "Zach," which Brad assumed was a pseudonym. No one signed his real name on GayNet. He read the profile. It sounded innocuous enough. Zach professed to like hiking and camping. Brad smirked when he read that. On screen, all the boys professed to like hiking and camping, but few turned out to have done either.

He read further. Zach also enjoyed most "outdoor pursuits." That sounded like a euphemism for sex. Brad clicked on the picture. It showed an attractive young man posed on a mountaintop in hiking gear. His legs were tanned and rippling with muscle. He looked like a pop-up poster boy for the great outdoors. That said something, of course, unless it'd been Photoshopped. You could be standing on top of the Pyramid of Cheops at Giza without ever having set foot in the Middle East, and no one would be the wiser.

With his sunglasses on, Zach had looked about twenty-six or twenty-seven in the photo. That was a decade or two shy of Brad's ideal but, *Hey!* It was a Friday night and he was horny. Wasn't that the purpose of being on GayNet?

A brief electronic conversation ensued, followed by an invitation from Zach. Brad was at his door in less than an hour. When it opened, the boy who stood there was considerably younger than he'd appeared in his picture. A lot of men Photoshopped their images to look younger, he knew, but almost nobody did it to look *older.* Just how much younger Zach was, Brad couldn't tell, but one thing was sure — he was *hot!* And what he lacked in age he made up for in sheer sensuality. Bradford quickly decided "Zach" would do for an evening's fun.

As it turned out, the sex was great. There weren't many younger men who could satisfy him the way an older and more experienced man could, but Zach had made all the right moves that evening. In fact, he was far better in bed than Brad had been at his age. Or perhaps he was just more comfortable in his skin.

Brad enjoyed playing the older aggressor role that evening. He hadn't been rough, but he'd taken advantage of Zach's submissiveness. He raked the boy's back with his chin stubble, giving him love bites and gripping him forcefully as he took control of his body, making Zach gasp and moan. He was a tasty meal and Bradford dug in for a generous helping.

All was going well until Zach responded to Brad's passion with an ardour of his own. *I love you!* Zach blurted out as he climaxed, clapping his hands over his mouth as though to shut out the offending words.

That was his first fatal error in Gay. Another quickly followed: the confession that he was only nineteen. *But almost twenty!* he'd added as an afterthought. All this had come on the heels of an admission that he already "sort of" had a boyfriend, though, as far as he was concerned, the relationship was all but over.

Brad left Zach's apartment that evening with a promise to call that he knew he'd never keep. For days afterward, he was plagued by the memory of their encounter, but as much as he'd wanted to repeat it he couldn't see himself as the partner of a nineteen-year-old who showed no emotional restraint whatsoever. Even Grace would have given pause at the thought.

Brad had long ago decided he would never let mere physical desire overcome his willpower. He saw himself as someone very much in charge of every aspect of his life. He needed to be in complete control. It was only beginning to occur to him now that it was the main reason he was always alone.

So how was it that a year-and-a-half later he found himself seated on the upstairs patio of an upscale restaurant in Province-town after a very enjoyable dinner, sipping wine with this same boy? But clearly this wasn't the same boy. Even his hair colour had changed!

Brad watched him across the table. The night they'd made love Zach's body had been every bit as superb as the wine they were now drinking. Except the wine was older. At that age, Brad knew, he probably forced himself to go to the gym once a week, at most. Muscles appeared spontaneously on kids like Zach and were the envy of every gay man over thirty. Himself included.

There was a decade between them, but Brad wondered if his

experiences in the last five years alone weren't an impassable chasm. On the other hand, he was having what amounted to a very intelligent conversation with this boy who was barely out of his teens. On the other hand again, the boy was truly irresistible. Zach smiled and Brad felt himself melting.

Now what? Brad wondered. Here I am sitting across the table from one of the world's sexiest twenty-one-year-olds. Do I turn him down again?

"So, are you a little more single these days?" he ventured.

Zach nodded. "Completely. I always seem to fall for the wrong type. Men are only after me because they find me attractive, but they don't want to know what's beneath the surface. They just want a sexy kid to hang with at the bars or sleep with once or twice and then dump."

Brad swallowed.

"Sorry, that was a bit pointed."

"You can't blame them for wanting to be seen with you. You're very beautiful," Brad said. "And as for the sex, I can vouch for that."

Zach smiled shyly. "Was that a compliment?" he asked.

"I think that was two compliments, actually."

Zach cocked his head as if a thought had just occurred to him. "You know, I'm glad I came tonight. I almost didn't."

"Oh?"

"Considering what happened the last time, I didn't know whether I should meet you again."

"You mean yesterday in the dunes or the night we slept together back home?"

"Both, actually. I realize it must be hard for you to sit across from me knowing I've said the 'L' word. I wasn't very experienced

133

then, but I definitely am now. You were only the second guy I'd ever slept with ..."

"*What!*"

Zach nodded sheepishly. "I think I was expecting too much. I didn't even want to have sex with you that night, but I couldn't help myself. When I saw you, I ..."

"... realized we'd spent eons together on Neptune's moon and thought, 'This has to be.'" Brad was grinning.

Zach stopped talking and sat watching Bradford. "You're making fun of me," he said.

It was true. It was something he did to distance himself from other men. He judged them, waiting for them to trip up and make a fatal mistake that would allow him to dismiss them. He didn't want to get attached to anyone.

Zach set his glass down. "Do you think we could just overlook those things and ..." He shrugged. "I don't know. Just get on with it, I suppose, and not get so awkward with each other?"

"And if I invite you to stay with me tonight, would that be making things awkward?"

Zach drew a breath. "I said I wouldn't sleep with you again even if you asked me to," he replied. "But sitting here across the table from you makes me feel weak in the knees."

The wine was getting the better of Brad. Something clicked in his head and said, *Do this!*

"Well, I think you should listen to your knees, young man. Why don't you down that wine and let me take you home so you can rethink things?"

Zach sighed. "I don't want another one-night stand with you," he said.

Brad sat back. "I can't promise anything," he said.

"On the other hand," Zach said, brightening, "I'd really like you to fuck me silly again." He picked up his glass and tossed down the contents. "Okay, let's go," he said.

IF BRADFORD THOUGHT they'd had good sex before, this time it was positively extraterrestrial. From the moment they shed their clothes it was as if their bodies had become one. Zach played virtuosic first violin to Brad's mellow cello, winding fine lines of fancy around him. Together they were sweet music, Mozart *ma non troppo* and "The Lark Ascending," while below the earth awaited their rapturous return. Not even the heights of passion he'd shared with Ross had been this blistering. Sometime in the night they fell asleep wrapped in one another's arms, their lips touching.

135

18

Brad woke to the phone's steely ring. Before he could open his eyes, it cut short.

"Fairfax House."

He rolled over to see Zach sitting naked on the floor, receiver in hand.

"Who may I say is calling?"

There was a pause. Zach stood, his muscles rippling coltishly as he passed the receiver up into Brad's extended hand.

"It's your grandmother," he whispered.

Brad groaned.

"Good morning, Red," came Grace's resonant voice. She'd returned as mysteriously as she'd disappeared. "Cat caught you napping?"

"Well, *you* caught me, that's for sure."

He slid down the ladder, wrapping a sheet around himself as he took the phone out onto the balcony. Dawn was just touching the tops of the dunes.

He gave Grace a synopsis of the events of the previous two days, including the news that the young man who'd answered the phone had rescued him from what would in all likelihood have been a nasty fate.

"Glad to know someone's looking out for you," she said. "Any idea who did it?"

"Not for certain. But I'm pretty sure it was Rosengarten or possibly one of his clients who murdered Ross," he said. "The man's got a propensity for taking out his anger on his houseboys. I got the impression he'd be capable of almost anything, if you pushed him."

"Keep that in mind while you're looking into things down there. We don't need him taking anything out on you. Have you managed to uncover a motive?"

137

"Rosengarten deals in fulfilling personal desires, which includes anything money can buy and maybe a few things it can't. It's possible the boys who work there are up for sale — dead or alive. It's also possible Ross spotted a closeted celebrity or politician who wants his identity kept secret at any cost. When I talked to him, Rosengarten seemed pretty concerned about discretion. Apparently he does a good job of providing it. The night I was there I saw a certain Senator Freeman of the Republican persuasion ..."

Grace let out a low whistle.

"Though why Rosengarten would kill one of his own just to keep up someone's reputation ..."

"Maybe it wasn't Rosengarten," Grace spoke up.

"I'll be surprised if it isn't," Bradford said. "He just feels like a killer to me."

"He may be a killer, but that doesn't make him Ross's killer."

"True."

"In the meantime, I'll run a check on him and Freeman, but your houseboy's story about his boss's background sounds credible. Anybody else we should check on, while we're at it?"

"Tall, thin fellow named Jeremiah Jones and an Asian body-guard called Johnny K."

"I'll see what I can do with that."

"When am I leaving for New York?"

"Not until you find out what's going on there. Upstairs thinks there's a connection to the New York problem somewhere on the Cape. So get out there and dig."

"Any clues as to where I should start?"

"Just sniff around for anything to do with His Holiness and you'll be on the way."

"Sniff around? I can't seem to avoid stepping in it. Did you know every other person in this place is a dyed-in-the-wool Buddhist?"

"The better to find your way home again, Red. Just remember to watch out for the big bad wolf."

That's if I don't turn into one first, Brad thought, glancing through the window at Zach, who sat practising his yoga. Grace clicked off and he went back inside.

"I've got to get going..." he began, but stopped when he saw Zach's lotus posture encompassed a whopping erection pointing due north.

"But not just yet."

"I WANT YOU to show me where you found me the other night," Brad said to Zach as they lay stretched out side-by-side. "Will you take me there?"

Zach smiled and rolled on top of Brad. "Only if you promise to take me to Tea Dance at the Boatslip this afternoon."

"All right," Brad consented, tousling his hair. There were worse ways to spend an afternoon than going to Tea Dance with a beautiful boy.

They turned right off Bradford Street onto Route 6, and then walked for a quarter mile. Zach pointed out the ditch he'd jumped in to avoid the oncoming car. Brad knelt and looked up and down the pavement. Cars passed, slowing to watch the pair who might have been checking for divots on a golf green.

There was nothing unusual to be found. Brad stood and brushed the dirt from his hands. He looked at the blue-haired boy waiting for him to finish, and felt a flush of tenderness thinking of the night they'd just spent together.

A loud cawing reached them from a nearby dune. A second crow joined in, followed by a third. Soon there was a veritable symphony of crowing that went on and on. Brad looked over at the tangle of brush leading from the dune to the beach.

"Something's making those crows angry. Think it might be someone in the bushes?"

Zach glanced over. "Could be a fox," he said with a shrug. "But they do sound pretty upset about something. Too bad I don't have my binoculars. That's what I use them for — bird watching."

Bird watching. That's cute, Brad thought. "I'm going to take a look," he said, jumping over the highway barrier and starting across the sand.

He reached the brush and began to part it with his hands, making his way up the rise. Zach followed him to the edge.

"There's probably poison ivy in there," Zach called out. "Or thorns. Maybe a snake or two."

Brad yelped. He'd just encountered the thorns. The crows — seven in total — flapped away at the sound, landing in another dune nearby. He recalled a nursery rhyme that someone, possibly his mother, had taught him:

One crow sorrow, two crows joy,
Three crows a wedding, four crows a boy,
Five crows silver, six crows gold,
Seven crows a secret, never to be told.

Just then he thought he saw a shape slip out of the trees at the far end of the dune. Or it might simply have been the shadow of a passing cloud, but he was too entangled in the brush to be sure. *Seven crows a secret!* he murmured, looking through the trees toward the beach where a number of men were moving about. No one appeared to be trying to get away or avoid being seen.

"Are you okay?" he heard Zach calling.

"Don't worry! I'm all right."

Zach elected to go around the dune and wait on the far side. Brad soon emerged, fighting off branches and tugging at vine leaves caught in his sandals. The pathway was well trodden, so there was no telling if any of the footprints had been made in the last few minutes.

"What did you find?" Zach asked.

"Not much. I think the crows were fighting over breakfast."

"Did you see anybody?"

"Hard to say. I thought I saw someone sneaking out the far side."

"What would anyone be doing in there?"

"Having sex, probably. I just wanted to make sure we weren't being spied on."

Zach looked at him skeptically.

"First you're thrown from a moving car, and now you think someone is spying on you. Does this sort of thing happen to you regularly?"

"It wouldn't be the first time," Brad answered, tight-lipped.

He scanned the ground until his eyes lighted on an empty bullet cartridge. He stooped and picked it up.

"Look at this," he said, rolling it in his palm. "Someone's been shooting around here."

"Were you shot at too?"

"No, but it's suspicious, don't you think?"

"Not really," Zach said. He looked down and scuffed a plastic tampon applicator with his toe. "This is a tidal marsh. The water comes in and goes out again. That shell could have floated in from Boston or Plymouth. There's no telling where it came from, or when."

Brad shrugged and pocketed the shell. "You never can tell."

Zach stared at him. "Is there something you're not telling me?"

Brad looked around where they stood on an open plain in bright morning sunlight a quarter of a mile from a beach where tourists gambolled in the waves. His story would sound absurd without the facts, yet he couldn't tell Zach more than he already knew without breaching security protocols and possibly endangering both of them.

"Call me suspicious, all right? Can we leave it at that for now?"

Zach eyed him again.

"All right," he nodded. "Until you decide to tell me what's really going on. Now can we go to Tea Dance?"

Brad smiled. "Just one more stop."

19

"Zach, this is Big Ruby. Ruby, this is Zach."

Ruby peered at Zach through her rhinestone glasses and reached across the counter. "Good to meet you, little feller," she called out to Brad's amusement, since Zach towered over her.

"Holy cool glasses!" Zach responded.

Ruby was alone behind the counter. She regarded them critically. "I know what *you're* having," she said to Bradford with a sly glance at Zach. "Now this boy looks like a coconut soy frappuccino to me. Am I right?"

Zach smiled. "Oh, yeah!"

"Looks like the front patio's free," she said. "Better grab it while you can."

They sat on a bench in the bright morning sun. Ruby came out and passed them each a cup, wiping her fingers on her apron.

Zach reached into his pocket, but Ruby stopped him. "First time, you're a guest," she said.

Zach looked perplexed. "Thanks," he said, "because I think I just lost my wallet."

He fished through the various pockets of his cargo pants. "It'll turn up," he said with a shrug. "It always does. I'll just have to retrace my steps over the last day and a half."

"Well," Ruby said, beaming. "You two certainly make a handsome couple."

Zach grinned. Brad blushed and nearly choked on his chai.

"Thanks," Zach said, licking the foam off his lips.

"You can always tell when two people are meant for each other," Ruby said, "because they look so right beside one another."

Halle arrived just then from around the corner, panting hard as if she'd been running. Her shaved head glistened and the tattoos gleamed in the sun.

She kissed Ruby. "Rue, hon, I'm sorry I'm late," she said in a husky voice.

"That's all right, galfriend."

Ruby winked at Brad and Zach. "See what I mean?"

She was right. The big butch Halle and the tiny perfect cowgirl made an oddly appropriate couple.

"This here's Halle," Ruby said. "And this is Brad and Zach."

Halle nodded gruffly at them, as if they were aliens landed in the front yard.

"You get in there and look after things while I talk to these boys," Ruby said.

She watched with a contented smile as Halle turned and went into the shop.

"That's one sweet gal, when you get to know her. She's a bit crusty on the outside, but inside she's soft and gooey as a cream puff."

"Kind of like Brad," Zach said with a grin.

Ruby laughed. "Where I come from, smack dab in the middle of cowpoke country, they don't make gals like her. Nothing but longhorn steers, a few coyotes and my clan. Halle's an entire different story. She comes from Tennessee. You ever heard tell of serpent handlers?"

"You mean the people who pick up poisonous snakes as proof of their belief in God?" Zach ventured.

"Those are the ones, little feller," Ruby said. "It's called the Church of God with Signs Following. 'In my name they shall take up serpents; and if they drink any deadly thing, it shall not hurt them.' Mark 16, verses 17 and 18."

"I'm afraid my knowledge of biblical quotations is a bit lacking," Brad said.

Ruby waved it away with her hand. "And that's the extent of mine," she said. "But Halle comes from a family of serpent handlers. When she went to church, like as not it was to watch some fool preacher pick up a handful of rattlers and shake 'em around. Couple of 'em died, as she can tell you."

"Some died of strychnine poisoning, too," Zach added. "If you're a good Christian, you're supposed to be able to handle snakes and drink poison and it won't hurt you."

"Gee," Bradford said. "Back home, we just had hymn sings."

Ruby let out a whoop. "Halle lit outta there as soon as she could. Figured she should see a bit of God's green earth before she died of a snake bite — which He'd probably appreciate, seeing how He'd gone to the bother of creating her and all."

Brad nodded to Zach. "You two have something in common," he said. "You're both Buddhists."

"No shit!" Ruby cried, taking a good look at Zach. "I should've known. You've got the light around you, little feller. Buddhists have that special glow."

"Are you going to hear the Dalai Lama speak next Sunday?" Zach asked.

"You bet!" Ruby cried. "Me and Halle are taking the bus all the way to New York. I've been waiting years to hear him!"

"I hope he won't have to cancel because of the hurricane," Zach said.

"Nah. It'd never happen. His Holiness wouldn't book a date if the future wasn't clear enough for him to see it through."

It was an interesting way of looking at things, Brad thought. To think you might know when to book something or hold off for a better time. The efficiency appealed to him. Then again, maybe the Dalai Lama's real date was with the bardo, and he just didn't know it. Though I guess that's why I'm here, Brad mused, to make sure neither sleet nor hurricane nor gloomy assassin stop him from giving his speech in Central Park.

"Have you ever been to Tibet?" Zach asked Ruby.

"Not yet. But I'm determined to get there before I die." Ruby suddenly looked sad. "My Rinpoche cries rivers of tears every day for his country — a country we have allowed to be lost in our lifetime! I have to get there for him, because he can't ever go back."

"I hope you do," Zach said. "It's the most amazing place I've ever been."

Ruby nodded to a spectacular pair of tanned lesbians walking up the steps hand in hand.

"Does your Rinpoche teach?" Zach asked.

"Not yet. He still gets a bit tongue-tied in English. That's why I call him my 'Reluctant Rinpoche.' He used to teach years ago, and he's promised to start again. I've asked him to teach me the hundred-syllable mantra."

"Wow! The hundred-syllable mantra — that's heavy duty," Zach said, impressed.

"You think that's heavy duty, try being a Catholic. For my first twenty years I bought into all that, 'O lord, I'm so unworthy' shit. 'Please dunk my head in rat crap and drown me in filth so I may understand Your glory.'" Ruby shook her head. "Now who makes up that stuff, anyway? Bunch of middle-aged geezers who aren't getting laid, most likely. The Bible's full of that kind of rot. No wonder the world's in such a mess, all these old guys making up crap like that, then trying to justify it by blowing one another up."

Brad smiled. "My family was United Church. We called it the 'Church of Anything Goes.'"

People strolled by, calling out greetings and continuing on their way as Commercial Street came to life. Ruby sighed contentedly. "I just love this town. Sometimes I doubt even nirvana could be better than this."

She turned to Brad. "You know," she said. "I haven't known you long at all, but I have this feeling like we've ..."

"... known each other before?"

"Not exactly." She laughed. "Unless you knew me as a little cowpoke out west, that is."

"I'm from up north," Brad said. "I was never west of Chicago till a couple of years ago."

The lesbian couple exited, joe in hand, smiling at Ruby as they went.

"Anyway," Ruby said, "what I meant to say is, I think we've been brought together for a reason."

"What reason?"

She shook her head. "I'm not sure yet, but there's something going on in this little town. Something not quite right. Maybe it's to do with that."

There was a scratching at the door. Halle came out with a small white dog jumping at her feet.

"Need a break," she said in her gruff baritone, stepping onto the patio. She held up a joint and winked.

"Hello, Bill," Ruby cried as the dog came shimmying and shaking and wagging its tail. After a quick once-around-the-patio, Bill jumped up on Bradford's lap.

"That's quite an honour," Ruby said, surprised. "Bill knows people and he's very choosy about who he takes to."

Halle lit the joint. They watched it flare up and then burn down to an orange glow. The pungent smoke wafted around the patio.

"That dog came outta nowhere, too," Ruby said. "Showed up on our doorstep about a month ago. We thought it might've been a lost tourist dog, so we put up signs all over the Cape. No one claimed him, though, so we took him in."

"That was nice of you," Brad said.

"Yeah. You'd make the effort for a dog, but not a human being, huh?" Halle said as she offered Brad the joint.

The others turned to look at her, but she seemed not to realize she'd said anything peculiar.

"If you want to give him a treat, little feller," Ruby told Zach, "there's a bag of doggie goodies over in the drawer beside the cash register."

Zach went in and opened the drawer. Brad watched him hesitate before placing his hand inside, gingerly removing a couple of bone-shaped treats before he closed the drawer and returned to the patio.

He held out a bone for Bill, who leapt from Brad's lap to accept a reward for his fickleness.

FOUR HOURS LATER they left Coffee Joe's, slightly stoned and highly caffeinated.

"You know," Zach said, looking at the sun sitting slightly off to the west. "If you're truly gay in Provincetown, you would have been in one of two places this afternoon: the Boatslip for Tea Dance or the dunes for sex. I feel compelled to point out we spent the entire afternoon smoking pot with lesbians."

"It was something, wasn't it?" Brad agreed, a silly smile on his face. "I think I learned as much about coparenting dogs and cloning weed plants as I need to know in this lifetime."

"*This* lifetime? Does that mean you believe you'll have others?"

"Not really, but I feel like I've lived three lifetimes in the past week alone."

Zach nodded. "It was strange to hear them talking about the Dalai Lama and Buddhism and then to open the drawer and see that big gun!"

Brad stopped and stared at Zach. "There was a gun in the drawer?"

"Sure, but it was probably only to scare off robbers," Zach reasoned. "Then again, Ruby's a cowgirl."

Reaching into his pocket, Brad fingered the empty shell he'd found on the dunes earlier. "Did you happen to notice what kind?"

"It looked like a Colt .45."

"That's a very powerful gun to scare off burglars." Brad put a hand on Zach's shoulder. "This place sure isn't what it seems, is it?"

They were in time to catch the last hour of Tea Dance before making their way back to Brad's house. They watched the sun set from the veranda, then spent the rest of the evening making love before Brad sent Zach home for the night.

"Are you sure you don't want me to stay?" Zach asked.

"I don't want us to get tired of each other," he said.

"That's not likely! Well, at least not on my part."

In fact, Brad had work to do and he didn't want Zach to know what it entailed just yet. *Just yet?* Why would he ever need to tell this boy anything about what he did?

He shook his head. It was a strange notion that had got hold of him.

20

An hour later Brad was crouched outside the Ice House in the shadows of the belladonna hedge. A handful of purplish flowers hung over his head, their sickly scent wafting around him as he peered through the leaves.

The curtains were thrown back, giving a clear view into the room where he'd sat among the other guests two nights earlier. It was empty now. Brad ventured a guess that the house wouldn't be open to the public that evening. That might make what he had to do a bit easier. On the other hand, without any distractions for the staff, it might make things a whole lot more difficult.

He made his way carefully through the hedge, taking care not to let it brush his skin. He scaled the fence and landed softly in a garden bed on the other side. Nothing moved in the darkness around him. As far as he could tell, no one inside had caught sight of him, either. He skirted a patch of moonlight and peered through the window. The table was bare. There were no place settings, voluptuous flower arrangements or expensive bottles of wine. It seemed there would be no dinner guests at the Ice House tonight.

Security seemed lacking, as well. The lugubrious Ichabod was noticeably absent from his post and the dining-room window was unlatched. Brad raised it a foot, keeping alert to sounds from within before lowering himself over the ledge.

The floorboards had been swept clear of the fallen plaster, but the bullet holes in the ceiling still gaped angrily down. Brad slid quietly along the wall toward the stairs. He nearly fainted as he turned a corner and almost collided with Ichabod as he stalked the halls with a candlestick holder.

"Polish the silverware, look after cook's orders, check the burglar alarms ... do this, do that," Brad heard him grumbling to himself.

Fortunately, the doorman hadn't heard Brad's footsteps. His tall, thin frame vanished down the hall and Brad slipped soundlessly up the stairway. He made his way to the Arctic Memorabilia Room and down the hidden passage till he was once again behind the wall of Hayden's study. Like the dining room, it too was empty, but Brad was prepared to stay as long as it took to observe the man in private.

He settled in and waited. Minutes turned to hours and slipped uneventfully past. By four o'clock he realized that nothing of importance was likely to occur in the house that evening. It'd been a waste of a night. Yet there would be others.

Tired and stiff, he made his way back down the stairs and out the window. The moon was long gone as he crept through the yard and retraced his steps to his residence, keeping careful watch over his shoulder to see that no one had followed him and no cars were racing silently toward him as he trudged along.

IT WAS GRACE who broke the news to him. Sometime during the night, while Bradford had been hiding out in his secret passageways, Hayden Rosengarten floated to shore in the Provincetown

Harbor. A beachcomber found the body just after 5 a.m.

"Bullet through the forehead at close range. We're checking on the make of gun."

Brad was silent.

"What are you thinking, Red?"

"I guess I was wrong. I was sure Hayden killed Ross."

"Doesn't mean he didn't do it. It just means that someone else killed Rosengarten in return. Maybe for the same reason, or possibly something closely related. Now tell me everything you heard and saw last night."

He described how he'd waited in the hidden passage behind Hayden's study for hours without seeing or hearing a thing. He went over his first visit again in detail, beginning with the $5,000 admittance fee and his exotic dinner in a roomful of highly privileged gay men. He described Rosengarten's explosive temper and his abuse of the clumsy server. He also recounted the phone conversation in which someone had threatened to kill Rosengarten.

"Now who'd want to kill a nice man like that?" Grace clucked.

When he described Senator Freeman's shootout in the dining room, Grace tsk-tsked. "Those Texans," she chided. "Maybe his trigger finger slipped again a little later."

Brad reached in the cupboard for a mug, flicking the On switch as he placed it in the automatic coffeemaker. "I already told you about the lesbian coffee-joint owner who hated his guts," he said over the gurgling sounds that filled the room. "Ruby threatened to kill him if she ever got her hands on him, which probably wasn't likely ..."

"You never know, Red."

"The female impersonator Cinder Lindquist mentioned a former houseboy named Perry who worked with Ross. Perry had been a favourite of Rosengarten's. Apparently he and Ross had a falling-out, and Perry left the guesthouse not long after."

Brad watched impatiently as the black liquid dripped into the mug. Caffeine was still a few minutes away.

"Cinder thought Perry might have been holding a grudge against Ross for getting too popular with Rosengarten. I took a spin by the bar where Perry works now. He claims not to remember Ross or even to know about the guesthouse."

"Go on."

"Cinder also mentioned a drug dealer who used to supply the guesthouse with party favours," he continued. "And by the way, the narcotics were very impressive at that place. They've got some flavours I've never heard of."

Brad eagerly tipped the mug, disappointed by the thin film of coffee covering the bottom.

"Anyway, Cinder claims the dealer had a grudge against Rosengarten, too. Ross's death might have been a revenge killing. I'm going to track down the dealer and pay him a visit."

Brad reached for the sugar, spooning it slowly into the cup in anticipation.

"There's also a rumour that Rosengarten screwed his former business partner out of a lot of money."

"The list is growing," Grace intoned. "Do you know who the former partner is?"

"Not yet. But during the phone call I overheard Rosengarten brag that a number of people wanted to see him dead."

"Looks like he was right."

Brad slipped the cup from the machine and replaced it with a second. He blew on the inch of steaming liquid.

"I'll pass this news along to the folks upstairs," Grace said.

153

"They'll locate whoever worked with Rosengarten in the recent past." She waited. "Did you ever consider the possibility that Ross committed suicide?"

Brad paused, mug to his lips. "Ross was a party boy out for a good time. Parties don't usually include suicide."

"But when the party ends, what comes afterward? You said yourself he died of a drug overdose. Long-term narcotics use might have affected his personality. You knew him as Mr. Smiley, but he could've become very depressed."

"Ross would've told me if he was going to end it. He'd want to say goodbye, though I doubt he'd let me talk him out of it if he'd made up his mind. I've seen him down before, but he always managed to pick himself back up."

"Sometimes even perfectly rational people start to fall ..."

"... only to learn there's no bottom," Bradford finished for her. "And they end up at a place like Hayden Rosengarten's, with their hopes shot and their future gone up in smoke. I know."

He took a sip. The acrid sweetness filled his mouth.

"Just thought you should consider it," the deep voice intoned. "By the way, we did a check on your usual-suspects list from the night of the dinner party."

"Can't wait for the credits," Brad said.

"The senator's well-known as a silent partner in illegal drug ops, even while he's been a very visible and outspoken member of government committees trying to clean them up. Apparently, a little hypocrisy goes a long way toward making a man rich. But it won't do him any good come election time if his opponents happen to find out what we know about him. *Oops!* You didn't hear me say that. Then again, no one on the other side's too squeaky clean either. It'd be like feeding Hannibal to the cannibals."

Brad gave a chuckle.

"Your other two guys showed up as well. Johnny K. is a small-time hood. He's suspected of being a hired killer, but there's no proof."

"What's his background?"

"Mongolian. There's our first possible connection with the New York operation. I gather he's an exotic-looking specimen?"

"Oh, yeah," Brad said, thinking of the bodyguard's almond eyes and solid build. "Why are all the bad ones *so-o-o* sexy?"

"Why do you think I hire gay agents to chase them? The other one, Jeremiah Jones, turns up as a horticulturalist."

"Orchids?"

"Yes, how'd you know?"

"Lucky guess."

Grace harrumphed.

"I can't find a thing on him, but that simply means he's been quiet till now. That's all I've got so far. Oh — not quite. I did turn up something interesting on Rosengarten's little operation. Apparently, there have been two high-profile suicides in connection with visits to his place in the past year. One was an up-and-coming 'family values' politician and the other a Roman Catholic bishop. Both turned up dead within a month of visiting the guesthouse. Now what could that mean?"

"Blackmail?"

"Sounds like it."

"That's where the closet gets you," Brad said, shaking his head. "Not to mention all that repressive fundamentalism."

"The bishop?"

"No, the politician."

"There's one other thing. Apparently Rosengarten didn't

always consider himself gay. There was a wife down around Chattanooga thirty years back. She died about a decade ago."

Brad whistled. "Married long?"

"Long enough to produce a daughter. We haven't found her yet, but we will. Guess what his profession was back then."

"Life insurance salesman?"

"Not even close. Itinerant preacher."

"You're kidding!"

"Not a word of a lie."

156

Well, well — you've come a long way baby, Brad thought. "It'll be interesting to see who turns up for his funeral," he said.

"Speaking of which, it's going to be awfully fast. The service is tomorrow."

"Sounds like someone's trying to get it over with quickly."

"That's what I think. See if you can find out why. Was there anything else on your end?"

Brad was silent. He thought of the gun Zach had discovered in the drawer at Coffee Joe's. Why would a coffeehouse owner need a gun in a peaceful resort town?

"What are you thinking, Red? It's so loud I practically have to hold the phone away from my ear."

"When I was at Ruby's café yesterday, the young man I was with said he saw a gun tucked in the back of a drawer."

"That so?"

"I didn't see it myself. In any case, I don't believe Big Ruby killed anybody. She talks tough, but she's a practising Buddhist and a very caring person."

"Look into it anyway."

The coffeemaker was gurgling through its final moments. The second cup was nearly full.

"I'd like to talk to her again. I have a feeling she knows something that she doesn't realize could lead me to Ross's killer — and possibly Rosengarten's, too."

"Assuming they're two different people. But if you talk to her, Ruby may figure out she's a suspect. We can't have her running away before this is properly looked into."

"If she *did* kill Rosengarten, she'll likely have run already, considering she told me she wanted to see him dead."

"Unless you're next on her list and she thinks she can bump you off before you find out about the murder."

There was a long pause.

"Bradford, are you listening to me?"

He was startled to hear Grace use his real name. She'd never done that before.

"I'm listening."

"Don't do anything stupid! That's an order."

"Don't worry."

"I *do* worry. And by the way ..." She paused. "In case you don't have enough on your plate, we're keeping an eye on Hurricane Isabel for you. The little lady seems to be heading right your way. We'll give you a day's warning if we have to evacuate you."

Brad hung up the phone and reached for the full cup of coffee. On top of everything else, now he had to worry about the weather too!

21

Brad took his breakfast out to the veranda. Nothing on the horizon suggested the approach of a hurricane. The sun had been up for only a couple of hours, but already people were making their way along the streets to the ocean.

He watched as they passed, sunk in curiosity — who were they and where had they been at the time of Rosengarten's murder? In such a small town, the killer was almost certain to be within a one-mile radius of where he sat eating scrambled eggs and toasted bagels. It could even be someone passing under his nose at that very moment on the way to the beach. Killer on the dunes.

A flock of seagulls winged overhead. Brad's mind drifted. He'd managed to get only three hours of sleep after returning from the guesthouse. He thought of Ruby. He had a gut feeling about most people, and it seldom proved wrong. He was ready to swear on the *Tibetan Book of the Dead* that Big Ruby was honest and reliable and the last person who'd harm another human being.

There was one sure way to find out.

On his way to town, he thought of Zach. He pictured the boy's angelic features. Where had he spent the night? He could imagine the kid showing up at one of the bars after they'd parted. With his good looks and unusual hair he would easily become the centre of attention. Any number of muscle hunks might have tried to pick him up. Maybe he'd gone home with one of them. Or several. He could even be on the beach with his binoculars right now. *Bird* watching indeed!

Then again, why shouldn't he? Brad challenged himself. After all, I was the one who sent him away. He's a sexy kid and at his age he probably loves the attention. Brad paused to wonder if he was jealous. Maybe a little, he admitted. It hurt to realize it, but it was true.

Yesterday, he and Zach had turned heads everywhere they went. An older man at Tea Dance stopped them to say how good they looked together. They were the kind of couple that others envied.

Coffee Joe's was bustling when he arrived. Big Ruby was alone behind the counter humming along to Melissa Etheridge's throaty growl blaring from the speakers. The place was cheery. In fact it almost felt like a celebration. Brad remembered Hayden's scathing comment about lesbian singers. For one paranoid instant he imagined Ruby telling him she'd finally got her hands on Hayden Rosengarten and shot him to death, and now she was celebrating. He needed to see that gun for himself.

"Howdy, friend! You're becoming one of my best customers," Ruby called out. "Where's your little sidekick got off to?"

"Zach's probably still sleeping. I think I wore him out."

She punched him lightly on the shoulder. "Good for you, cowboy. We gotta give the young 'uns their workout!"

"Ruby, could I talk to you in private?"

"I'm mighty busy," she said, nodding toward the throngs lined up for their joe. "Is it something serious?"

"I'm afraid so."

Ruby wiped her hands on her apron. "You haven't been back to that hellhole and got yourself beat up again, have you?"

Her face showed genuine concern. Brad dreaded having to tell her about Rosengarten.

"No, it's not that. But it's important."

She looked at him sideways. "If you say so. I'm going to have to close up, then. Halle didn't come in to work this morning, either. Another youngster who can't keep up with her elders."

She walked across the room and flipped the OPEN sign to NEARLY OPEN.

"Sorry, folks," she announced to the room. "I've got a bit of an emergency. I'll have to ask you to leave."

She waited till the last grumbling customer had left, then locked the door and turned to him.

"What is it?"

"Hayden Rosengarten was murdered last night. He was shot in the head."

For once Ruby had nothing to say. She stared at Brad in dumb incomprehension. "That's awful!" she managed at last.

"I was hoping you'd say something like that ..."

"What do you mean?" Ruby said, confused.

"I'm just glad you didn't react with joy when you ..."

"Well, in a way I am glad, but ..." Ruby's face took on a look of realization. "Are you sayin' you thought I mighta had something to do with it?"

Brad could feel her bristling.

"Ruby, when I was here yesterday, Zach opened a drawer to get a treat for Bill. He found a gun inside. Could I see the gun?"

She looked hard at him. Her eyes narrowed. "You're a cop,

ain't ya?" Ruby's face showed betrayal. "I should throw you off my property, you goddamn turncoat."

"But you won't ..."

"No, you're right. There's something about you I still like. And trust ..."

"Thank you."

"... even though you think I killed him."

"I don't think that, but I need to see the gun."

Ruby's mouth screwed up into a tight ball, then she shrugged. She walked over and opened the drawer. It contained only a hand-ful of dog treats and a bag of dope. She looked up worriedly.

"This doesn't look good, does it?"

"Any idea where it might've gone?"

Her eyes widened. "Halle closed shop last night. Maybe she took it home with her ..." She brought her hand to her mouth. "But, my god! That girl wouldn't hurt a puppy!"

"What about a human being?

Ruby's face was strained with worry. "I don't know what she's done with that gun, but she'd never kill anybody!"

She looked around the café desperately, as if she might find either the gun or Halle sitting innocently at one of the counters.

"Who do you think might have wanted to see Hayden dead?" Brad asked. "Particularly somebody who would benefit from it."

Ruby rubbed her head. "That could be lots of people."

"There was a business partner he screwed out of a lot of money, wasn't there?"

"Yes, there sure was," Ruby said forcefully. "He screwed his partner out of half-a-million dollars."

"Do you know who that person was?"

Ruby looked down. Finally, she sighed and said, "That partner was me, pardner."

Now it was Bradford's turn to be surprised.

"We met in a bar one night and he seemed all right, if a little smooth. He had lots of great ideas. Plus, he had the cash. We went halves on an art gallery that was up for auction. Things went okay for awhile."

She smiled ruefully.

"People like Rosie O'Donnell put their work in the gallery to help raise money for charity. It was mostly terrible stuff — canvases splattered in paint and covered in Cheerios and whatnot, but people bought 'em 'cause celebrities made them. We raised thousands to give to different causes ... or so I thought."

Ruby's shoulders slumped.

"It turns out he embezzled most of the money. When the charities came looking for the cash, he declared bankruptcy. He bought his guesthouse with the money he stole. If it hadn't been for Halle, I couldn't even have afforded this little place."

Brad watched Ruby's face as she looked around at the café she'd worked so hard to create. She turned to see him watching.

"As much as I hated Rosiegarters," she said. "I'd never've killed him for real."

"I believe you, Ruby," he said.

She shook her head. "You're probably the only person who'll believe it after me running off at the mouth about him all over town. There must be a thousand people who heard me say I wanted him dead."

"Apparently someone else felt the same. What do you know about the clients who went to his guesthouse?"

"He made lots of connections while we ran that gallery. Rich

people. Famous people. Not just politicians. Some of them probably went to the house. You never know who might get worried
if he thought Rosiegarters was trying to out him."

Brad mentioned the beefcake movie star he'd seen at dinner.

Ruby snorted. "Cream puff! Off screen, a guy like that couldn't
break a breadstick in half. He wouldn't know what to do with a
gun!"

"What about locals? Anybody else around here sore at either
him or Ross?"

"Little town like this? Oh, yeah! There's plenty. His ex-drug
dealer, for one." Ruby shook her head. "Man brought him the
best fair-trade weed this side of Puerto Rico. Pure and smooth.
Not the kind that gives you that awful pot hangover. It's what we
smoked the other day. I doubt he'd kill Ross, but he had plenty
of reason to give it to old Rosie."

Brad thought it sounded like the same drug dealer that Cinder
had mentioned.

"No one can prove it, but Rosiegarters hijacked this guy's
shipment of weed as he drove down the Cape one day. It's not
the kind of thing you complain to the authorities about, either.
And Fred got beat up real bad."

"You think he might have killed Rosengarten?"

"Ah, honey! I don't think anybody did anything!" Ruby shook
her head in disbelief. "It's too hard for me to picture it."

"Well, somebody murdered him, I can tell you that."

Ruby's eyes brimmed with tears. "I just can't believe it!"

"Is there anybody else?" Brad asked gently.

She looked away. "There's the bartender over at Purgatory."

"Perry?"

Ruby nodded. "He's one of my regulars. He used to work for

Rosie. Rosie assured him all his clients were safe and clean, but ..."
She bit her lip. "Perry swore he'd kill Hayden if he ever ..."

Ruby stopped.

"... if he ever got sick?" Brad said, recalling the lost look on
Perry's face.

Ruby sniffled and wiped at a tear. "I don't know if I should be
telling you these things."

"It's okay," he said, resisting an urge to hug her. "I know
Rosengarten abused the boys who worked for him. I saw it
happen the night I went there."

Brad already knew where to find Perry. He took down Fred's
name and address, assuring Ruby of complete discretion. "Better
for him to tell me about it than let the local police get it out of
him," he said.

"So you *are* a cop."

"No, I'm more like a peace enforcer, but I have the power to
make an arrest, if need be."

Customers were peering in the window and knocking on the
door. Ruby looked defeated.

"You'd better open up before you lose all your customers,"
Brad said.

She wiped away another tear.

"You've got my number," he told her. "Call me if you think
of anything. And let me know the minute you find out what
happened to that gun. I'm sure Halle will turn up soon and
everything will be fine."

Even as he heard himself say it, he knew it wasn't likely.

22

He found the drug dealer's house without a problem. It was located in the Portuguese neighbourhood, beyond the fish market and almost out of sight of the road.

The unkempt garden was a rarity in property-proud Province-town. The building seemed to be hiding in shame. The stain was peeling badly and the side windows were covered with heavy shutters. What he could see through a broken slat revealed little apart from an untidy living room lined with shelves of figurines. Brad knocked on the door and four huge German shepherds sprang to life, teeth bared, barking furiously through the picture window.

Brad waited. The barking continued. He was about to give up when he heard a bolt slide to one side. The door opened a crack and the dogs disappeared from the window. They reappeared, ferocious and silent, behind the face staring up from waist level.

"Hi, how are you today?" Brad said, feeling like an out-of-place Jehovah's Witness. "I was told I should talk to you, uh, about an upcoming party I'm planning?"

Boy, that was pretty feeble, he thought.

"Who told you I have anything to do with parties?" the face asked through the crack.

"Cinder Lindquist," Brad said.

"Ah, Cinny!"

The door opened to reveal a man in a rumpled dressing gown seated in a wheelchair. Obviously, thought Brad, he couldn't have been running around shooting people the night before.

"Come on in," the man said, wheeling his chair about.

Powerful arms and shoulders propelled him through the room. Brad followed as the dogs whined and sniffed at his crotch.

"Selma! Patty! Homer! Marge!" their owner called. Reluctantly, the dogs left Brad and went over to sit by the wheelchair.

The man reached over to a side table and picked up a can of beer. He tilted it at Brad. "Don't mind me," he said with a wink. "I'm just finishing breakfast."

Brad looked around the room. Rows of action heroes stared menacingly from knick-knack shelves. These were the figurines he'd seen through the windows, guarding the place from above almost as fearsomely as the dogs guarded it from below.

"X-Men," the man said with a deep laugh. "Each one of them has special talents and abilities. Like me." He looked down at his wheelchair. "Anyway, they're good company. Almost as good as the dogs'."

He wiped a hand across a greying beard, watching Brad with small black eyes. "Name's Fred," he said finally.

"Pete," Brad said.

"You a local boy, Pete?" Fred asked.

"Just got in last night from Chicago."

"City of Wind," Fred said with a guffaw, amused by what passed for wit in his mind.

He indicated a lumpy armchair. "Have a sit, Pete."

Brad sat on the edge of the cushion. The dogs watched him,

drool-covered tongues hanging out of their mouths.

"I keep the kids just a bit hungry," Fred explained. "It makes them eager."

Fred reached over and stroked one of the dog's ears. As he did so, Brad glimpsed the handle of what looked like a Colt .45 tucked into a shoulder holster covered by his dressing gown. It vanished as he sat upright. Then again, Brad thought, he needn't have been *running* last night.

"So, Pete, what can I do you for?"

"I hear you've got the best fair-trade dope this side of the rain forests," Brad said.

Fred smiled. "You've been talking to Big Ruby. No one else calls it that."

Oops! thought Brad. That definitely was not cool! He smiled sheepishly. "You mean that short dyke at Coffee Joe's?"

"That would be her."

"Come to think of it, I did overhear her telling somebody you had the best stuff in town."

Fred swelled with pride as he took another swig of beer. "Best stuff on the Cape!" he boasted.

"You must be a major party supplier," Brad said.

Fred nodded. "The biggest around."

Small-time criminal, Brad thought. Thinks he's flying low enough under the radar that he can brag about it and not get tagged.

"Do you supply that house up a-ways from here, the one with no name?"

A scowl passed over Fred's face. "I never go near the place."

Brad mustered a look of surprise. "I heard it was the wildest place to party on the Cape, bar none."

Fred's eyes narrowed. His fingers gripped the arms of his chair. "Bastard ripped me off," he said. "I had a big shipment coming in about a year ago. He was the only one who knew about it. When I drove in, a cop was sitting waiting for me outside of Truro. Busted me up real good. That's why I'm sitting in this chair right now."

"You saying a cop did that to you?"

Fred nodded. "At least he was dressed like a cop. Big fellow — dark. Coulda been Chinese."

Or Mongolian, Brad realized with a flash.

"Took my dope and tossed me out of his car halfway back to town. Left me lying in the road."

That sounds familiar, Brad thought.

"Doctors say I'll never walk again in this lifetime."

One of the dogs whined as though at the memory. Another barked skittishly at the noise of the first.

"It's okay, Patty," Fred said, patting her head. "Lucky for me I'm a Buddhist, so I know I'll get to walk again in my next life."

Yet another Buddhist, Brad noted curiously.

"But old Hayden Rosengarten's not gonna trouble us again."

"How can you be so sure of that?" Brad asked.

Fred smiled. "Because he ain't around anymore. They fished his sorry carcass out of the harbour this morning."

"Really?"

"Really, dude. He got what he had coming to him for a long time now."

"Kind of a harsh punishment, don't you think?"

Fred scowled and looked down at his chair. "Maybe you can't see things from where I sit."

Touché, thought Brad, though it doesn't give you a licence for murder. "I guess you'd like to have gotten even with him for what he did to you."

"Even? I'd've liked to get more than even. I wish I'd had the chance to turn him into roadkill, the kind that takes forever to die. He'd be chanting *Om-mani-padme-hum* for years."

"Any idea who got to him?"

Fred brought his beer down onto the table with a crack. "Listen, dude. You're making me nervous with all these questions. Did you come for dope or town gossip?"

The dogs were whining again. One of them came over to sniff Brad's leg, drooling on his shoes.

"Dope," Brad said. "Sorry for making you nervous."

"It's all right. It just gets my guys a little worried when they hear so much talk. Usually a customer comes and goes inside of sixty seconds."

Fred wheeled his chair around, turning it with remarkable agility. It wouldn't be hard to believe he could get around almost as easily as a fully-abled man.

"Tell you what," he continued, wheeling himself over to a desk. "I don't have much of a supply right now. Here's a joint — it's on the house. If you like it, come back in a few days and we'll talk."

Bradford pocketed the joint and stood. "Thanks," he said. "I'm much obliged."

23

Quentin's business card was burning a hole in Brad's pocket. He took it out and looked at the address again. From the start, it had sounded familiar. It was time to discover why.

He was sure the chatty houseboy had some connection to Ross's killer. Tom Nava's tip about Ross and the drowned boy sharing similar tattoos drew a line straight to the snake coiled on Quentin's chest, if not the one in his pants. There had to be something about the Ice House itself that related to those markings. If he could find out what, it might lead him to Ross's killer. It might also shed light on whoever had killed Hayden Rosengarten.

He followed Shank Painter Road across Bradford Street and down to Commercial. From there he turned right and walked west. The properties here were dazzling. The address on Quentin's card lay just around the corner from Tremont Street. Brad recognized the place the moment it came into view.

He was standing before one of Provincetown's ritziest guesthouses. He well remembered the antebellum mansion with its full-length veranda running along the ground floor and Juliet balconies above. It was among the most highly sought-after places on the Cape. As a young twink, Brad would never have dreamed of staying in such a place, but then again, Cinderella hadn't planned on meeting a prince, either.

It was by accident that the house found a place in his personal history. One night, after hours of sweaty dancing beside a boy who looked like he'd come fresh from his own private Olympic trials, Brad was suddenly presented with the opportunity. It turned out that the boy, Trevor, worked there. Trevor brought Brad back to the legendary house at four in the morning with the promise of wild sex. True to his word, Trevor's capabilities were feral as well as gymnastic. Their escapades encompassed an outdoor pool, several veranda chairs, a hammock, three bar stools and a Japanese garden. Afterward, Brad looked up to see that they'd provided entertainment for the inhabitants of the rooms overlooking the common area. A half-dozen men clapped and cheered before closing their doors and returning to bed.

By then it was nearly dawn. Trevor lit a joint and lay back at the edge of the pool.

"Will you get in trouble for this?" Brad asked.

Trevor laughed and nearly choked on the smoke. "Nah," he said. "But if I get a bonus, I'll treat you to lunch."

What Brad had yet to learn was that in P-Town, the houseboys ran the show. And in a house like this, reservations were often made a year or more in advance because no one — *absolutely no one* — wanted to risk being left out in the cold come summer. And *yet!* No matter how high your hair or how deep your pockets, and regardless of how capable your secretary was at booking in advance, you could still find yourself left *without.* For sometimes even wealth, personal connections and early booking arrangements were no match for Fame and Sex, as one Money Gay discovered.

Like the Wise Queen, every professional houseboy knows that in the inevitable Hierarchy of Gay, Fame comes first, then Sex, followed by Money. As Trevor told it, Money Gay had booked months in advance, laying out his conspicuously impressive VISA Super-Plutonium Plus card to stay in the best-of-the-best, as Money Gays always insist on doing. At the last minute, however, he arrived in P-Town to discover to his complete horror that overnight his much-anticipated harbour-view suite had been downgraded to a mere "town view."

172

Thinking of the loss in prestige it would entail, he threw his bags down on the imported marble tile floor of the lobby. "What do you mean I've been *moved?*" he raved. "I made these reservations last fall!"

The weight of Money Gay's social standing loomed over him. He owned a Mercedes, a Jaguar and a yacht, as well as a house in Palm Springs, a cottage in the Hamptons and a *pied-à-terre* in Manhattan. He was CEO of an internationally acclaimed fabric manufacturer that catered to the *crème-de-la-crème* of interior designers. Revered celebrities like the Olsen twins and powerful fashion mavens around the world were dependent on choices made by his company. He held degrees in business management, interior decorating and law from universities noted for the pre-eminence of their graduates. He had his hair cut regularly in Beverly Hills and his fingers manicured in Boston. He was even a very thorough magazine reader. And all of this, he reasoned, did not count for nothing.

"I'm sorry, sir," the houseboy informed him without the slightest hint of a cringe, for the houseboy was wise in the ways of the world and used to dealing with Every Sort. Moreover, he

had great power in that he knew the one truth: Money respects
only what it can't buy, and hence this tale.

"If you like, sir, I can offer you an alternate suite one floor
below. It's got access to the pool and the gym and ..."

"I don't care! I booked the top floor and I want it!"

Money always insists on having what it wants, despite reason
or logic to the contrary. And in this case the only logic seemed to
lie in the hands of what was, all things considered, an absolutely
Spectacular Houseboy.

Houseboy spectacularity notwithstanding, Money Gay
demanded his chosen suite. Things went on in this vein till
Money Gay decided to take matters into his own hands. Ignoring
the houseboy's protestations, Money Gay tore up the stairs and
pounded on the door of the very room he'd been denied.

"Open up!" he screamed. "This is *my* room!"

Where Wise Queens see beauty and Spectacular Houseboys
see power, Money Gays see only ownership. For this reason, they
miss the best of what life has to offer. But that's another story.

Inside, a voice called out politely. "Who is it?"

"Open this door!" screamed Money Gay. "Whoever you are,
you can't possibly be able to afford this room any more than I
can."

The door opened. Calvin Klein stood before him. "I'm sorry.
Is there a problem?" he asked.

Money Gay was faced with *echt* Fame. He backed off, one step
at a time, and allowed himself to be led quietly back downstairs
by the Spectacular Houseboy who made sure not to gloat when
Money Gay eventually accepted the second floor — and second-
best — suite. And for that, the houseboy also made a handsome

tip later that evening by assuaging Money Gay's deflated ego and other particulars of his being.

As with any fairy tale, endings must be just. And so, Fame got what it wanted: the top floor of a guesthouse renowned for its spectacular view of the town and its harbour. Money got what it could afford: in this case, being on the second-floor suite just below Fame. And Sex got what it deserved: both money and respect, without losing any of its power.

Why then, one might well ask, is Money lesser than the other two absolutes of Fame and Sex? Because, as Trevor and all house-boys know, Fame and Sex *are* power. Both can walk naked across a crowded beach and turn heads. But ask a mere Money Gay to walk naked across those self-same sands, and chances are he would run away in shame.

And that, as they say, was the end of that.

Bradford smiled, remembering his long-ago tryst with Trevor as he stood looking up at the house. He climbed the stairs and rang the buzzer. In the lobby, he asked to see Quentin. The desk clerk's eyes widened noticeably.

"Are you a cop?" the man asked.

Brad shook his head. It seemed strange to be asked that question twice in one afternoon, but he let it pass. After all, he was calling on the massage equivalent of a prostitute. Even in Provincetown, the law had to be considered sometime.

The man jerked his head toward the back of the house. "Back there," he said. "Room 24."

Brad followed a path till he came to a red door. He had raised his fist to knock, when he saw that the door was ajar. He pushed it open. There stood Tom Nava.

"Looking for me?" the cop asked from behind his mirrored glasses.

"Actually …"

"Don't tell me — you just dropped by for a massage."

"Well …" Brad's mouth gaped.

"I don't think you're going to get one," Nava said, indicating the unoccupied room. "Your masseur has flown the coop. And in quite a hurry, from the looks of things."

The bed was unmade. Clothes lay strewn around the floor. The room looked as though it had been host to its own minor Hurricane Isabel. Brad looked back at Nava.

"Care to tell me what you're doing here?" the cop said.

Brad swallowed. "Actually, I wanted to ask him about his tattoo."

Nava grunted. "That so?"

Brad couldn't tell if Nava was being sarcastic. He licked his lower lip. "You see, I have this theory …" he began.

"Go on."

"It's, uh … those snake tattoos. Ross had one. And James Shephard. So did Quentin …" he looked at the card in his hand. "Morrow. Quentin Morrow."

"Were you a friend of Mr. Morrow's?"

Brad smiled nervously. "I met him at the Ice House. A couple of nights ago."

"The *Ice* House?" Nava pulled out his pad. He shook his head and began jotting down what Bradford said. "There was a murder there last night. I suppose you know nothing about that, either."

"Just what I heard locally."

Nava looked up from his notes.

"You sure are one for being in the thick of things, aren't you, Mr. Fairfax?"

"What happened to Quentin?" Brad said.

The cop took off his glasses and looked around the room as though hoping it would speak for itself. Then he turned his unwavering gaze on Brad.

"I don't know what happened to him," he said, "but I intend to find out."

24

Brad wasn't surprised by the houseboy's disappearance. He had no way of knowing what had happened to Quentin after he was knocked unconscious, but obviously he'd been witness to the attack. Perhaps that was why he'd fled. Or did Quentin have something to do with Rosengarten's death? He hadn't seemed the murderous sort. Then again, most murderers didn't, until viewed in hindsight.

As far as Brad was concerned, there was already a sizeable cast of suspects. He could simply add Quentin to the list. On the other hand, attractive young men — especially those bearing snake tattoos — seemed to be on P-Town's endangered species list lately. Something drastic might have happened to the boy, but for the moment Brad didn't know what, if anything, he could do about it.

At three o'clock he made his way to the Gifford House. It was still early, which meant it was a good time to have a conversation with a certain bartender of extraordinary sexual appeal. He reached the imposing guesthouse and walked across the outer deck, his footsteps echoing behind him. The circuit-party boys from the previous day were gone. In their place, as if time had simply jumped a few decades, sat a gathering of older men in stuffy shirts and cravats, drinking mint juleps and bearing the optimism of a bygone era. They reminded Brad of Amanda Wingfield and her hordes of gentlemen callers. He nodded to them as he passed.

He tried to organize his thoughts as he headed down the steps of Purgatory. He hoped Perry would talk to him this afternoon. That is, if the hunky bartender was even working today. He wasn't sure what he'd do if Perry refused. He could hardly force him to talk. Despite his claims, Perry was clearly connected with Hayden Rosengarten and the Ice House.

178

On the bottom step, Brad froze and pulled back abruptly into the shadows. There, talking intently with Perry, was Zach.

They knew each other!

Brad heard Zach laugh and saw Perry flash his smile in return. For one paranoid instant, he imagined they might be talking about him. Paranoia gave way to jealousy. So this was what Zach did with his free time! It was a slap in the face. Suddenly he felt a surge of fear. Did the boy know Perry was infected?

He tried to shake off the thought. Get a grip, he told himself. A simple conversation did not a sexual relationship make, even in Gay. And even so, he reminded himself, he hadn't married Zach or asked whether he was seeing anyone else. What right had he to be jealous? If Brad got possessive over every man he slept with he'd have no time for anything.

Brad crept quietly back up the stairs and sat at the bar in a seat obscured by an overgrown fern whose leaves trailed to the floor. His suspicions continued to plague him. Every few seconds he turned to look over his shoulder at the doorway. What on earth was Zach doing here? Were he and Perry both somehow connected with the deaths of Ross and Hayden?

He shook his head at his own stupidity. How could he have been so blind? He didn't know a thing about Zach! The first rule in his work was to trust no one. It had been drilled into his head repeatedly. Anything could be arranged to look like an accidental meeting: find a lonely young agent, discover his weakness for attractive men and set a trap. Zach had been a sexy duck decoy just waiting for him to light on the pond.

Another godlike bartender flirted with Brad as he took his order. Brad ignored his overtures. Other customers came in and the man turned his attention elsewhere.

Twenty minutes passed. Brad's curiosity was killing him. Finally, Zach came up the stairs and left without looking around. Brad finished his drink and went downstairs. He leaned on the bar.

Perry looked up. "G and T, my friend?"

Brad nodded. "You've got a good memory."

"Only for the good-looking ones," Perry said as he reached for a glass and filled it with ice.

Still flirting, Brad noted, but there wasn't much sense in asking for a date now.

"So how's the invention business?" Perry asked.

"Thriving, thanks. How are the boys?"

"Getting cuter and cuter," the barkeep replied with what might have been a smirk.

Brad's paranoia returned with a jolt. Was Perry taunting him? Did he know Brad had been seeing Zach? Even if Zach had mentioned him, would Perry connect Bradford the golf pro with Frank the inventor? Only if Perry had already seen him with Zach, Brad realized. And in this tiny town that was highly probable!

"I heard there was a little excitement down by the harbour this morning," Brad said, watching Perry fill his glass with tonic.

Perry whistled. "The murder? News must travel fast when tourists hear about such things the day they happen."

"I gather the gentleman in question was well-known around town."

Perry gave a small laugh. "Well-known, yes, but not much of a gentleman," he said, placing the drink in front of him.

Brad flipped him a bill. "If you knew Hayden Rosengarten, then you must have heard of his guesthouse."

Perry smiled innocently. "Is that the place you were asking about the other day?"

"That's it."

"Ah! Of course I knew about it. I wouldn't call it a guesthouse, though. It's more of a whorehouse."

"Really?"

Perry's smile vanished. "I should know — I worked there."

Brad leaned forward.

"But not for long," Perry went on. "Just long enough to regret it. I have that bastard to thank for the fact that I'll be stuck on meds for the rest of my life." He caught Brad's look. "Yeah — I'm positive."

"Sorry to hear it."

"Whatever." Perry shrugged. "I should've known better, but they filled my head with all sorts of crap about how beautiful I was. What they meant was how 'fuckable.' Those rich bastards didn't give a goddamn about me."

Brad sipped his drink. The mix was just right. Perry had remembered even that.

"Funny you don't recall a guy named Ross Pretty. He worked there, too."

Perry shot Brad a look. "Can I assume you were a friend of Ross's?"

Brad nodded. "I'm his ex-lover. I've come to claim his body."

Perry looked at him appraisingly, as though suddenly seeing him in a different light. "I warned Ross to get out of there before something happened," he said. "Something bad like what happened to me. Now it's too late. The only consolation is that he won't have to suffer a long miserable death like the rest of us."

Brad considered this. "You ever argue with Ross?"

"Argue about what?"

He shrugged. "Anything."

Perry looked at him long and hard. "You're not really an inventor, are you?"

Brad shook his head. "No, I'm not." He thought for a moment that would end the conversation, but it didn't.

"Yeah, we argued. More than once, for what it's worth. Ross didn't know what he'd got himself into. He wouldn't believe me when I told him Rosengarten was using him."

"Were you in love with Rosengarten?"

Perry looked at him scornfully. "I'm not into daddies. Not even the sweet type. I prefer good-looking guys like you."

"Did you and Rosengarten ever have sex?"

Perry shrugged. "Everyone did. It was part of the hiring policy. Anyway, the bastard's dead and gone. And I say 'good riddance.'"

"Do you know who killed him?"

Perry leaned forward over the bar. "Could've been me," he said. "But then again, it could have been a hundred guys in this town. If anyone confesses to it, I'll buy him a drink. Hell, I'll buy him ten drinks!"

"I take it you won't be at the funeral tomorrow?"

Perry smirked. "Oh, I'll be there," he said. "I want to see them put him in the ground and cover him over. That's the only way I'll believe the bastard's really dead."

"Harsh words," Brad said.

Perry's face twisted into an unpleasant snarl. "Man, you have no idea. That man was a monster! He didn't care for anyone."

"And what about you?"

"What about me what?"

182

"Do you care for anyone?" Brad said. "All these cute guys who come in here and drool over you day after day. You ever take any of them home and coax them into a little bareback?"

Perry slammed his fist on the bar. "No one should live with what I've got! I'd never do that to anyone!"

"Not even if you didn't like the guy? What about that cute kid with blue hair who left a few minutes ago? Maybe he's a younger version of those rich bastards you despise. Would you infect him to get back at the rest of them?"

Perry released his grip on the counter and leaned back. His eyes narrowed. He seemed to be calculating something.

"Hey! Life's rough," he said with a shrug. "What a boy does with his body is his concern, not mine."

In that moment, Bradford hated the handsome barkeep more than he'd ever hated anyone. He downed his drink and stood.

"Thanks for the drink," he said, turning.

"Nice to see you again, Frank. Come back any time."

25

Brad didn't hear from Zach that evening. He hadn't really expected to after seeing him chatting with Perry, but some part of him still hoped Zach would call. Brad's visit to the Gifford House and his angry accusations to Perry hadn't allayed his fears any, though he knew he shouldn't have asked those questions. All the more reason why someone in his position should never have personal connections, he reminded himself. It only upset him to think about it now.

He sat on the veranda and watched the sun set. The once-promising bottle of Château de Beaucastel did nothing to assuage his feelings. He barely tasted it. Afterward he flung the empty bottle into the darkness of the marsh where it disappeared without a sound.

At ten o'clock he took a shower and went to bed, tossing on the mattress as the clock's luminous dial changed slowly: 10:30 ... 11:50 ... 12:45. Zach's face hovered in the air before him. Kids like that thought they were invulnerable because everybody loved them, Brad knew. And then one day they ended up in bed with the wrong guy, and a promising life was compromised.

He had nightmares that night. Zach turned up in most of them. Together they were running from someone they couldn't see. Whenever Brad looked over his shoulder, all he could make out was a dark car. As it got closer, he saw that it was a Porsche. *A rich man's car.*

At one point they were running downhill when the rim flew off one of the wheels, rolling after them like a saw blade threatening to cut them to bits. Losing sight of Zach, Brad jumped out of the way just in time to avoid its jagged teeth.

He fell face down, finding himself staring at a large red gem. *That's a very big ruby,* he told himself, picking it up. As it lay in his palm, the stone twinkled and dissolved into a drop of blood.

Brad woke with his heart palpitating. It was just past 2 a.m. He tried to recall the car that almost hit him the night he'd met Ruby. Had it been a Porsche? He couldn't be sure.

Outside, wind buffeted the house. He walked naked out onto the veranda, the cool wind whipping his body. Waves crashed in the distance. He shivered. Was this solitude or loneliness? One was a cool drink of water, the other an attack of sciatica. It shouldn't be that hard to know the difference.

Suddenly he tensed. Was it a shadow or had someone just slipped into his yard? He couldn't make anything out in the darkness. He withdrew silently inside, grabbing his shorts and racing down the stairs. Out in the yard, everything was in motion — the trees, the marsh grass and even the street signs wobbling on their posts. He waited ten minutes, then gave up and went back up to bed.

He lay awake for another hour listening to the wind and the distant surf. He remembered his dream of the Porsche. Had it been a warning for him not to trust Ruby? He hoped not. He still couldn't believe she'd hurt anyone.

Images of Zach drifted through his mind, plaguing him with the memory of how perfectly their bodies had merged. Yet the very next day he'd discovered Zach secretly meeting with Perry. Perry, who was a possible suspect in Ross's murder. Perry, who was an even more likely suspect in Rosengarten's murder. Just how much did Zach know and what exactly was his involvement in P-Town's ugly little secret? It made Brad doubt everything Zach had said, including his claim that when they'd met a year-and-a-half earlier he was a sexual novice. *Bullshit!* Brad thought. That kid had all the right moves, and you don't pick those up overnight!

He fell into a fitful slumber just before dawn.

THE MORNING WAS overcast. The sky and the dunes stretched in an unbroken line of grey as far as the eye could see. Provincetown in the rain was a dismal place. It was fitting weather for the funeral of a man who'd been despised by so many people.

In the mirror, Brad saw the dark circles beneath his eyes. He let out a sigh. He was definitely becoming a candidate for early wrinkles. He deliberated over his wardrobe for some time before deciding what to wear. He wanted something that would seem suitably solemn, yet with a hint of casual elegance. What exactly was that? he wondered. A priest with a sprig of lilac in his hair?

It wasn't till he was leaving that he discovered the note pinned to his door. He'd missed it in the darkness last night. It was from Zach. So he *had* seen someone after all! Why had Zach come by at two o'clock in the morning? Fearing he'd be late, Brad tucked the note into his pocket to read later.

From a distance, the grave markers looked like giant chess

pieces. Your bishop may take my queen, Bradford mused, but my knight definitely prefers your king. Check and mate, Mr. Hayden Rosengarten, entrepreneur.

He was surprised to see several dozen people standing around the open grave. They weren't the people he'd expected to see. For the most part, they looked like regular townsfolk. There were no hard-ass mobster types come to pay their last respects to a fellow criminal. By all appearances, this would seem to be the funeral of an ordinary and fairly popular man.

Perry stood off to one side, under a tree. The barkeep paid Brad no attention. A few minutes later, Fred rolled up in his wheelchair without his canine escorts. He looked surprised to see Brad there. Brad watched as Perry walked over to the drug dealer and the two spoke briefly. All the pieces were connecting.

A tall shapely blond wept quietly into her handkerchief. There was something familiar about her, Brad thought. She looked like Cybill Shepherd. What on earth would Cybill Shepherd have to do with an ex-drug lord and brothel owner?

Brad recognized another familiar face, that of Hayden's spectacular bodyguard, Johnny K. He remembered how Rosengarten had pointed him out at dinner, claiming the stud had his name tattooed on his penis. Would that be Sebastian O'Shaughnessy or Bradford Fairfax?

At Johnny K.'s side was the cheerless Jeremiah, whose eyes roved icily over the crowd. The thin man caught Brad's glance. He nudged his companion, who glared at him across the grave.

Brad nodded and smiled. Bet you thought I was dead, he mused. He watched to see if the pair would acknowledge Perry or Fred, but no one gave anything away. Maybe Johnny K. wasn't the cop who assaulted Fred on the highway outside of town, after all. Then again, a man would look pretty different dressed in a uniform.

Two Asian men in burgundy robes, heads shaved, stood to one side of the gathering. Every few minutes they raised conch shells and blew a mournful sound over the gathering. There were other people in colourful costumes as well. These people were all Buddhists, Brad realized with a shock.

A short bespectacled man in a saffron gown began to chant. Brad stood listening to what sounded like a Tibetan funeral ceremony. He looked up to see Cybill Shepherd standing beside him in tears.

"I'm so sorry," Brad said. "Were you related to him?"

"No, you silly goose. It's me — Cinder."

Brad did a double take.

"Don't be so obvious," Cinder chided.

Bradford resumed his stare at the coffin.

Cinder sighed. "Funerals are wonderful, don't you think? There's something about them I just can't resist. Thank God for waterproof mascara!"

"Who are all these people?" Brad asked, surveying the crowd.

"Buddhists," Cinder replied, as though it were obvious to everyone but Brad.

"Yes, I know they're Buddhists, but why are they here?"

"Hayden was a Buddhist. Didn't you know that?"

"No!"

"Oh, yes! Big time! He even willed himself his own estate when he's reincarnated. I think the big boys are still working on that one."

"I noticed some of his bitterest enemies among the mourners," Brad said, glancing across at Fred and Perry.

"I wouldn't doubt it. They want to be sure it's really him going into that hole. Wouldn't you?"

"I'd rest contented with whatever the coroner's report said."

"It didn't do Ross much good," Cinder reminded him.

Brad noticed a man in a brown suit standing quietly off to one side. He was Asian Ivy League, if there was such a thing. For a moment, Brad felt he knew him. Then he recognized the face — it was the visiting Tibetan spiritual leader in the poster he'd seen in town. Hayden must have been a very big deal to Buddhists, Brad realized.

Cinder looked over to see what Brad was watching.

"Oooh! Isn't he nummy?" Cinder gushed.

The ceremony appeared to be coming to an end. The shell-blowers emitted one long final gasp as the coffin slowly sank into the ground. At the last moment the winch slipped. The box jerked and dropped the remaining few inches, landing with a thud. Perry smirked. Fred pulled an oversized joint from his pocket and threw it in after the box.

"Cheers, you bastard!" Brad heard him yell. "Here's something to keep you company while you roast in hell!"

"What a waste," Cinder declared through tears.

It seemed like half the town had come to the funeral of a man everyone hated. The only one crying was Cinder. For a moment Brad imagined the murder might have been a group conspiracy, but that was just small-town America getting to him, he reasoned. Pull into a gas station in rural Georgia, and you'd think Stephen King had dreamed the place up. Surely an entire town wouldn't conspire to kill one of its own citizens, no matter how hated he was? Still, Hayden Rosengarten was a blemish on Provincetown's fair complexion. More than one person had thought so.

Brad had almost convinced himself his conspiracy theories were downright loony when he turned and saw a figure in purple trudging toward them with a small white dog trailing behind. The missing piece!

Ruby came over and planted herself beside him. "I was afraid I'd missed it," she said.

"Hi Ruby," Brad said. "You're the last person I expected to see here today."

Ruby looked sheepish. "I know," she said. "I'm the last person *I* expected to see here today, too."

"Hiya, hon," Cinder said, bending to kiss Ruby on the cheek and reaching down to pat Bill, who licked his hand affectionately. "Love the dress."

"Thanks. Only one I own. I keep it for funerals and weddings."

"I didn't realize you two knew each other," Brad said, surprised.

"Honey, the whole town knows each other," Cinder replied. "There's not a soul here today who doesn't know everyone else."

"My Rinpoche talked me into coming," Ruby told him. "He said it would be good for my karma if I could forgive Rosie-garters as he leaves the earth plane."

"That's a noble sentiment," Brad said.

She smiled. "Isn't it? That and the fact that the bastard's in the bardo right now. When a soul dies, it contemplates the light for four days. If it enters into the light, it never returns. If it doesn't enter, it gets reborn as something else. I'm going to try to stand between his soul and the light. In his case, I think he'll come back on a lower rung of the ladder."

Brad cocked his head inquisitively.

Ruby winked. "I wanna make sure he gets reborn as a cock-roach so I can step on him when we meet again. Come to think of it, he already was one in this life. I'll try for an ant."

She nodded toward the handsome Asian in the brown suit Brad and Cinder had noticed earlier. "That's my guy over there. My Reluctant Rinpoche."

Brad had always thought of religious devotees as physical blobs, but here was one who positively radiated a hearty sexiness. Then again, he reasoned, both Ross and Zach could hardly be called slackers in the physical fitness department, even if they were just trainees. Maybe it was a Buddhist thing.

The Rinpoche walked over to greet them exuding power and well-being. Brad extended his hand. The man had a handshake like a trucker's. Brad felt his hormones twitch. He looked forty, tops. Perfect daddy age, Brad thought, as he stared into the man's deep-set eyes. Here was major sex appeal.

"Thank you for coming, friend," the Rinpoche said in heavily accented English. "It is good to see so many people at funeral."

"Death is a terrible thing, isn't it?" said Ruby.

"On the contrary," the Rinpoche replied, his voice soft and calming. "Death very beautiful. It return us to where we come from."

Despite his poor English, Brad had no problem understanding the man.

"Important to remember, we begin to die as soon as we are born," the Rinpoche intoned like a malevolent fortune cookie.

"Then we should be very practised at it when the time arrives," Brad said.

The Rinpoche nodded and said, "Dying very easy for those who know how."

"But funerals are so much more fun!" Cinder exclaimed.

Everyone turned to look at him. "I'm sorry," he mumbled.

"All that separate this life from next is single breath," the Rinpoche went on, looking at Bradford. "A skilful death is most desired when the time come."

"It's so beautiful when he talks about death," Ruby gushed.

Clearly, Ruby thought her Rinpoche was a god on earth, but when Brad looked at him all he saw was a muscle dude in a brown suit. Guess I'm just not the enlightened sort, he mused.

Brad watched as Bill lifted a leg and peed on the man's shoe. Good aim, he thought. Boy, sometimes it pays to be the little guy!

Oblivious to the insult, the Rinpoche reached down to tug Bill's ears. "Animals very fond of me," he said, smiling.

Brad looked around the graveyard where the assembly was breaking up. Ruby turned to look at the coffin. She shook her head. "He'll never hurt my loved ones again," Brad heard her whisper fiercely.

The chanting had resumed. There was probably little else for Brad to learn there.

"I'm afraid I've got to take my leave," he said. He shook hands with the Rinpoche again, letting his grip linger while he gazed into the man's eyes. "I've got a duty of my own to perform."

Cinder took that moment to have a mild breakdown. His chest heaved with sobs. "It's all right, honey," he said, waving off Brad with a hanky. "I'll be okay in a moment."

At the gate, Brad nearly walked into a wall of sex as a figure stepped out of the bushes directly in front of him. It was Johnny K., with the ghostly Jeremiah standing behind him.

"Mr. O'Shaughnessy," Jeremiah intoned icily. "How nice of you to come to our patron's funeral. We're touched."

JEFFREY ROUND

"Life has its surprising turns, doesn't it?" Brad said. "You must be very broken up by the loss."

"It was a terrible shock," Jeremiah said, his eyes rolling heavenward like Mary Pickford portraying Sorrow.

"What will happen to the guesthouse now?" Brad asked.

"I hope we'll be able to continue with our patron's traditions," the man said solemnly.

Brad shrugged and said, "Why kill a good thing?"

"Precisely," Jeremiah said, with no indication he'd caught the irony.

Johnny K. was silent, as usual, but the hand inside his jacket pocket might well have been clutching a gun. Brad remembered Grace's warning about his suspected past as a hit man. He wasn't going to risk making it a double funeral.

"If you'll excuse me, gentlemen, I must be on my way."

The bodyguard's eyes bore into him as he passed. A block from the cemetery, Brad turned and looked back. The pair were still watching him.

He continued walking. On the next block, he remembered the note he'd tucked into his pocket. He opened it.

To the World's Most Beautiful Man:

I've been lying awake all night thinking of you! I just realized I don't have your phone number! I'm dying to see you again. Meet me at Café Edwige for breakfast around ten, if you get this. My treat!

xoxox
Zach

That's quite an appetite, Brad thought. You had me for supper two nights ago, Perry for brunch yesterday and now you want me again for breakfast today. Clearly, the young man was not all he seemed. Brad folded the note and carefully returned it to his pocket. It might be useful later for fingerprints, or even DNA sampling, if it ever came to that. He checked his watch. It was past eleven — too late to meet Zach even if he'd wanted to.

Besides, Ross was waiting for him.

26

Brad picked up the earthenware urn with Ross's remains and carried it to the edge of town. Ross had wanted to see fireflies coming through the smoke. Only Bradford could give him that. He walked all the way to Race Point with the vessel tucked beneath his arm. By the time he arrived the afternoon was nearly over, but he wasn't ready to let go. He sat on the sand and waited for the sun to finish crossing the sky, while a handful of beach-combers straggled back to their cars and dune buggies. He watched as they climbed into their vehicles with cheers of farewell before heading on their way.

Seagulls wheeled overhead, crying raucously as they searched for a silvery glint of fish in the dying light. As the sun set, the air grew chill. Dusk gathered as evening slowly turned to night. Still, he waited.

In the distance, headlights of passing cars gleamed along the interstate like roving lighthouses. The moon rose over the water. Brad could feel the cold. He was starting to wonder if it would ever happen. Finally, he saw what he'd been hoping for. Ghostly wisps of fog began to come in off the sea, creeping over the sand and rocks.

He stood, clutching the urn as he walked. The fog grew denser till he could no longer see the water or the rise of dunes off to his right. He was cut off from both land and sea as the fog enveloped him.

Here's your smoke, Ross, Bradford said silently. *Now let's see if we can find your fireflies.*

He remembered a joke Ross had told him about a dying lama who'd gathered all his students around him to say he was leaving them forever. *This is my last hour on earth,* he proclaimed. The monks were stupefied. *But Master! How will we go on living when you are dead?* The lama smiled. *These two things are both the way of all things,* he answered calmly. *What do you mean, Master?* they cried. *Well,* said the lama, *you know what they say: when it rains, it pours.* And with that, he died.

Brad smiled at the memory as he trudged along. He might have been the only living creature for miles in any direction. At last, when he'd gone far enough, he looked down and scuffed the sand. A ghostly glint flashed. He walked on, keeping his eyes trained on his shoes. With each step-*flash!* step-*flash!* the phosphorescent algae beached in the sand ignited on contact with air.

Look, Ross! Here are your fireflies! Tears fell from Bradford's eyes. *I set you free for the last time!*

He put the urn down and unscrewed the lid. His fingers dipped in and brought out a handful of coarse grains. Here was all that remained of the body he'd loved, of the man he'd loved. He flung the ashes upward into the wind.

And so departs the soul, a voice said somewhere in the back of his head. Whether it was his own or someone else's, he would never be sure.

ZACH WAS HUDDLED on the step waiting for him when he arrived back at his guesthouse. Brad wiped his cheeks with his hand, hoping the tear tracks weren't noticeable.

Zach stood at his approach. "Hi there!" he called out.

"Hi," Brad responded flatly.

"I was beginning to worry that something had happened to you. Given your recent history of unusual occurrences, that is."

The memory of seeing Zach laughing and talking with Perry rose before his eyes. "I had things to do," he said, setting the urn down on the stoop.

"What's that?" Zach asked.

"A duty I needed to perform."

Zach watched him without approaching. "They're Ross's ashes, aren't they?"

"Were," Brad answered. "They *were* his ashes."

Zach hesitated. "This probably isn't a good time for me to be here," he said.

Brad didn't reply.

"Do you want me to go?"

Brad nodded.

"I'm sorry," Zach said, reaching out a hand to Brad's shoulder.

Brad stepped back. "Look!" he snapped. "Don't fall in love with me. I can't be there for you!"

For a moment, Zach looked crushed. "I understand," he said, then rushed down the walk and around the corner.

Brad picked up the urn and entered the darkened house. Instead of turning on the lights, he went directly upstairs and set the empty container on the window ledge facing the sea. He lit a candle and placed it beside the urn.

If you're here, Ross, give me a sign, he asked silently.

Nothing happened.

Blow out the candle, Ross.

Still nothing.

Figures, Brad thought. Serves me right for believing in spooks.

OK, Ross. Wherever you are, I still believe in you. And I still love you. You don't need to give me a sign.

An instant later, a crash splintered the glass as a softball-sized object flew through the window, knocking over the candle.

Jesus! thought Bradford. *Couldn't you have just flickered a bit?*

He ran over to the window and looked out. There was no one there. Once again he raced down the stairs and into the yard, but whoever it was had disappeared in the black of night. He tore down the drive and across the road. Nothing moved over the marsh or along the street. It had been a hasty retreat, if whoever it was had even gone that way. Someone could just as easily have slipped between the houses and across the neighbouring yards.

Brad hoped it hadn't been Zach. Could the boy have done something like that in a moment of rage at being rejected? He didn't know Zach, he reminded himself. He could be capable of a lot of things.

Walking back, Brad saw he'd left the front door open. He cursed himself for being so careless. It was the perfect opportunity for someone to get inside while his attention was diverted.

He stopped in the hall and listened carefully. Nothing. Slowly, he made his way upstairs in the dark, ears and eyes alert for danger — a creaking floorboard, a moving shadow. The fallen candlestick lay on the landing. He picked it up to use as a weapon, in case he needed it.

He crept quietly across the living-room floor, careful to avoid the shards of glass that lay glinting in the moonlight. Finally, satisfied he was alone, Brad turned on the lights. The urn lay on the floor beneath the window. He picked it up and set it on a table, then looked around for the rock that had shattered the glass. Instead, he discovered a package wrapped in brown paper. He unwrapped it and found himself holding a miniature video-cassette.

The package had been weighted so it would break his window. He fished around for the other object, holding it to the light. He'd seen something like this before. In fact, he'd seen this very globe of plastic with a starfish at its centre on the desk of Hayden Rosengarten. *Shades of Andy Warhol!*

Brad set the globe on the windowsill and retrieved his camcorder. He patched it into the video network and inserted the tape. On the screen, a blurry image flickered to life. The camera was focused on a set of lips and what looked like a whole lot of whipped cream. No — it wasn't whipped cream, he realized. They were bubbles. Someone was sitting in a bubble bath up to his chin in suds.

He watched as a glass was raised and lowered again. The camera zoomed out slowly as the face came to life. It was Hayden Rosengarten, looking for all the world as if he were still alive!

Hayden reached over the side of the tub and grasped a bottle of champagne, refilling the glass. His other hand lifted a joint to his mouth and took a toke. Brad was seized with the urge to run out and scour the neighbourhood again, but whoever had thrown the package through his window would be long gone. He watched the dead man drinking and smoking dope as he smirked at the camera.

Hayden burped. "Is that for me?" he asked someone standing offscreen. "It's awfully big!" There was no response as Hayden's eyes remained focused on the other person.

Brad caught a flicker of movement behind Rosengarten where smoked-glass tiles framed the tub. This looked like the bathroom he'd peered into from the secret closet. In the glass, he could make out the rustle of a robe like the one he'd worn on arriving at the guesthouse.

"Oh, baby!" he heard Hayden say. "Come to Daddy. You need a spanking."

The robe fell to the floor and a muscular shoulder moved into the frame, revealing what looked like an out-of-focus birthmark.

The focus returned to Hayden's face. "Is that thing real?" he exclaimed. "What are you going to do — shoot me? Do you even know how to use a man's toy?"

"Does Daddy want to die?" came a familiar-sounding voice.

"Oh, yeah! Shoot me with your big gun! *Bang-bang!* I dare you!"

Something glinted in the mirror just before the screen went black.

He was shot in his own guesthouse! Brad realized with a shock. Someone pulled a gun on him and Rosengarten called his bluff. Whoever killed him must have dumped his body in the harbour later that evening.

Brad rewound the tape and played it back. He waited for the robe to fall and the shoulder to reappear. He backed the tape up again and watched it in slow motion, finally freezing on the birthmark. Only it wasn't a birthmark. It was the blurry tattoo outline of a snake!

"Would you look at that," he mumbled. "A genuine clue!"

He backed the tape up to the last few moments of Hayden alive in the tub. The man seemed fearless as he watched the gun being trained on him. His eyes betrayed no hint of the tragedy that was about to occur. Either that or the alcohol had numbed him to the point of not caring.

I don't know about a skilful death, thought Bradford, but I bet it was swift.

27

Brad put in an emergency call to Grace. The tape was still rewinding in the camera as she answered. Brad told her everything that had transpired in the last day and a half, omitting the tiny detail that he'd actually gone to talk to Big Ruby against her orders.

Grace didn't seem surprised by any of it. "I'll check with forensics to find out if he had a blood-alcohol level consistent with half a bottle of champagne," she said. "And by the way, the bullet that killed Rosengarten?"

Brad inserted a blank tape into a neighbouring machine as he waited.

"It was fired from a Colt .45."

He clicked the door shut and pressed *Record* and *Play*.

"I've seen at least two in the last week," he said, mentioning Senator Freeman's and Fred the drug dealer's. He hadn't actually seen the gun in Big Ruby's drawer, so he couldn't say for sure what it was, though Zach had thought it looked like a Colt .45. So had Nava's gun, come to think of it.

"Assuming the tape's real," Grace said, "do you think it was one of his guests who killed him?"

"If not, then someone made it appear to be," Brad reflected.

"Whoever it was is wearing one of the robes that Ice House guests are issued on arrival."

Hayden had said that discretion was the key to keeping his clients' trust and, as far as Brad could tell, he'd run his organization very discreetly. Except for when it came to dying.

"What I want to know is when the murder occurred. I sat there from half-past nine till nearly five in the morning and I didn't hear a thing the entire night."

"Forensics will come up with an answer," Grace said. "But that still doesn't tell us who tossed the tape through your window."

"It had to be someone who knew about the video camera in the bath. And that would most likely be someone who worked there."

"That's a logical assumption," Grace said. "But then we need to ask why."

"There'd be two reasons to send me the evidence," Brad said, watching the tapes winding simultaneously as one duplicated the other. "First, an employee might have sent it to me out of loyalty to his deceased employer hoping I'd catch the killer. Admirable. Or, second, someone may want to get the murderer out of the way for his own reasons. Very devious."

"You said both Jeremiah Jones and Johnny K. were at the funeral. Do you think one of them killed Rosengarten and wants to pin the murder on the other?"

"Or maybe they both killed him. They weren't exactly broken up during the ceremony."

"Whoever sent the tape obviously knows who you are and where you're staying. Could someone have followed you home from the graveyard?"

The clip finished recording. Brad stopped the machine. "I was very careful about that, but it's possible," he said, removing the original tape and inserting it into its case.

"I want to see this tape as soon as possible," Grace said.

"I'll see to it," Brad replied.

"My guess is whoever sent the tape knows who knocked you out and left you on the side of the road. That was meant to look like an accident, of course. As your friend Ruby pointed out, you weren't very careful wandering around those roads at night. The real accident was that you survived."

Brad removed the duplicate tape and replaced it in its case. He was listening carefully to Grace's words. What he was thinking, but wasn't willing to voice, was that the only people who knew where he stayed during his assignments were the people he worked for. That meant there was a third possibility: the person who found the tape was also the murderer and had sent Brad the evidence simply to throw him off track. It wouldn't be the first time an agent had been betrayed in such a fashion. He took a pen and wrote *D-U-P-E* on the second tape.

"At this point, you have to assume the murderer could be anyone you've met and possibly even someone you haven't met yet. Someone is keeping track of you, that's for sure."

Brad slid the duplicate tape into a drawer. Apart from Ruby and Cinder, no one in Provincetown knew he was actually looking into Ross's death. Cinder's involvement was an open question but, as far as he could see, Ruby had no access to the Ice House. He'd told both Zach and Perry he was in Provincetown to claim Ross's body, but that was all. Given the recent turn of events, he couldn't be sure they didn't know or at least suspect that there was more to it than that. In any case, the only other person who knew where he was staying was Zach.

As if she'd read his mind, Grace said, "What about this boy who rescued you? That could easily have been set up. How likely was it that he happened to be cycling down the interstate after midnight? Do you know for sure you can trust him?"

Brad winced. The answer was a resounding "*No!*"

"Have you even seen this bicycle he was supposed to have been riding?"

The answer was again "no," Brad had to admit.

"Someone's on to you, Red. I'm not saying you've been careless, but someone has already tried to kill you at least once — who knows whether the first incident with the car was accidental. At this point it's hard to tell if the person who tossed the tape through your window is friend or foe. You can't trust anyone from now on."

"Don't worry," he replied, turning the lock on the drawer. "I have no intentions of becoming somebody's next murder victim."

"Neither did Rosengarten, I'm sure. And by the way, the bullet casing you sent us was fairly recently fired — probably at a duck, though. It came from a shotgun. Very likely it floated in on the tide. Didn't you say you found it on a salt marsh?"

Bradford recalled Zach's words. He had found it on the marsh, he admitted. Grace gave him a brief update on the hurricane's approach before ending the call.

BRAD WOKE WITHOUT feeling the least bit refreshed. The face in the mirror revealed the restless night he'd just spent. His fears had plagued him through his dreams and would doubtless pursue him all day as well.

He decided to go for a run to clear his head. It was the release he sought whenever work got to be too much for him. He found solace and solitude in the hours he spent moving faster than everyone else around him.

Provincetown's bike trails were perfect for a long-distance jog. A path wound through dense scrub and sand at the tip of the Cape. As he jogged, Brad pondered the recent events and possible identity of whoever was behind them.

Zach's declaration that he came to Provincetown every September sounded plausible enough, and it would be easy to check. Brad's trip hadn't been pre-planned, but it would be simple enough for anyone following him to get here from anywhere in the country in less than a day. What did Brad know of Zach apart from a few intimate details of his body and the fact that the boy could be compulsively emotional?

There was also his unexplained connection with Purgatory's sexy barkeep. Were Perry and Zach having an affair? Or could Perry be using Zach as a go-between for himself and the Ice House? And if so, why? Brad wasn't sure which of the two scenarios he preferred.

Perry had admitted his past connection to the guesthouse. Had it resumed with the death of its owner? And where did Fred the drug dealer fit in? He'd once been the Ice House's official drug supplier. Could he have had a side deal going with someone who worked there even after his accident? Maybe Perry had been helping him all along, and somehow the pair had found an opportunity for revenge on the house's hated owner. It was plausible.

Trees zipped past Brad's visual field as his feet found their rhythm. The sky was cloudless. Coming around a curve, he was momentarily stunned by the blue vista dotted with sailboats. Things didn't get much more idyllic than this. The view disappeared as he thudded past.

And then there was Cinder, the man of a thousand faces and voices. He'd recognized Brad from the start and had even tipped him off to Ross's murder. He also worked at the Ice House. Had he known about the camera in the bathroom? That wasn't difficult to imagine. Cinder clearly made the short list of suspects. But that begged other questions. Why not just give Brad the tape instead of throwing it through his window? He could simply have said he found it in the guesthouse. Then again, that might implicate him in Hayden's murder.

Whoever threw the tape through Brad's window knew both who he was and where he was staying. That was particularly bad news, no matter how you read it. Again, the trail pointed right back to Zach. He'd definitely been in the neighbourhood at the time. And no one else had been to Brad's residence. Maybe Zach had assumed others knew where he was staying, not realizing he'd been the only one.

A thought struck him. Tom Nava had escorted him home the first night. And Tom knew he was looking into Ross's murder! Now that he thought about it, Nava could easily be the dark cop who stopped Fred on his way into town with a drug shipment. Corrupt cops were a dime a dozen. Maybe that was why he hadn't shown up at the funeral!

Grace might very well be right in saying someone had followed him home from the graveyard. It didn't necessarily have to be someone who attended the funeral. Halle had been the other notable absentee that day, along with Ruby's gun. Suddenly the suspects were everywhere.

One thing was clear in all this mess: despite his precautions, someone was clearly onto him. But why try to kill him one night and then deliver taped evidence of a murder the next? Surely that pointed to two different perpetrators? His thoughts went on in much the same vein till his feet returned him to the trail's starting point.

Exhausted, he headed home and soaked in the Jacuzzi until a buzzing at his front door interrupted him. He scampered downstairs in a towel, half hoping it would be Zach, but it was the repairman coming to replace the window.

Brad was momentarily elated when he opened the door to the man in the checkered shirt and goatee. He'd had any number of fantasies about hot encounters with service men, but he quickly realized the man standing in his living room was straight by the way his eyes discreetly avoided Brad's midriff wrapped in its towel. Clearly, none of his fantasies would be coming true today. He wondered for the tenth time that week if he was becoming a sex addict. He was still wondering by the time the man replaced his window and left.

All day long, doubts about Zach and the others clouded his mind. His instincts said he needed to talk to Ruby. She might at least be able to tell him if the person in the tape was one of the houseboys. She might even know who'd thrown the tape through his window.

He waited till just before closing to return to Coffee Joe's. To his surprise, the café was locked and dark. The NEARLY OPEN sign hung across the door. As far as Brad could remember, the café never closed early during tourist season. He banged on the door and heard Bill whine.

"Ruby?" he called out, his senses alert.

Someone or something shuffled about inside. A door opened and closed. Brad was about to rush around to the back of the building when the front door opened slightly. Ruby stood before him.

"It's you," she said in a tone that wasn't the least bit welcoming.

"Closing early?"

"I wasn't feeling well," she said. "I worked all day by myself and I was afraid you were a pesky customer who wouldn't take 'no' for an answer."

"You still might think that," he said with a forced laugh. "I was hoping for some chai and conversation."

Ruby hesitated, then opened the door. "Come on in," she said. "I can still whip you up a cup."

The café was empty except for Bill, who skidded around the floor at breakneck speed. I bet *you* could tell me what's going on, Brad thought. He realized it must have been Halle he'd heard leaving by the back door. He'd just missed her.

"Any news from Halle?" he asked.

"No ... well, yes. She called to let me know she's all right," Ruby lied, and not very convincingly.

"Did you find out if she took the gun?"

"Uh-huh." Ruby nodded. Her hands fumbled nervously as she placed a cup under the steamer. "She said she was trying to protect me."

"Protect you from what?"

Ruby looked sheepish. "She said she heard me threatening Rosiegarters one time too many and didn't want to take the chance I'd follow through on my threat, though God knows I wouldn't."

Brad nodded.

"You hear anything more about the murder?" she asked over the sound of frothing milk.

"I think we have a pretty good lead on who killed Hayden," Brad said. "I thought you might help me figure something out."

Ruby brought the cup over to him. "How's that?" she asked.

He took a sip and smiled. *"Ahh!* Perfect every time."

Ruby sat beside him at the counter. Bradford held up the cassette. He'd brought his camera. He plugged it into the café's monitor and they sat and watched the tape together. Ruby held her breath as the shoulder passed in front of the lens and the robe slipped to the floor.

209

She turned to Brad. "I can't tell you a thing," she said, perplexed. "It's just some guy in a kimono."

"Let's watch it again," Brad said. "This time in slow motion."

They watched to the point where the second figure stepped in front of the lens. Brad stopped the tape.

"You know everyone in town," he said. "Anybody have a tattoo like that on his right shoulder? Or maybe hers?"

Ruby's face was a pale moon reflected in the light of the screen. She bit her lip. "It wasn't me and it wasn't Halle. That's all I care!" She looked as though she might cry.

Brad knew not to push things. It wouldn't be a good time to suggest that Halle had a few well-placed tattoos on her body, and that she'd have no problem passing for a man if she wanted to, though probably not enough to fool Rosengarten. And certainly not once her clothes were off. If she really *was* a woman, that is.

"Did Rosengarten's taste run to women?" he asked casually.

Ruby started, fearful. "Not that I ever knew of."

"All right," he said, disconnecting the camera. "Thanks for taking the time to look at this with me." He stopped at the front door. "If you think of anything, call me. You have the number."

"I will," she said, diminished. She hesitated. "Did you find out what kind of gun killed him?"

"It was a Colt .45," Brad answered. "What was yours?"

"I think it was a Smith & Wesson," Ruby said. "I don't know much about guns, really."

And that, thought Bradford, is the third time you've lied to me tonight.

28

He'd just entered the house and locked the door when his phone rang. Brad recognized Cinder's rasp instantly.

"Darling, you may not believe this, but I think it was an inside job," Cinder squawked into the phone.

"What makes you say that?" Brad asked, setting his camera case on the floor.

The burglar alarm indicator blinked a warning at him. He walked over and reset it. He was clear on what he and Grace had discussed, that he could no longer trust anyone.

"I've been doing a little investigating at the Even-Less-Than-OK Corral," Cinder answered. "Everyone was nice as pie till after the funeral. Now they're all accusing one another, lest the fickle finger of blame be pointed at them first. The tall, skinny guy at the door is first among all the finger pointers."

"What do you know about him?" Brad asked as he sat on a chair and pulled off his sneakers. "It seems to me he held a pretty high position of trust with Hayden. In fact, he seemed to be second in command when Rosengarten wasn't there."

"You're bang-on, hon. He did most of the hiring and firing around the place. Old Rosebud didn't do much of anything without his say. But I don't think they were business partners."

"Why's that?" Brad asked.

"Because there was no end to his grumbling about how little he got paid for all his hard work."

Brad recalled overhearing the man's litany of complaints the night he'd broken into the Ice House.

"To hear him go on," Cinder continued, "you'd think he moved heaven and earth to keep old Rosie-o happy."

Brad threw his shoes into a corner and peeled off his socks. "Was that true?"

"He did a lot around the place, that's for sure. Still, I'd be surprised if Hayden left him anything in his will."

"By any chance do you know who receives the bulk of the estate?"

"I just heard. The monks spent the last twenty-four hours meditating to determine where Hayden is going to be reincarnated. They've come up with the answer and most of the money is going there."

This, Brad thought, might be the clue he was waiting for. If the estate had been designated for anyone affiliated with the Buddhist group, or anyone among the employees at the guesthouse, it would be a cinch to figure out who murdered Hayden Rosengarten. On the other hand, if it was some whacko plan to give his money away to a third-world family who'd never heard of him, in the ridiculous belief he'd be reborn there, it wouldn't help things much. Fitting, perhaps, but not much use as motives went.

"So," he said. "Who's the lucky recipient?"

"The Boston Zoo. Apparently Rosebud's coming back as an orangutan."

There was a notable silence on Brad's end.

"It's a kind of monkey, I think. That's just how it goes if you're a Buddhist," Cinder said. "If you don't live your life doing good deeds, you have to come back as a lesser animal and get kicked around till you realize what it's like to be low species on the totem pole."

"Gee," was all Brad could manage. He tried to imagine Ruby kicking an orangutan.

"Aren't you glad you're not a Buddhist?" Cinder said.

"I guess there's something still to be said for Presbyterianism, even if all you get for Christmas is walnuts and oranges."

"You betcha! On the other hand, those Buddhists get to wear some pretty kitsch outfits!"

Brad interrupted him. "Listen, Cinder. How much do you know about what went on in that house?"

"Well, I'm not a nosy queen for nothing, hon. I've had a good look around that place in my time. And believe me, I've had far better times in far worse places."

Brad reached into the camera case. "What do you know about the cameras?" he asked, holding the tape up in front of the new windowpane.

"The ones over the bathtubs, in the guestrooms, down the polar bear's snout, or behind the aquariums? Or were you referring to the ones in the hallways, perhaps?" Cinder asked.

Brad tucked the cassette into its case and locked it back in the drawer. "Let's start with the bathtubs."

"Well, that Hayden sure was one for kink. But more than that, he had business smarts, too. Remember, he was no Eve Harrington ..." Cinder did what amounted to a double-take on the phone. "Or was he? Anyway, he always said if his guesthouse went tits-up he could go into the video business."

"So the cameras were there to help out with that?"

"Hayden kept tapes of all the big-name clients who came to the establishment. And I think he meant what he said. If things went wrong for him, he'd find a way to get money out of some of those guys."

"Blackmail?"

"Sure, why not? Some of those guys are still in the prime of their careers. He could've wrecked more than a few public profiles with his private records. Remember Rob Lowe?"

"He went there?"

"I cannot tell a lie."

Brad rolled his eyes. "Do you think one of the clients found out about it?"

"That's exactly what I think. You sure are a smart little cookie. I think somebody discovered what old Rosetta had up his sleeve. I guess he told the wrong person ..."

"Who in the house knew about the tapes?"

"Just about everyone," Cinder said. "There wasn't much that was a secret. When Hayden got drunk he'd go around saying all kinds of things. He just never drank when the clients were there. It was his golden rule."

Which says a lot about the champagne in the bathtub, Brad thought. "So you're saying everybody who worked there had access to the tapes?"

"Oh, no!" Cinder said. "No one knew where they were at, except for one or two of his most trusted staff."

"And who was that?"

"Well, Johnny K. for one — you must've seen him at the funeral yesterday. He's the rough-looking one. Johnny K. was Hayden's chief bodyguard. I never got too close to him. He'd step on a girl's hem as quick as pick it up for her."

"Anything else?"

"I hear he has a legendary cock, but I never laid lips on it myself."

"Big?"

"And how! Apparently it was the biggest of the lot in that place."

"Do you know if he has a snake tattoo on his right shoulder blade?"

"Oooh!" Cinder trilled. "I *love* phallic symbols! I'm sure that boy has tattoos all over his body, but whether one of them is a snake I can't be sure."

"Would he have had any reason to kill Hayden?"

"Johnny K.? Nah — he knew which side his dick was buttered on."

"But if he thought he could get away with it and be better off ...?"

Cinder thought for a moment. "Maybe, but I doubt it. Why bite the hand that feeds you when you can eat out of it?"

"Cinder, do you have any idea who would want to kill Hayden?"

"Maybe Mozart?"

Brad hung up and peeled off his T-shirt. He was checking the outline of his tattoo in the mirror when the phone rang again.

"Bradford? Ruby here."

His ears picked up immediately. "Hi, Ruby."

"Listen, can we get together? I got somethin' to tell you."

Brad sucked in his breath.

"I don't want to say much on the phone, but I think I know something you should know."

Bingo! he thought. "I'll be right over."

"No," she said. "Meet me on Bradford Street, all right? You walk toward me and I'll walk toward you and we'll meet somewhere in the middle."

"Give me five minutes."

"Fine, but I'm leaving now. It gives me goosebumps to stay here knowing what I think I know."

Brad grabbed his socks and shoes. He was back out on the street in under a minute. All along he'd had the feeling that Big Ruby might lead him to the killer, and at last it seemed to be happening.

29

Bradford passed the bicycle rental shop and the cheery café where he sometimes stopped for breakfast before the rest of the world came to life. Both were dark and empty now. He'd gone only three blocks when the car came racing toward him down the hill. With its headlights off, it was a mere shadow moving at lethal speed.

Without thinking, he flipped himself over a hedge as the car went careening by at breakneck speed. As he lay there in the dirt he remembered his dream about the Porsche. It'd happened so fast he hadn't even had time to notice what type of car it was.

Whew! I sure as hell don't want to end up dead on Bradford Street, he thought, remembering Ruby's words the night they met. He picked himself up and dusted off his clothes. Then he felt the twinge in his ankle. He tried out a few careful steps — it was painful, but he could walk.

He looked down the street as far as he could see. No Ruby. An awful thought occurred. Suddenly he began to run, oblivious to the pain. As he rounded the hilltop he saw the crowd gathered by the side of the road near the bottom. He ran till he reached them, pushing bystanders aside until he stood over the crumpled body lying half-on and half-off the sidewalk.

Oh, God! he thought. *Please don't let it be!*

But by the murmuring of the people gathered around, he knew Ruby was dead.

"It was a terrible accident," he heard one man say. "The car didn't even stop!"

Accident? Bradford thought. This woman knew about safety on the streets!

He stood and walked on in the direction Ruby had come. He passed several houses before he saw something glittering in the dirt at the side of the road more than a hundred feet from the body. He picked it up, turning it in his hands. This was no accident, he thought. She was running for her life!

He looked back at the crowd. He could be of no use to Ruby now. Nor she to him, sadly. Whatever she had to tell him, she'd taken with her to the bardo.

BRAD COULDN'T FACE going back home and he didn't see any point in returning to Coffee Joe's. No doubt the news of Ruby's death would get around town within hours. And he certainly didn't want to be the one to tell Halle, despite what he suspected about her.

He wandered down to the harbour where the shushing of waves reached his ears. He crossed the darkened beach to the remains of an old pier that hadn't been used in years. The rickety structure extended forty feet into the ocean before collapsing in a heap of disuse and broken boards.

With his arms outstretched for balance, Brad stepped onto the pier. He walked out as far as he safely could, leaving the outermost end to the pelicans and seagulls perched there watching him with curiosity.

With his legs dangling over the edge, he sat and stared across the harbour. The lights of town surrounded him from behind, gleaming over his shoulders like a glittering cape. He was very close to where Hayden's body had been fished from the harbour two days earlier. Would he ever discover who had killed Rosengarten and Ross and now Ruby?

Beneath him the water slapped at the barnacle-covered pillars and withdrew again. A thought came to him: *The sea giveth and the sea taketh away again. These two things are both the way of life.* His eyes followed the darkened outline of the Cape out where it disappeared under twinkling stars. Somewhere beyond this bare reef of sand lay the outer world. From where he sat it all looked so simple and uncomplicated, as if nothing could ever change or challenge him. But in truth it had been years since his life had been simple. Loneliness only looked easy to the untrained eye.

The tower bell struck eleven. The ringing tones brought back the bells of his childhood. Whatever sense of belonging he'd known then had been ripped from him with the deaths of first his mother and then his father. So what did it mean for him to have no allegiance to anything other than truth? That's what Grace had asked when she'd interviewed — no, *interrogated* — him for the position. Could he offer that kind of allegiance to her organization? Yes, he'd told her. He could do that and more. But what had he meant?

What he'd meant was that he was alone in the world and had no allegiance to anyone beyond a handful of friends he could easily abandon, if need be. And he'd proved it by abandoning Ross. Or had he? Maybe he'd simply proved he had no allegiance to anything whatsoever. Not even to truth. What good was an agent who functioned perfectly but cared for nothing? Was he that heartless?

No!

Hadn't he come to Provincetown out of allegiance? No — allegiance be damned! It was out of *love!* Ross might have been the only one he'd loved since his father, but Brad knew what love was and what it could make him capable of doing. And that's why it was dangerous. That was why Box 77 had wanted his allegiance to be with them, and them alone, because when you loved someone you would do anything to protect them!

Rope and tackle clanged softly against a metal mast. His gaze wandered out over the water and up to the stars. All he wanted was an answer, something to tell him he was doing the right thing, and that his actions were for a purpose, despite appearances. But there were no answers out there.

Finally, when he'd had enough salt air and remorse, he stood and headed back. Even the impersonal company of a bar would be better than this misery and self-doubt.

Brad found himself sitting in the semidarkness of the Atlantic House. He stared at a photograph of the young Eugene O'Neill hanging over the bar. O'Neill had come to Provincetown to make his name as a dramatist. An unknown when the picture was taken, he eventually became a man of monumental accomplishments. Yet he too would face his share of tragedy.

Brad thought of his first visit to P-Town, when he'd encountered the drunken queen and her entourage. She'd stood three feet away from where he sat now, hands on her hips, accusing him of not knowing the importance of the guesthouses in Provincetown. And, by association, of not knowing what it meant to be gay. She was speaking of self-knowledge. What she'd meant was, he hadn't known who he was. He'd been an unformed lump, an unshaped piece of clay. If he did nothing to shape himself, fate would intervene and do it for him in ways he might not like. But had his experiences in the intervening years made any difference? All he felt was loss and regret.

He steadfastly wished he could go back to those times now, as he downed his third gin and tonic and signalled for another. How many more would it take to forget that Ruby was dead? And how many more to forget that he was the cause? Grace would have his head for disobeying her orders. Now, at last, he could see the consequences of his actions. Why did he never listen? She'd given him a directive and he'd disobeyed. He wouldn't be surprised if he lost his job over it.

My *job!* he thought with scorn. Grace and her shadowy lot could all go fuck themselves! He'd done what he thought was right! There was nothing he could do or say to justify it now. But no one could tell him he was on the wrong track, either, given the awful turn of events. Nor could anyone make him feel good about it.

Brad felt a hand on his shoulder. He turned to see Zach looking down at him.

"I wasn't following you!" Zach exclaimed before he could say anything. "I was passing through and saw you sitting here. You looked so miserable. I just wanted to see if you were all right. If you want me to, I'll leave."

Brad took a deep breath. He recalled his suspicions about Zach's possible involvement in all of this. The idea suddenly evaporated.

"Sit," Bradford said, indicating the stool beside him.

Zach sat and looked into his face. "Why so sad?" he asked.

"Big Ruby died a few hours ago."

Zach's mouth fell open. "What happened?"

"She was run down by a car."

"Was it an accident?"

"It wasn't an accident. Someone chased her and deliberately ran her down. She saw it coming and she was running for her life." He pulled out the rhinestone glasses he'd found lying on the road. "She dropped these about a hundred feet before the car got her."

Zach took the glasses and turned them in his hands. Brad realized the time had come to make a choice. Either he had to trust Zach fully or forget him entirely. He already knew which it would be.

"What I'm going to say is probably the most confidential thing you will ever hear," he said, then stopped, realizing how pompous that sounded.

"Is this what you wouldn't tell me the other day on the salt marsh?"

Brad nodded. "Once I tell you this, there's no going back," he said. "Are you sure you want to hear?"

"I want to hear," Zach said.

Brad had already told Zach he'd come to Provincetown to claim Ross's body. Now he told him the rest of his story. Choosing his words carefully, he explained how he'd discovered the drowned boy and the next day learned that Ross's death was a murder, only to have it followed by Rosengarten's and now Big Ruby's. Then he told Zach how he'd abandoned Ross five years earlier to work for the secretive Box 77. When he finished, Zach sat there watching him.

"That's about it," Brad said. "But I want to say I'm really sorry for getting you mixed up in all of this."

"That's what you really do?" Zach said. "You work for an

organization that safeguards against threats to global security and has no name?"

Brad nodded.

"Whew!" Zach said. "I think you should stick with the golf pro story."

Brad managed a smile.

"And I'm really sorry about Big Ruby," Zach continued. "I adored her, but you aren't to blame. Obviously, somebody has it in for the people of this town. If we could just figure out why, then we'd probably know who."

223

"That's what I've been trying to do for the last week."

Rather than be scared off, Zach jumped into the story with zeal.

"I'm not an expert in international espionage, but it seems there's a common thread running between Ruby, Ross, and Hayden. And maybe even the guy who drowned the night you got here. There must be some deep, dark secret we haven't figured out."

Brad nodded. "Ruby knew Ross as a customer, but she didn't know he worked at the guesthouse until I told her. As for Hayden, Ruby claimed she hadn't spoken to him since their art gallery went bankrupt a few years ago."

"What about the drowned guy? Did he live here, too?"

"According to the police he'd been living here since the beginning of the summer."

Zach held up a finger. "Then this is what we know for sure: one, they all lived in Provincetown. And, as we know, everybody who lives in Provincetown knows everybody else." He raised another finger. "Two, they all had connections to the guesthouse, although Ruby's was admittedly from a distance."

Brad added a third finger. "And they all smoked dope. There's number three."

Zach looked sheepish. "So do we, but it doesn't add up to much, does it?" He thought for a moment. "What about a drug dealer?"

"I'm ahead of you there. I talked to him the day before yesterday. He was at Rosengarten's funeral. He's in a wheelchair, though."

"It doesn't mean he can't drive a car. Or that he's not faking his injury!"

"You sound like Grace," Brad said.

"Who else is there?"

Brad mentioned Perry the barkeep, watching for Zach's reaction.

Zach laughed. "I know him. He works at Purgatory. I meant to tell you." His hand went into his back pocket and fished out a wallet. "They called to say they found this. Perry tried to pick me up when I went in to get it."

Brad remembered Zach's missing wallet. He could've kicked himself for all the unfounded suspicions that had gone through his mind about Zach and Perry in the last day-and-a-half.

Zach saw the turmoil in his face. "Don't worry. He's sweet, but not my type," he said. "You're my type."

"I'm glad. I hate to tell tales out of school, but he's also HIV-positive."

"I know — he told me."

Brad hoped he could trust what Zach was telling him. He'd have to.

"What was Perry's connection with the guesthouse?" Zach asked.

"Perry worked there at one time, and apparently he knew Ross. They had a fight, but Perry says he was only trying to warn Ross to leave before anything bad happened to him. Unfortunately, Ross didn't listen."

"Whatever else he may be, I doubt he's a killer. I can sense these things. He's more like a wounded animal. But there's got to be something else that ties all these people together."

"Whatever it is, it's nothing obvious that would make them all potential murder victims." Bradford downed his drink. "I'm exhausted," he announced. "And I've got a lot of explaining to do in the morning."

225

He stepped down from the stool and nearly tumbled to the floor. Only Zach's quick reaction kept him from falling. Brad hadn't thought of his ankle since he jumped the fence to avoid the speeding car.

"I'm taking you home," Zach declared.

"No," Brad protested. "It's dangerous for you to get any more mixed up in this than you already are."

"I can't have you run over or falling down in the street," Zach reasoned. "Just let me walk with you. Besides, I already am mixed up in this. How much worse can it get?"

30

With his arm over Zach's shoulder, Brad was able to keep the weight off his ankle. At the door to his guesthouse he turned to Zach and held him. Their lips met. Brad broke off the embrace.

"I can't invite you in."

"Why not?" Zach pleaded.

"I'm afraid for you. I can't put your life in peril."

Zach pressed himself closer to Brad. "It's too late now. We've already slept together. We're both a part of this."

Brad felt his resistance weakening.

"Are you telling me you're going to let me walk home alone in the dark?" Zach pressured.

Brad considered. "And you just thought of that now?"

"Well, not exactly," Zach admitted. "But you didn't think of it earlier, and now it's too late to send me home."

Zach's eyes begged to be let into his house, into his life. Brad hesitated. There'd been too many years alone, and Big Ruby's death had snapped something inside him.

"All right," he relented.

They went up the stairs together. Zach helped Brad out of his clothes and into the loft bed where they tumbled into one another's arms.

"I know I shouldn't say this, but it feels awesome to be with you," Zach said.

"It feels right," Brad agreed. "Somehow it just feels right."

He rolled over on top of Zach, his erection pressing itself between Zach's legs. The boy gasped and slipped his arms around Brad's chest.

"Oh, God!" Zach blurted out, wanting to say more, but he held back.

He shifted and Brad suddenly found himself lying beneath the boy, whose own erection now snaked between Brad's legs.

"You're a wild ride, little buckaroo!"

"Save a horse — ride a cowboy instead. That's my motto!" Zach beamed.

Zach's erection nudged him. Brad suddenly realized how big the boy really was.

"Whoa!" he cried. "Nice and easy, now. That's practically virgin territory and I believe you need a passport to enter."

He reached over to his bedside kit and handed Zach a condom. He held onto the boy tightly as he entered, adjusting to the burning sensation. Then, just as suddenly, it turned to indescribable pleasure. Zach rocked gently till an urgency overtook him. He began to thrust more and more wildly. Brad looked down to see Zach's horse head tattoo join with his own to create a winged stallion.

"We're flying!" Zach roared as they rocked in unison till their heads were banging on the side of the loft.

"I love ... *your hair!*" Zach gasped, and let out a laugh as they both came at the same time.

Zach collapsed, spent by his exertions. Brad cradled Zach's head against his shoulder, running his hands through the boy's blue locks. He was thinking for the tenth time that evening how right it felt to be with Zach, when sleep intervened. He woke in the night to find arms wrapped tightly around him, as though they would never let him go.

IN THE MORNING Brad was awake and out of bed first. He felt a dull pain in his ankle, but it was no match for the one in his head. He found he could walk gingerly if he was careful. He popped some painkillers and took his coffee onto the veranda where he sat looking over the awakening salt marsh. Everything was peaceful, as if there were no troubles anywhere in the world.

He thought of Ruby, and then he tried not to think of her. How could he live with the knowledge that he'd led her to her death? Any moment now the phone would ring and he'd have to face Grace. What would he say?

Lying in Zach's arms all night, he kept thinking how much he wanted out of this cat-and-mouse game of international espionage. He longed for a normal life. Or at least as normal as any gay man's life could be. Did he even know what normal was anymore? Probably not, if he ever did.

What would he do now that he'd seen the world from the inside out: not the bank, but the money-laundering cartel that bribed the bank's president to overlook its activities; not the accident victim lying crumpled on the side of the road, but the conspiracy behind her death that had already led to at least two others? Where do you turn after seeing the world without protective glasses?

He'd been warned he would hit this wall sooner or later. Everyone does, he was told. Once you've put on your safety belt, you can't stop the ride, they'd said. You began to see things you might not want not to see, things you'd never forget. Your mind stretched to accommodate facts it never imagined possible, if it imagined them at all. And suddenly all of life seemed up for reassessment. You couldn't trust anything you'd ever assumed or relied on.

This was the frame of mind Bradford was in when the phone rang. He grabbed it in the middle of the first ring.

"It's Grace, Red. I understand you've had a bit of trouble down there."

"You could say that."

"I'm sorry to hear about Ruby."

"She's going to be missed by a lot of people," he said, suddenly thinking of his own father. "She was the kind of person who becomes a fixture in other people's lives."

"Obviously she wasn't the one ..."

"I never thought she was."

"So you said. I wish I'd believed you."

"And I wish I'd listened to you. Ruby might still be alive today ..."

"You were doing your job."

"Not last night. I stepped out of line ..."

She stopped him. "Listen to me, Red. There are no rule books for what we do. Every day brings new decisions. *Tough* decisions. No one can tell you what's right and what's wrong. You have to trust your gut and do what you feel is right. Otherwise you'll be the one who ends up dead. It's the same for you and for me and for all of us, every single day."

She was trying to convince him what he'd done wasn't wrong. She'd guessed at his fragile state of mind and knew he needed bolstering more than he deserved reprimanding for having ignored an order.

"Ruby knew something about someone. Even if you hadn't been there, that person would have figured it out sooner or later. It had nothing to do with you personally. Do you understand that?"

Brad hesitated. Could he afford to believe it? He had to.

"Sometimes you've got to take risks to get things done," Grace went on. "And sometimes you're going to think that those risks aren't worth it, but they are. You're much too valuable for us to lose, Red. Do you hear what I'm saying?"

"Yes."

"Now pull yourself together. You've got important work to do in the next forty-eight hours. The Dalai Lama's talk is in three days. I'll be damned if you're going to run off now and let whoever's trying to ruin his little party blow his head off with a long-range rifle. I don't want another 'grassy knoll' incident on my hands."

"I'm with you all the way."

"And, Red ..."

"Yes?"

"That blue-haired boy you're with?"

Brad felt a lump in his throat. He waited.

"He checks out. As far as we can see, you can trust him on all counts. Just ... look after him."

For a moment he couldn't speak. "Thanks," he croaked.

He put the phone down and sat looking out across the marsh. Had he really suspected Grace had something to do with it? He had. When she didn't return his call the night before Hayden was murdered, he wondered if she'd slipped away to arrange to have someone put a bullet through Rosengarten's forehead and leave Agent Red holding the bag. She'd have no problem justifying it to the organization. Now he saw how idiotic that was.

He stepped onto the ladder and stood watching Zach breathe. You're such a beautiful guy, he thought. Zach turned his face toward him and murmured.

"What was that?" Brad asked.

Zach's eyes opened. He smiled. "I dreamed I fucked you last night," he said. "It was the most wonderful dream I've had in ages."

"I'm glad you stayed last night, but I have to say you're about as stubborn as a donkey."

"I'm hung like one, too," Zach replied, raising his eyebrows and pulling back the covers to reveal a whopping morning erection.

"You are *so* twenty-one," Bradford said, climbing back in beside him as a bell chimed the hour.

31

An hour later they were on their way to the Pilgrim Monument, the granite monolith that glowered over P-Town's landscape. Erected three centuries after the arrival of the pilgrims, the tower commemorated their effort to bring the ideals of freedom and democracy to the new land. In its dedication ceremony, however, no mention was made of the people who were displaced by those ideals. As the Indians learned, democracy is one tough cookie.

"I need a day off," Brad declared when Zach asked the occasion for the visit. "I think it only right I should celebrate getting plundered by a donkey with a pilgrimage to Provincetown's biggest phallic symbol. Though I have to say you were only able to take advantage of me last night because I was drunk."

Zach snorted. "If your legs point due north every time you get drunk, I'll gladly pay for the shots whenever we go out."

At the museum entrance they startled a sleepy-looking attendant. She handed over their tickets and change, reminding them to save time for the museum's displays after their climb.

"We currently have a very exciting pictorial history of Provincetown's sand dune formations," she enthused. "As well, you'll find a compelling who's-who of fashion in pilgrim times."

Inside, the tower was eerily silent, the air cool and undisturbed. No one else seemed to be braving the hundred-and-sixteen-step ascent that early on a sunny morning. Markers embedded in the stone bore the names of Massachusetts's earliest communities. As they climbed, an occasional window slit allowed brief views to the outside.

Before they reached the halfway point they found themselves panting with the exertion. "And we call ourselves 'young,'" Zach scoffed.

"Speak for yourself," Brad said. "I'm over thirty."

233

They stopped to peer over the railing to the ground below. Brad lurched back and gripped the wall behind him. He took a deep breath and looked up at Zach's inquiring face. "Fear of heights," he explained sheepishly.

"You're kidding," Zach said, leaning over the railing and looking down. "We're not even that high yet."

As he stepped back a shot tore up the centre of the tower and pinged off the stairs above, sending a shower of stone and mortar dust into the air.

"*Holy crap!* Was that what I think it was?" Zach exclaimed.

They turned to face one another at the sound of pounding footsteps from below.

"Let's go!" Brad commanded quietly.

They raced upward, taking the stairs two at a time. "What will we do when we get to the top?" Zach whispered loudly.

"I don't know," Brad answered. "I'll think of something."

Another shot rang out, echoing inside the tower's hull as they lunged the last few steps to the top. Brad pushed Zach through the doorway. Hesitating a moment, he leaned over and looked back down the stairwell. A pair of gloved hands gripped the railing several floors below as a hooded figure raced swiftly upward.

Brad burst through the door and into the tiny stone maze high above the town. The Cape's tail stretched as far as the eye could see. In the blue distance, boats crisscrossed the harbour, while the streets of Provincetown slumbered below. If he'd had time, Brad could have identified every landmark in the town. But there was no time. Their pursuer would reach them in seconds.

Birds fluttered past in the clear air as he searched for a way out. The tower's giant bell hovered overhead. If they could climb onto it, it might afford a momentary hiding place. Unfortunately, it was enclosed in mesh. Cutting through the wire would take too long and any movement of the bell would alert whoever was after them.

The only way out was down. With his fear of heights, Brad wasn't much of a candidate to leap over the tower wall and cling to the stonework by his fingernails in a merry game of cat and mouse with the killer till one of them eventually fell to his doom and the other climbed victoriously back to the top. It might happen that way in the movies, but he wasn't Tom Cruise. He wasn't even short. And chances are it wouldn't be the hero who survived in real life.

There were many ways to die, most of them unpleasant. And this was surely one of the worst. But at least it was P-Town, he reasoned, watching a sailboat glide over the horizon. While it might not make for a skilful death, it promised to be aesthetically pleasing.

Brad looked at Zach, who stood waiting for him to make a decision. He might be able to rush the killer and grapple with him as he entered, giving Zach time to run down the stairs and save himself. But he already knew Zach well enough to know the boy wouldn't abandon him. He'd stay and they'd both be killed. Or maybe with luck they could overcome the assailant together. But it was risky.

Think! Bradford commanded. How could they escape? In his dreams, he'd merge with the blue alien and they'd fly across the harbour. But that wouldn't cut it in the waking world.

Silence reigned as the wind blew through his hair. They had seconds at most. Brad pressed against the wall and peered around the corner. He watched as a gloved hand slowly pushed the door open and the hooded figure emerged. The pursuer's other hand was sunk deep in his pocket, bulging with readiness. Don't tell me, Brad thought. There's a gun in your pocket *and* you're glad to see us.

He motioned silently to Zach and they slipped around the stone partition. And that's when they discovered they weren't alone! A crowd of expectant faces stood before them, mouths open in silent wonderment. At precisely that moment the bell tolled and the choir of nuns, those gentle penguins of goodwill and innocence, broke into song.

"*I know that my Redeemer liveth ...*" came the glad tidings.

Bradford looked up. *Hallelujah!* he thought. Saved by the bell!

From somewhere deep inside the tower came an antiphonal response. Assassination in stereo! Brad and Zach ducked behind the choir with barely a ruffle of feathers or misplaced note. The movie had switched from *Mission Impossible* to a Dick Lester caper featuring the zany antics of two of the Fab Four.

Brad peeked through the black and white folds to see their

235

would-be assassin skirting a corner of the maze. The figure turned with deadly agility, working his way around the choir and its unexpected musical accompaniment to the scene.

Brad and Zach took advantage of the moment to sneak along the row of frocks to the tower's farthest end. It would be a matter of seconds before their pursuer realized they were hidden in the nunnery. Even worse, whoever it was might have enough ammunition for the entire group, and Brad couldn't take that chance.

They crept toward the door as the hooded figure skirted the chorus in search of his prey. With the would-be killer's back turned, Brad and Zach ducked toward the stairs. Dick Lester had just given way to Buster Keaton and an entire troupe of Keystone Cops.

Brad held back, waiting behind the exit while Zach raced down the stairs. From outside came shifting, fleet footsteps as the killer approached. At the last second, Brad threw himself full force against the door, slamming into the body on the other side. Someone let out a roar and Brad heard metal skidding across concrete.

He raced down the steps two at a time, keeping far from the open stairwell and out of target range. He caught up with Zach and they made their way through the second choir slowly climbing to join their singing sisters above.

The door at the top opened and slammed shut again. The boom echoed through the cavernous interior, a glorious bass note resounding with the lilting chant wending up the stairs. Their would-be killer was now book-ended by a double choir of holiness proclaiming the arrival of the Saviour.

At the bottom, Brad and Zach raced through the museum entrance toward the front door.

"Don't forget the displays!" the ticket seller shouted after them. "They're included in the admission price!"

Brad placed Zach in a waiting cab. "Don't go home," he instructed. "Meet me at the A-House. You'll be safe in a public place. I'll get there as soon as I can."

He turned and strode back inside.

32

Zach was waiting at the bar when Brad came in. His face showed pure relief.

"Are you all right?" he cried as he sprang up and crushed Brad in a hug.

"I'm fine." Brad held Zach at arm's length and looked him over. "Are you okay?"

"I'm okay, but scared shitless. What happened back there?"

"Give me a minute."

Brad turned to the bar. A young dolphin of a waiter came toward them, all eyes and limbs. Brad ordered a gin and tonic and the boy returned to the bar.

"When I went back, I waited till whoever was shooting at us left the tower. I hid in the bushes, but I didn't get a clear view of him. He wore his hood up like some skater punk. He jumped into a waiting car and took off before I could catch the licence."

"It had to be the same guy who murdered Ruby and Ross and Hayden!" Zach said. "But what connection do I have with the guesthouse?"

"Your connection is through me. I'm the one they want, though I have no doubt they would have killed you, too."

"But why?"

"It has to be because of someone I met there, but I still can't figure out who."

"Who else did you meet?"

He told Zach briefly about the Hollywood megastar who'd recently separated from his wife and kids.

Zach shrugged. "Everyone knew he was gay. Even his wife."

Right, thought Brad. Everyone but me. Why do I always learn these things standing in line at a supermarket checkout?

"There was a singer." He tried to remember the name. "Rufus somebody or other ..."

"Wainwright? Skinny, grungy guy about twenty-seven or twenty-eight, looks closer to sixty?"

"Sounds right."

"He's about as queer as Bush is ... well, *challenged*. Nobody on earth would be surprised to hear it. Nobody on any other planet, either. His songs are like a gossip column about his life. He's all sex and drugs and bad affairs. I doubt he's got anything left to hide."

"All right, so he's a worst-case-scenario candidate," Brad said. "And I think the senator, for all his gunslinging homophobia, isn't really much of a candidate, either. If you're running for president, usually you wait till after you win the election to start killing people, don't you?"

Zach shook his head. "All those closet cases! Are the rich and famous really that scared to be themselves?"

"Scared enough to kill, apparently," Brad said, looking around the bar. "Hayden said discretion was an absolute necessity for making his clients feel safe."

"If you include every gay man who's been there," Zach said, "there'd probably be no B-list celebrities left."

"True enough."

"What if it's someone who went to the house that we don't know about?" Zach asked.

"Then why come after me?" Brad said. "I wouldn't have seen him, so I couldn't tell anybody about him."

"Maybe Ross knew who it was. And Ruby and Hayden, too. And maybe the killer knows you're going to figure it out eventually."

"Hayden mentioned having entertained what he called a 'very queer fish' the night Ross died. I gather he was talking about someone important."

"Maybe Ari Fleischer was in town."

Brad's gag reflexes kicked in. "If he's gay, I'll go straight!" Zach started to speak, but Brad put his hands over his ears. "Stop! I don't want to hear this. I pray you're wrong!"

The waiter returned with his drink. Brad tipped the boy and sent him on his way.

"What about one of the employees?" Zach asked.

"There was a thug named Johnny K. He was Hayden's body-guard. Come to think of it, he's about the same size as whoever followed us to the tower. Grace said he's a suspected killer-for-hire, although there's no proof. Yet."

Zach sat listening. "Go on."

"I now think it was Johnny K. who killed Ross, but I don't know why yet," Brad said. "I also think he killed Hayden. The night you were waiting for me outside my house, someone tossed a videocassette through my window. It showed Hayden sitting in his bathtub when someone came in and pulled a gun on him."

"A snuff tape!"

"Whoever it was had a tattoo of a snake on his shoulder."

"Does Johnny K. have a snake tattoo on his shoulder?"

"That remains to be seen. My guess is that Hayden found out Johnny K. murdered Ross and became worried about his house's reputation for discretion. You can't have murders happening at a place like that. If he roughed up Johnny K. the way I saw him do to another guy, Johnny K. might've been angry enough to kill him."

Zach was staring at Brad. "There's still something you haven't told me about all of this, isn't there?"

Brad sighed. Grace had said he could trust Zach, but just how much could he tell the kid before he was no longer safe? *Safe?* After that morning's excursion, it was already too late.

"Come on — out with it. I think I deserve to be told why someone just tried to murder us."

Brad looked cautiously around. There was no one within earshot. In a whisper, he told Zach about his real mission to make sure the intended killer of the Dalai Lama didn't complete his objective.

Zach was incredulous. *"Holy crap!* Who would want him dead?"

Brad cocked his head. "Think about it," he said. "Which government is indicted every time the Dalai Lama appears in public as the real spiritual leader of the people of Tibet?"

Zach nodded. "So they're going to kill him in Central Park? You can't be serious!"

"I'm very serious," Brad said. "Grace believes that whoever's murdering people here is connected with the assassination plot."

"Why?"

"Because they all knew something that we obviously don't."

"But what could that be?"

Brad shrugged and sipped his drink. There were so many things that *could* be. But what he really needed was a solid lead. It might be the videotape, but then again it might not. There was something odd about how it just stopped. If it was truly the tape of a murder setup, then why not show the actual killing?

He remembered his father's words of advice: *Everyone has a reason for the things they do.* Someone was being blackmailed, Brad thought. That was the reason for the murders. It had to be. Hadn't it? He needed to get back into the guesthouse for one last look around. Then he might have something concrete to go on.

"Well, this is all kinda cool!" Zach enthused. "At least, now that we're not being shot at."

"How's that?"

"Well, it kind of makes you Batman, which kind of makes me Robin," he said, grinning. "I always wanted to be someone's Boy Wonder."

"Okay, you can be my Boy Wonder. But you've got to promise to be very careful every minute of every hour from now on. I got you into this, and if anything happens to you like what happened to Ruby I'll blame myself for the rest of my life."

Zach's eyes grew large. "Then I'd better stay with you at all times so you can protect me."

33

Brad and Zach stopped in front of a house on the outskirts of town. From outside it appeared fairly ordinary but for the sign over the front door designating it a Buddhist temple. Inside, they were met with the smell of incense and the murmur of solemn voices. Ruby's wake had commenced.

They stood in a crowded room lit by dozens of gently flickering candles. People sat or knelt on the floor, chanting quietly before a pallet where Ruby's body lay like a broken bird. Monks in purple cloaks and saffron robes intoned throaty sounds. Brad was touched to realize that all these people were Ruby's friends, customers and fellow Buddhists. *When it rains, it pours,* he thought.

He recognized Ruby's Rinpoche sitting cross-legged on the floor to one side of the body, facing the gatherers. His voice was solemn as he read from texts laid out before him. Bill was there, too, standing guard on the other side of the pallet, the Rinpoche's canine twin.

"What are they chanting?" Brad whispered.

"The Rinpoche is reading from the *Tibetan Book of the Dead,*" Zach said. "Buddhists believe that the dead can hear. He's telling Ruby that she has died and needs to move on instead of clinging to the past. The reciting of sacred texts helps the soul on its journey through the bardo."

A woman seated nearby suddenly broke into tears, her sobs welling up loudly. The Rinpoche stopped chanting and gently raised a hand.

"Please not to cry," he said. "Crying only confuse the dead one and pull her back. The mind must stay clear and untroubled to cross over successfully."

Brad saw Halle kneeling in the midst of the mourners. She glanced up and caught his gaze. He hadn't seen her since Ruby's death. She didn't look surprised or frightened to see him. Nor did she seem as distraught as he would have expected. During a break in the chanting, she rose and came toward them. They offered their condolences.

"Thank you for coming," she said in a subdued voice. "You didn't know Ruby long, but she liked you both."

Well, if that isn't downright composed, Brad thought. "I only wish I'd got to know her better," he said.

"There is still time," said a gentle voice at his side. He turned to find the Rinpoche smiling at him. "Mr. Bradford, so happy to see you again."

The grip was strong as they shook hands. "I'm sorry the circumstances of our rejoining have to be so sad," Brad said.

The Rinpoche smiled again. "Not sad. Buddhism teaches that death, like life, only one aspect of things. One path of many that all must walk eventually."

Was it really so simple for these people? Brad wondered. First you're here, then you take a right turn and you're invisible? How does that make it all right to lose a loved one?

The Rinpoche seemed to have sensed his doubt. "You are like ..." he began, his hands describing something oval-shaped in the air between them. "Like egg," he concluded. "Need to crack." He smacked his palms together and his face took on an expression of relief, as though showing Bradford what the experience would bring.

Brad smiled stiffly and introduced Zach to the Rinpoche. They bowed formally to one another.

"Please to join ceremony," the Rinpoche said. "It help Big Ruby's soul reach its sacred destination." He turned to Halle and took her hand. "In my country, things not so rushed. But here, we adapt. In Tibet, people chant many days for departed soul. Here, chant only few days. Westerners always in big hurry."

Brad turned and whispered to Zach. "I need to talk to Halle alone. Can you distract his Holiness?"

"Sure thing," Zach said. He turned to the Rinpoche. "I've been looking for a master. Is it true that when the student is ready, the teacher appears?"

The Rinpoche held up a finger. "To find good teacher very hard, but to find good student even harder."

Brad took Halle off to the side. He was reluctant to pressure her in her time of grief, but he needed some answers.

"Let me say again how sorry I am, Halle. I can only guess how much you'll miss Ruby."

She smiled sadly. "I prefer to think that I'll have one less body to sleep with, but one more spirit looking after me from the other side."

For a moment, Brad wondered whether Buddhists were really advanced in their thinking or just daft. He didn't have time to follow the thought.

"Halle, did you know Ruby was coming to meet me the night she died ... ?"

Halle looked startled. "No, I didn't."

"I went to see her that night just after she closed the café. I thought I heard the two of you inside, but when she opened the door she was alone."

Halle shook her head. "I was out late the night Ruby died," she said. "She didn't even tell me you'd been there."

If you were out late, Brad thought, then you wouldn't have seen Ruby before she died. How could she have told you anything at all?

"I asked Ruby if she could help identify someone in a videotape implicating Hayden Rosengarten's murderer. At first she said she didn't know the person on the tape, but later she became disturbed by something she knew or perhaps something she remembered. Not long after I left, she called to say she wanted to see me. I agreed to come right over, but she was afraid to stay at the café till I got there. I don't think that's like Ruby ..."

Halle let out a low whistle. "That's not like Ruby at all," she agreed. "Something must've scared her good!"

"Or some*one*. And I think that someone also killed her."

Halle's hand flew to her mouth. She shook her head in disbelief. The reaction seemed entirely genuine. "You mean it wasn't an accident?"

"I know it wasn't an accident. Someone deliberately ran her down."

Halle's face contorted with grief. Tears came to her eyes, but she said nothing. Whatever she was turning over in her head, Brad knew she wasn't likely to share with him.

"That's terrible," she said at last. "I hope you're wrong, but in either case it won't do Ruby any good now."

"Are you sure?" Brad asked. "It might give her spirit some peace to know her killer has been caught. It might even help her get through the bardo successfully."

Halle seemed to think this over. "And you think ... I can help?"

"There was a gun in your shop the day Zach and I were over. The next day it was gone. Do you know where it ended up?"

Halle wiped a tear and sniffed. "I didn't know it was missing. I'll check when I get home tonight."

Brad wasn't buying it. Grieving widow or not, he had to press her. "Ruby said you took it."

Halle's face went white. "She said that?"

"She said you hadn't come home the previous night, and that you took the gun to protect her."

Halle shook her head. "I didn't take it!"

Her eyes glazed over. She seemed suddenly withdrawn. Brad recalled her comment about helping a dog but not another human being. With her dissociative, antisocial behaviour, he realized, she was a prime candidate for schizophrenia.

"By the way. Do you know anyone with a snake tattoo on their right shoulder?"

Halle's eyes flickered back to the here and now, but her voice was oddly distant. "Yeah, now that you mention it. There was a guy who came in once or twice. He had some kind of animal on his shoulder. I never talked to him and Ruby didn't like him much. His name was Johnny K."

Bingo! thought Bradford.

"Halle, thank you very much. I think you've told me exactly what I needed to hear."

She looked relieved. "Ruby was really fond of you. I hope you know that."

"Thank you. I know."

Brad watched her turn back to the roomful of chanters. Suddenly something clicked. He recalled Ruby's curious comment at the funeral about Hayden not being able to hurt her loved ones again.

"Halle!" Brad called out.

She stopped and turned warily.

"I was just wondering why you didn't go to Rosengarten's funeral with Ruby the other day."

Her eyes flashed like a feral cat trapped in a barn. Brad knew he was right. He knew why Ruby had looked so panicked when she realized the gun was missing.

"Why would I?" she asked.

"He was your father, wasn't he?"

Halle's hands curled into fists. Suddenly her defiance crumpled and she ran from the room. Serpent handler's daughter, he thought. If he looked, he knew he'd find the tattoo somewhere on her body. It might not be on her shoulder, but he was willing to bet it would be a snake coiled and ready to strike. A serpent as described in the Bible passage Ruby had quoted. Hayden Rosengarten had liked his kids marked. *Suffer the children,* indeed.

Brad turned back to find Zach locking eyes with the handsome Rinpoche. He felt a tingling of jealousy to find his lover so engaged by this other man.

Whoa! Brad told himself. You've slept with him twice — well, three times, if you count last summer — and you're calling him your *lover?* Zach was simply the boy he intended to get to know better. Okay, so he'd practically fallen for him already. But what word should he use to describe him? Partner? Companion? Boyfriend-in-Training? He couldn't decide.

In any case, here was a very attractive Asian man locking eyes with Brad's *new friend*. And he was definitely feeling jealous over it. Zach's eyes disengaged from the Rinpoche's. He came over to Brad.

"Mission accomplished?" he asked.

"Yes — and you?" Brad asked, trying not to sound accusatory.

Zach smiled. "I asked him about the hundred-syllable mantra. He offered to teach me. It's something I've been dying to learn."

In private, no doubt, Brad thought. He envisioned the two of them sitting cross-legged on the floor in saffron robes, knees touching as they chanted over a stick of incense. Did Rinpoches even wear underwear?

"We're going to start the day after tomorrow," Zach said. "Hope you don't mind if I abandon you for a few hours."

"Not at all," Brad said, somehow relieved at being given a choice in the matter of minding or not minding. His jealousy eased a bit. It would also afford him time to go back to the guest-house and see what he could see.

"Thanks. I knew you'd be cool about it."

34

Zach stayed with Brad at his guesthouse that night. The next morning as they parted, Brad admonished him to be on his guard at all times. He watched Zach's blue hair turn a corner, and then headed for the police station.

Nava was off duty till the afternoon. If there was any news about the Ice House's missing houseboy, it would have to wait.

Returning home, Brad discovered another note pinned to his door. He tore it open to find a few words scrawled in a shaky hand: *The gun is in the water off the end of the old town pier.* It was unsigned. Tellingly, it had been left in broad daylight sometime after he and Zach went into town. Was someone getting desperate? At least his window had been spared this time.

Brad immediately relayed the news to Grace, who promised to check out the tip.

Just before dusk, Brad headed for the Ice House and settled in across the street to watch. He wasn't sure what he was waiting for, but he hoped it would soon become clear. He didn't have to wait long. Within fifteen minutes, a familiar figure emerged from the front door. It was Perry the bartender!

He'd been right in thinking Perry's connection with the Ice House had resumed with Hayden's death. But what was he doing there? Did he have anything to do with Hayden's murder, or had his ex-boss's death merely made it possible for him to return to the place where he'd once worked? In either case, it bore investigating.

Brad watched the barkeep disappear down the hill with a small package tucked under his arm. He'd love to have known what was in it. He was tempted to follow, but he needed to get inside the guesthouse. Stealthily, he crossed the street and slipped through the hedge. In his zeal, his arm caught on one of the belladonna branches.

"Damn!" he said, flinching. He watched carefully to see if it would bleed, but he didn't appear to have broken the skin.

He crept forward until he crouched beneath the dining-room window and peered in. The table had been stripped bare except for a neglected vase of orchids. The thin man's cherished flowers had wilted and drooped. Had Jeremiah fled the Ice House?

This time the window was locked. Brad took out his Swiss Army knife and jimmied the edge, but the latch held firm. He gave up and went around to the back of the house. Here he had better luck. The lock pulled free of the rotted wood with ease.

Brad raised the window and peered inside. Someone had been in the house since his last visit. Empty champagne bottles were scattered around the room, while dirty dishes sat on the table and the floor was unswept. It seemed no one cared any longer what the place looked like. Either that or the staff had been let go. It hadn't looked like this the night Hayden was murdered. In fact, this appeared to be the aftermath of a mammoth celebration.

Brad hauled himself over the sill and into the room, then crept along the hall and up the stairs to Hayden's door. He turned the handle.

The room was empty. The desktop looked much the same, except for the missing paperweight. The desk drawers, however, were open and their contents scattered on the floor as though someone had gone through them at breakneck speed. Fishing through the filing cabinet, Brad discovered some old phone bills and bank records, along with a property deed. The document itself had no street address. Even to the bank, the estate was known simply as *The Ice House.*

Inside a walk-in closet Brad found what he'd been looking for: a bank of video monitors with views of all the different rooms in the house. Obviously, he'd been watched as he stood in front of the mirror practising his persona of Sebastian O'Shaughnessy on the night he visited. While it might have tipped off the staff that he wasn't who he claimed to be, it could never have told them his real name. Someone had known about him beforehand.

He looked around. Where were the tapes? They'd be somewhere the guests would never go. The Arctic Memorabilia Room? Possibly. Cinder had said there was a camera inside the bear's snout. The secret passages? Not likely. It was too dark and inconvenient to store anything there. Maybe in the cellars, if there were any. Then he snapped his fingers. *Of course!*

He raced past the landing, down the hallway and up the ladder. The hatch swung upward. Inside, the cupola was surprisingly large and completely weather-proofed. Along with its view of the harbour and the entire town, it housed a video playback unit, several monitors and a solid steel cabinet. He broke the lock and wrenched open the door. He'd just hit pay dirt!

Inside were hundreds of tapes labelled only by date. He inserted one in the machine and watched the monitor. He slipped in a second and then a third. He'd been right! The screen filled with actors, singers, politicians, televangelists, military brass, Mafia dons and even Salvation Army band leaders. Here were all the favourite stars commiting all their favourite sins. Whatever Hayden's purpose in making them — whether to use as blackmail or reality TV with a twist — this went way beyond the hijinks of Paris Hilton and Nicole Richie or Sharon Osbourne tossing ham and bagels over the fence at her neighbours.

It was a cornucopia, a veritable sex-a-thon of the rich and gayly famous engaged in trysts with houseboys, pool boys, altar boys, pizza delivery men, world-class hustlers and cowboys on crack. Here, at last, was motive! He was witnessing a spectacle for which the price tag would be inestimable to some and simply unimaginable to others.

Most important, the tapes could probably tell him who'd been at the guesthouse the night of Ross's murder. That was the proof he needed! Brad quickly looked through the entire cabinet, but realized with a jolt that all the tapes from that evening were missing. Someone had removed every single one, along with a number of others at periodic intervals. *A very queer fish, indeed,* he could hear Hayden say. Who had been there that night?

He still didn't have the evidence he needed to collar Ross's killer, but it was time to call Tom Nava all the same. His role in the P-Town escapade was nearly done.

He closed the cabinet and reached for the ladder. Halfway down, he gripped the rungs and paused to rub his forehead. His legs felt weak. His vision was clouded and his heart beat like a tom-tom. *Whoa!* Too much caffeine, he told himself. He waited till the sensation abated before continuing.

At the bottom he turned and found himself staring down the barrel of a Colt .45. At the other end stood Johnny K.

253

35

Brad waited, but nothing happened. Either that or death meant you were frozen in time with your mind focused on the last image you saw before you croaked. Slowly, Johnny K. lowered the gun until it no longer pointed at his head. This was no bardo.

"I guess you're wondering how I got into the house," Brad said.

"Not really," the muscle stud said in a raspy voice that was the vocal equivalent of a carrot grater. "I just wondered why you came in the window when the front door was unlocked."

Brad blushed. He hadn't even thought to try it.

"What I'm really wondering is *why* you're in the house, but I think I've got that one covered, too."

Johnny K.'s voice grated harshly in his ear. Brad recognized it. This was the voice that had told him over the phone about Ross's death! It was also the last voice he'd heard before being hit on the head and dumped on the highway! One mystery solved, Brad thought. But will I live to solve the others?

Johnny K. tucked the gun in its holster. Clearly, he didn't think he was going to have to use it. Brad started to swoon again, feeling the same dizzy sensation he'd experienced on the ladder, as Johnny K. wavered in and out of his field of vision.

Brad shook his head. "It was you who called me about Ross, wasn't it?"

Johnny K. smiled. "I knew you'd come to fetch the body when you heard about it. Ross always said you were such a *faithful* friend."

Brad sensed an ironic tone he didn't care for.

"But I never thought you'd be stupid enough to get so involved in things here. You made it very uncomfortable for all of us."

"So why even call me at all?"

"I tried Ross's family, but they wanted nothing to do with him, being good Christians and all. Seems they didn't think he'd gone any place they'd be meeting up with him again soon. But we couldn't have his body traced back here. And the longer it sat, the likelier that would have been. That's where you came in handy."

A pounding filled Brad's ears. His mouth was dry. "Why did you kill him?"

Johnny K. laughed. "What makes you think it was me?"

"Who else could it be? I already know you killed your boss. I have a tape that incriminates you in his shooting."

Johnny K.'s face clouded. "There's no such tape!" he snarled.

"There surely is," Bradford said.

"Prove it!"

Well, Brad realized, there's only one way to find out if I'm right. "The video shows you with a snake tattoo on your right shoulder blade."

"Fuck you!" screamed Johnny K. "Who the hell gave you that tape?"

"You tell me," Brad said. "It came sailing through my window the other night. It must have been a friend of yours. Maybe someone wants to get rid of you."

"Jeremiah!" Johnny K. sneered. "He thinks he can run this place by himself with me out of the way. And he's counting on those tapes to help. It's called 'blackmail.'"

Bingo! Brad thought. "Is that why you killed your boss?"

Johnny K. shook his head. "I didn't kill him. But that won't matter to you soon. You'll be in la-la-land in another minute," he said, flexing his powerful fingers. "And then I'm outta here."

Stall for time! Brad told himself. He noticed a swelling in the bodyguard's pants. It seemed Johnny K. got a little hot over his killings.

"I have to say, I'm mighty intrigued by what I've heard about you," Brad said. "Considering that you've been written up as a legend in your own time."

"What kind of legend is that?" Johnny K. asked, coming closer.

"A very big one," Brad said, feeling his knees buckle. He reached out to steady himself against a wall.

"Tch-tch. You seemed to have scratched yourself on our hedge," Johnny K. said. "That could be a problem."

Brad looked down. An angry red welt showed where his forearm had brushed the belladonna bush.

"A problem for you, I mean." Johnny K. smiled like Stanley Kowalski cornering his pesky sister-in-law, Blanche. "I think we've had this date from the beginning," he said as Brad slumped to the floor.

Brad felt himself being picked up and carried down the hall where he was unceremoniously dropped onto Hayden Rosengarten's oak desk. Through bleary eyes he saw the lens of a camera pointing at him.

"Time for your close-up," Johnny K. said.

He stood back and tugged on his T-shirt, pulling it overhead like a man born to take his clothes off. A large "K" was tattooed on his chest. And there was the snake coiled on his right shoulder. *It was him!*

"How do you feel?" Johnny K. asked. "Is your mouth dry? Vision a little cloudy? Those are the first symptoms. Heart palpitations should follow."

Brad tried to speak, but no sound emerged.

"You'll probably experience a few hallucinations, too," Johnny K. said as he unhooked Brad's belt and slipped off his pants. "Pretty soon you'll fall into a coma and your vital signs will cease," he said. "Poor you."

He held up a vial of white powder and sprinkled some on the back of his hand. "Too bad you're not a drug user," he said. "All it takes to counteract belladonna is a little opium ... like this." He sniffed sharply and the powder disappeared up his nose.

He placed the vial on the desk a few inches from Brad's head. As much as he would have liked to, Brad couldn't coordinate his muscles to reach out and grasp it.

He tried to concentrate, focusing on the "K" on Johnny K.'s chest. "Nice tattoo. What's the 'K' stand for?" he gasped.

Johnny K. smiled. "Karma," he said. "Meet your fate, Bradford Fairfax."

His hands ripped open Brad's T-shirt, exposing the wings on his abdomen. "Hey! Nice tattoo, yourself."

Brad heard the slither of leather against skin as Johnny K. stepped deftly out of his pants.

"I think this has your name on it," Johnny K. said, grabbing Bradford's legs and hoisting them over his shoulders.

Brad looked down. The letters Y-O-U-R N-A-M-E were etched from base to tip on what was truly a magnificent piece of equipment.

Not exactly B-R-A-D-F-O-R-D F-A-I-R-F-A-X or even S-E-B-A-S-T-I-A-N O-'S-H-A-U-G-H-N-E-S-S-Y, but hardly a disappointment, Brad thought, watching it disappear one letter at a time. Maybe dying wasn't so bad after all.

"You fuck real good," Johnny K. said with a sneer. "But I bet you hear that all the time."

The words came to him through a haze. Brad tried to focus, struggling for clarity.

"In fact, you fuck better than your dead boyfriend."

Ross's face rose before him. Something powerful reared inside him as Brad's mind clicked back to full consciousness.

"Bastard!"

With one solid blow Johnny K. flew backwards into the filing cabinet and slumped to the floor.

Brad quickly had the top off the glass vial and took a sniff. Johnny K. was right — a snort of the white powder cleared his head of the last vestiges of fogginess.

He soon had the bodyguard's arms secured with his own belt. Then he dragged him toward the wall and felt around for the hidden panel. Sure enough, a door slid open.

"I'll let you know when it's time to come out," he called to the groggy figure bound hand-and-foot and lying on the floor of the secret chamber.

Brad went over to Hayden's desk and dialed the police. Tom Nava came on the line and Brad explained where the murderer could be found, along with an intriguing library of videotapes.

"You doing my job for me now?" Nava grunted.

"Consider it a favour," Brad said.

He hung up and got dressed, and then walked over to the camera. He rewound the tape and pushed *Play.* On screen, his limp body appeared at the mercy of Johnny K. Brad couldn't help notice the smile on his face.

He watched for a moment longer, then turned off the camera. If he destroyed the tape, he reasoned, he'd be tampering with evidence. Then again, did he really want this shown in court? He stuffed it into his pocket. It would make a nice little addition to his collection of autoerotica.

36

Sometime during the night Hurricane Isabel slammed into the North Carolina coast at more than one-hundred miles an hour, leaving a trail of havoc in her wake. She then headed inland, turning north and away from Cape Cod before beginning her inevitable descent into a tropical storm and finally to a wisp of a breeze that would be scarcely a memory for most people within a week.

That night Bradford slept a dreamless sleep. When he woke, he checked his answering service but there was nothing from Zach. He felt let down. He would've liked some small reminder of Zach's presence, especially since they'd spent the night apart. Maybe Zach was already getting cold feet. Either that or the seriousness of the situation had dawned on him and he'd been scared off at last.

The only message was from Grace. She congratulated him on capturing Johnny K. and said the tip about the gun had panned out. They'd located it off the end of the pier in about ten feet of water. It had turned out to be a Colt .45, as they knew it would. All that remained to be seen was which gun the bullet had actually been fired from — Big Ruby's or Johnny K.'s. The gun had been surprisingly easy to find, Grace added, almost as an afterthought.

Brad was left to read into that last remark as he brought his breakfast out to the veranda. He looked down at his abs, remembering the bodyguard's magnificent body, and pushed aside half a bagel covered in cream cheese. Time to get back to the gym, he told himself. That's how it always starts. You take your mind off it for a day and *bingo!,* flab starts forming like ice crystals on a window. At first it's a thin coating, then next thing you know it's so thick you can't see out.

He watched his abdomen expand and contract with each breath. These days, just dieting wasn't enough. You could be out at the gym feeling great about yourself when some muscle queen with a three-percent body fat ratio catches your eye and paranoia strikes a home run. Do I have love handles? Wobbly thighs? Why do I stay home watching TV when I could be in here pumping iron another five or six hours a day?

The phone interrupted his self-reproach.

"Care to take your sugar to tea?" It was Cinder.

They confirmed for a pleasant little seaside café, then Brad phoned Zach's guesthouse. There was no answer. He left a message saying where he could be found.

Cinder was waiting outside the café in a frilly knee-length skirt and bobbed platinum wig, his arms covered in silver bangles. Was this Marilyn? Brad wondered. It wasn't trashy enough to be Madonna.

"Neither. I'm Renée Zellweger in *Chicago,*" Cinder announced when he asked.

"Thoroughly Postmodern Cinder," Bradford said. "And just about as up-to-date as a girl can be."

At that moment a gym queen strode past in a thong and sleeveless T-shirt. Brad's eyes wandered over the man's flawless physique.

Cinder shot him a glance. "Fashion Rule Number One: a thong is always wrong," he stated categorically. "Remember that, handsome."

Brad brought Cinder up to date during lunch, mentioning that he'd been able to ascertain the validity of Johnny K.'s status as a legend, without going into too much detail.

"You lucky tart! Well, now that you've got things all wrapped up here, I suppose you'll be going home soon," Cinder said.

"That's likely, but I come back once or twice a year, so I can catch your show again some time."

Cinder reached across the table and touched the back of his hand. "So sweet," he said. "But I still find it hard to believe it was Johnny K. I mean, I know he was a vicious thug but I didn't think he was a killer, too!"

"Appearances can be deceiving," Brad said.

"How did you end up fingering him?"

"Someone sent me a tape of Hayden sitting in a bathtub. In the mirror I could make out a figure threatening him with a gun. When I slowed the tape, I saw a tattoo on the killer's right shoulder."

Cinder grabbed Brad's arm. "You don't mean the 'Oh, it's so big, shoot me!' tape?"

Brad started. "How do you know about it?"

"Honey, we all had to audition for Hayden. That was his favourite scenario. He liked his boys big and deadly. I'm pretty handy with a gun myself, if I may say so, though I doubt I'd ever match Johnny K.'s stupendous nether regions ..."

Brad was staring at him. "Are you saying the tape isn't real?"

"No, honey, I'm sure it's real, if you saw it. What I'm saying is, we all made a 'bang-bang, you're dead' tape with Hayden. I think he wanted it in case anyone tried to blackmail *him,* so he'd have something on each of us."

Brad's head was reeling. It had all been a dress-up game! "Then who ... ?"

Cinder was shaking his head. "I think you got the wrong killer, hon. Now who do you think would've sent you a tape like that?"

"I've been trying to figure that out."

"Well, it had to be someone with access to the Ice House."

"I've been wracking my brains to think what Ruby and Ross and Hayden all had in common ..."

"They were all Buddhists ..." Cinder said, with a wave of his highball glass.

Brad smiled. "Very funny ..." Suddenly his smile vanished. He snapped his finger. *"They were all Buddhists!"*

"I just said that."

"And who would they have had in common?"

"Well, there was that car guy. Come to think of it, he was at the house the night Ross died. I was sure surprised to see him there, but he's quite the hotcha-hotcha hunk with his clothes off, let me tell you."

Brad was perplexed. "The 'car guy'?"

Cinder's forehead scrunched in concentration. "Yeah, you know," he said, shaking his bangles. "That nummy guy at the funeral. The Rim-Porsche-something-or-other."

"Oh, God!" Bradford said, recalling his dream where the rim flew off the Porsche and chased him and Zach down the hill.

And that's when he remembered Zach saying he was going to learn the hundred-syllable mantra with the Reluctant Rinpoche that afternoon.

"Zach's with the Rinpoche!"

37

Cinder was a surprisingly good runner in women's flats.

"It's all that marathon training," he shouted, as they raced toward the Buddhist temple. "I just hope we get there in time!"

That thought was uppermost on Bradford's mind as they ran. Once there, however, he was less sure what to do. From outside, the building appeared sedate. The Asian characters above the door probably said *Welcome, Fellow Buddhists,* but at that moment they seemed much more dire in their directive.

"This is no good," Brad said. "We can't be seen standing here." He thought for a moment. "Look, I've got to get around back and see if I can get inside. Can you do something to distract attention away from me?"

"Honey, my entire life is about distracting attention away from other people and onto myself. Just leave it to me," Cinder said, already approaching the front door.

Brad waited a beat before slipping into the yard. It was cut off from the property next door by a large and very full hedge. At least this one was only honeysuckle, he noted. Brad passed a side window as a fierce-looking Asian man came into view. He ducked behind the hedge and the window slid to a close. No further alarm was sounded. He hadn't been seen.

A knocking reached his ears. "Hel-l-o-o-o?" he could hear Cinder call out. "Is anybody *homo?*"

Good boy! Brad thought as he moved toward the back of the house. The yard yielded little coverage as he crossed the overgrown garden. A wind chime tinkled at his approach. He tried the porch door. It opened and he slipped inside.

Brad proceeded cautiously down the hall, keeping his eye open for a hideaway in case anyone approached. He heard Cinder at the front door asking to see the "Rim Porsche."

"He no here," a man's voice replied.

"I'm having a crisis of spirit," Cinder cried. "I need guidance and you could be just the man to help me."

Brad took advantage of the distraction to slip upstairs. He searched quickly. The second floor was unoccupied. It wasn't until he reached the third floor that he smelled incense coming from under a closed door. It opened onto a dim interior. Bookshelves flanked a window at the far end and curlicues of smoke encircled the room. A body lay stretched beneath the window.

Zach!

Brad ran over and shook him.

"Zach!"

He was breathing, but he didn't move.

"Ah! Mr. Bradford," said a voice from behind him. "Don't worry. I haven't harmed him."

Brad whirled to see the Rinpoche seated on the floor, completely at ease in a lotus posture.

"You, on the other hand, may be in for some rough treatment."

"Your English has improved," Brad said.

"Thank you. I wish I could say the same for my Tibetan. I can't speak a darn word of it apart from a few phonetic readings from that illustrious fairy tale, the *Book of the Dead.*"

"You won't get away with this," Bradford said. "There are four people at this very moment who are aware of the fact that you offed Hayden Rosengarten, Ross Pretty, Big Ruby and James Shephard."

The Rinpoche laughed. "And are those people Marilyn Monroe, Judy Garland, Bette Davis and Renée Zellweger, by any chance?"

The sarcasm stung, but Brad decided to overlook it.

"You see, Mr. Fairfax, this meeting isn't by chance. I've known all along that you would stumble onto the truth. I've even prepared for it."

"And what truth is that?"

"That your friends were getting too close to something for their own good, which is why, as you so cleverly put it, I 'offed' them."

"The P-Town murderer," Brad said.

"I humbly accept the honourable title," he said, with a slight incline of his head.

"Why Ross? He could never have hurt you!"

"So true! But an eager young proselyte who discovered his Rinpoche at a house of disrepute might speak about it sooner or later. I couldn't take the chance it might be sooner. I was as surprised to see him there as he was to see me, but the damage was done. I'm sure the bardo must have looked lovely on an overdose of ecstasy."

"And James Shephard? The boy on the beach? Is that why you drowned him?"

"Precisely. Both knew me as the Reluctant Rinpoche. And both were such promising young students, too."

Brad drew a breath. "So why Big Ruby?"

The Rinpoche shrugged. "Regrettable, I must say. She made the best lattes on the Cape. But I couldn't have her telling you that I'd borrowed her gun, could I? For ceremonial purposes, of course. At least, that's what I told Halle the night I came over. Halle would never suspect me, but you'd already spoken with Ruby."

"So you sneaked into the Ice House and shot Hayden Rosengarten in the forehead, then vanished with the tape of your own visit the night you killed Ross. And on the way home, you tossed Ruby's gun into the ocean in a place that would be convenient to find — with a little tip-off."

"Precisely."

"And was it you I overheard threatening to kill Rosengarten on the telephone a few nights before?"

The Rinpoche's face showed surprise. "My, but you do get around."

"You're the 'queer fish' he threatened to expose to the world."

The Rinpoche smiled. "Yes. I need to maintain my status as a visiting Rinpoche for a while longer. As you may have guessed, I have important work to do in the next day or two."

What work could that be? Brad wondered as his father's words returned with a vengeance: *Everyone has a reason for the things they do. You don't have to like or agree with it, but you'll be better off if you understand it.* Here was the *real* motive. He was standing before the intended assassin of the Dalai Lama!

In a flash, the Rinpoche flew through the air, landing on one foot while lashing out with the other. Brad ducked in time to avoid a vicious kick, but the Rinpoche's hands transformed into whirling blades of destruction.

267

I thought that happened only in films, Brad mused as he assumed a defensive posture. Hands flew swifter than the eye. Feet kicked out with brutal savagery as blows were countered and returned with infinite precision.

"I see you've mastered a few of our martial arts skills," the Rinpoche noted as they circled the room. "I will enjoy this. To conquer one worthy opponent is better than vanquishing a thousand weaklings."

As the man spouted philosophy, Brad saw his opportunity. His foot flew out and connected with the Rinpoche's shoulder, but he received a swift blow in return. He struck again immediately, causing the Rinpoche to double over in pain. Brad's knee came up and caught him square in the jaw. The Rinpoche's face contorted in surprise and anger.

"You're not that good!" he snarled.

Big mouth, Brad thought. You can't talk and fight at the same time. You're using both sides of your brain and one of them has to take precedence. But while Brad was thinking, the Rinpoche was also busy looking for a point of weakness. His heel connected with Brad's thigh, sending him reeling. He followed up with a kick to his side. Brad staggered and fell.

This wasn't a Kung Fu movie. They both knew an accomplished fighter could kill an opponent with a few swift blows. Brad looked over at Zach's unconscious form and felt a surge of love. *I have to save the kid!* he thought, staggering to his feet. One good strike was all he needed to deliver.

But Brad's strength was nearly gone as the two parried and danced around in what was more a John Woo *ballet-de-violence* than a Bruce Lee *tour-de-force*. He might never land that final blow.

Just then the door opened and Thoroughly Postmodern Cinder came cracking down on the Rinpoche's head with a heavy metal frying pan. It should have been a wok, but it was a mere skillet that left Renée Zellweger crying tears of joy over the expensive oriental carpet.

In a true martial arts tale, it would never have happened that way. It must be the hero who triumphs against all odds, never the blond femme fatale and especially not the blond-devastato man wearing a frilly *oop-she-bop* dress and size thirteen women's flats. But this wasn't a movie, and so be it. Happy endings sometimes came true in the most unexpected ways.

269

The hero strode — limped, actually — over to his beloved and awakened him with a kiss. Zach stirred and rubbed his head.

"Holy Hollywood, Bradford! I dreamed we were fighting a dragon and you were almost winning when Renée Zellweger came in and stole the scene."

Brad smiled and tousled Zach's hair. Cute kid, he thought. Maybe I'll keep him.

38

Grace called twice before noon and then again at the crack of two before Brad finally managed to open his bruised eyes. Zach passed the phone up to the loft where he lay sprawled, wings fully revealed to sky and dune.

"Good work, Red. We're all very proud of you. The Dalai Lama should rest easy now, if he even experienced a moment of doubt or dread. When I met with him last week he seemed to think there wasn't a worry in the world. Do you think he really is omniscient?"

"You met with the Dalai Lama? When?"

"Right before Rosengarten's murder. That's why I wasn't able to call you back. We'd set up a security meeting to discuss alternate plans for his talk in case his would-be assassin hadn't been captured, but he wouldn't hear of it. He would speak in Central Park on Sunday, come hell or high water. He's almost as stubborn as you."

"At least he's safe," said Brad, grinning at the thought of the colossal forces brought together. Hurricane Isabel probably had nothing on those two.

"In fact, I believe he's about to begin his talk any minute."

Brad looked over at the clock, noting the time with a start.

"As for the others, I understand the local authorities are dealing with them. Your Officer Nava had a particular zeal to bust Johnny K. for impersonating an officer while causing bodily harm to a certain drug dealer in his jurisdiction."

"Poor Fred," Brad said. "What about Jeremiah Jones?"

"No crime in growing flowers, as far as I know. That's all he's guilty of, unless he admits to contemplating blackmail. Halle, as you so skilfully figured out, was Rosengarten's daughter. Apparently Ruby bought the gun to protect them from him. It's ironic it ended up being the weapon that killed him, but by someone else's hand."

271

Bradford cleared his throat. "Well, I guess that's nearly everybody ..."

"Oh — that missing houseboy turned up in Key West. He got frightened when Johnny K. knocked you out and he simply ran away."

Just one person left, Brad thought. But I'll get to him later.

"We have more precise theories on the who, what, when and how much of it, but that can wait till you get back. How are you feeling, by the way?"

Brad rubbed the back of his head. "Alive — mostly."

"Zach tells me you didn't sustain any major injuries. And apparently you're responding well to his healing techniques. Not that we won't ante up for the medical bills, if need be. But it must be nice to be in the hands of a genuine healer."

Brad wasn't sure what to say. "He's good, I guess."

"Good?" Grace snorted. "That boy's the best thing that's happened to you in a long time. And don't you forget it." She paused. "Just an opinion, mind."

Brad handed the phone back to Zach, who climbed onto the

ladder, looking down at Bradford lying before him.

"See something you like?" Brad asked.

"Oh, yeah," the boy said, running his hand over Brad's tattoo.

"Is that your hot hand or your cold hand?"

"You tell me."

"Feels pretty hot. Wanna make like the winged stallion?"

"Oh, yeah!"

BRAD MADE A quick stop at Purgatory later in the afternoon. He just needed to confirm one thing with the handsome barkeep, now that he knew Perry wasn't the killer.

"G and T?" Perry asked when he entered.

"Not today," Brad said. "But a little information would be appreciated."

Perry gave him a wary look. "Shoot," he said at last.

"I saw you leave the Ice House yesterday."

Perry waited, expressionless.

"Did you by any chance leave with some videotapes?"

After a moment, Perry nodded. "Yes."

"Have you destroyed them?"

Perry nodded again. "I was in them. So was Ross."

Brad thought for a moment. "They've already got Rosengarten's killer," he said. "So I guess the tapes aren't necessary now."

"I had nothing to do with his murder," Perry interjected.

"I know that now, but you'll forgive me for having wondered. Ruby told me you claimed you'd kill him if you ever got sick."

"I've said a lot of stupid things, but the truth is I'd just swim out to sea till I disappeared beneath the waves."

"I hope you won't ever have to do that," Brad said. "Were you and Ross ...?"

"Lovers," Perry said, nodding.

"You tried to claim Ross's body at the morgue."

Perry smiled sadly. "They wouldn't even give me that much," he said.

"I'm glad to know he found someone like you before he died."

"I wish I could've saved him," Perry said.

"So do I." Brad extended his hand. "I hope things work out for you."

AS BRAD AND Zach made their way out to Race Point, they passed a gaggle of younger boys. One turned and whistled after Zach.

"Hey, cutie! Dump your father and come with us to Tea Dance," he called out.

"Never," Zach called out, grabbing Brad's arm as they trudged over the sand.

"I guess you must have *It*," Brad said, mildly miffed.

Zach smiled. "I may have *It*, but you've got *me.*"

They walked barefoot, the sand cool between their toes. Brad was thinking about all that had happened in the past week.

"Grace tells me you think my injuries aren't lethal," he said.

Zach smiled. "You'll live, but it probably hurts right here." He pressed the back of Bradford's neck.

Brad winced. *"Ow!"*

"Don't worry, I have a cure for that."

"Is that so?"

"I have the cure for nearly everything. Just put yourself in my hands."

"I'd like to."

"Then do it. It requires no thinking."

"That's where you're wrong. Everything in my life requires thinking ... For instance, I was just thinking about my late partner. Work partner, I mean. Two years ago he was knifed to death ten feet away from me. I couldn't get to him in time."

"Brad ..."

"It wasn't my fault, but I still feel if I'd been *thinking* it might have been prevented. Only how can you *think* about something before it happens?"

"Brad ..."

"For instance, if I'd been *thinking* I would have realized the 'Reluctant' Rinpoche was too young to have left Tibet with the Dalai Lama in 1959, as Ruby claimed."

"We could think for each other," Zach replied.

Brad was silent for a moment. "And I hate New York," he said. "I'm probably the only gay man who does, but I'd never go there willingly."

"New York's okay," Zach told him. "You just have to learn to pace yourself. I could teach you."

"I'm a whiner and a complainer ..."

Don't settle for me. I'm far too much trouble, he seemed to be saying, like the seller who tried to lower his cost when the buyer accepted at too high a price.

"Take this sand, for instance. As much as I love this place and its beauty, all I can think right now is that it's rubbing my feet completely raw."

"It *is* pretty coarse," Zach agreed. "But things can't always be perfect. You have to take that leap of faith."

"Faith?"

"I'm talking about the L-word."

Brad was silent. The L-word was not something he was comfortable with. He stooped to pick up a shiny stone, rolling it between his fingers as they walked.

"Every time I come here I like to bring back something to remind me of my trip," he said. "I have a whole collection on a shelf at home. Sometimes it's a shell, sometimes a colourful rock ..."

Zach stopped and turned to him. "What are we to each other?"

"Huh?"

"You and me. Who are we?"

"Why, I'm your Man of Steel ..."

"Uh-huh. And what am I to you?"

"Robin to my Batman?"

"Okay. Anything else?"

Bradford turned the stone in his fingers, letting the light catch on its glittering surface.

"Sometimes you just have to go with it and see what happens," Zach said.

Brad walked on. "I've seen what happens and I don't approve," he said over his shoulder.

"It's not something you approve or disapprove of," Zach said, following behind. "It's just something you accept and learn to appreciate over time."

"Like good wine?"

"Like good wine."

They trudged to the top of a dune and stopped, looking out over the ocean as though their walking had taken them to this spot where conclusions might be drawn. There was an unspoken peace about it all, standing at the edge of the world looking backwards into history, the Where-We-Came-From of this once-Brave New World.

"Ross used to come here," Brad began. "It was his favourite place in the world ..."

"I almost forgot!" Zach exclaimed. "I dreamed about Ross last night! I'm sure it was him!"

Brad looked over.

"Boy, was he handsome! He was tall and dark haired, with this gangly smile that could just about break your heart ..."

"That sounds like Ross, all right," Brad said. A look came over him. "Why did he visit you instead of me?"

Zach shrugged. "Probably because I'm easier to get through to. While he was visiting he said something odd. I didn't understand it."

Brad was watching the waves. "What did he say?"

"I'm trying to remember. It was like, 'Tell Brad thanks ...'"

Brad turned to him.

"'... for the fireflies.'"

Bradford's eyes misted over. He rubbed a hand across his face.

"You really loved each other, didn't you?" Zach said.

"Yeah," he said. "We really did."

Zach leaned close and hugged him as the wind blew past.

"Did he say anything else?" Brad asked after a while.

"Just one other thing."

Brad waited.

"He said, 'I hope you'll be happy together.'"

"Did he really say that?"

Zach nodded. "Scout's honour."

"You're a Buddhist, not a Boy Scout."

Zach smiled. "I know. And I can't wait to take you home to

meet the folks. 'Hello, Mom, Dad? This is my husband, the spy.'"

Bradford turned and looked into those calming eyes that were like seeing into the depths of the ocean. He was thinking about Zach's blue hair and the way his lips curled optimistically upward at the corners. He stood watching Zach a long time, as though weighing something invisible between them.

The sun was setting over the water. If they started walking now, the sparks would soon be flying up with their footsteps. He looked at Zach, and then down at the stone in his hand. He raised his arm and threw it out across the waves where it skipped once, twice, three times, before it sank.

"I guess I'll need another souvenir of my trip," he said finally. "Got any suggestions?"

Zach smiled. "Just one."

Acknowledgements

Thanks to Shane, Janice Hill and Uppinder Mehan, Sharron Campeau, Wanda Underwood, Regina Binder, Charlie Fulmer, Megan Johnston, Margaret Hart, DR and Bob, Marietta Hickey and Lawa Rinpoche, Uli Menzefricke, and Jay Quinn. Thanks also to Jessica L. Smith, Mary Beth Madden, and all the Working Girls (and Boys) of Haworth! Special thanks to Ned Bradford, in whose Provincetown house this book was conceived, and of course to Greg Herren, who, in the midst of Hurricane Katrina, took care to see that it wasn't forgotten. Nothing has astonished me so much in years! I also extend my appreciation to Agatha Christie, Ethan Mordden, Mae West and all the good people of Provincetown. Live long and fare thee well!

For the Cormorant edition, I'd like to thank astute readers Dean Gregory and Richard B. Olson for pointing out my sins of omission and commission in the book's original edition, and Marc Côté for taking on Brad and the Gang.